PLAY WITH ME

DIAMOND IN THE ROUGH 1

REBEL HART

1

RAELYNN

"No! Please! Somebody, help!"

The car skidded out of control and tires burned their rubbered tracks into the road. I gripped the 'oh shit' handle in the car, feeling us careening out of control. I screamed for help as I saw a car going over the edge. Sounds of metal crunching against metal sounded helplessly in my ears as I cried out a name I didn't recognize. A name that sounded unfamiliar, even as it fell from my lips.

Then the world muted itself around me.

Our car came to a stop just beyond the impact point. The mangled guard rail in front of us ignited into flames as I pushed out of the car. I stumbled around, feeling my stomach upheaving its contents onto the road. I couldn't regain control. I couldn't see straight. Between motion sickness and worry bubbling in my gut, my dinner didn't stand a chance of staying down.

"Help!" I roared.

I stumbled to the guard rail and peered over the edge. I gazed into the darkness below, watching it undulate, as if it were laughing at me. I looked around for the car I knew had plummeted over the edge. I tried to gaze beyond the darkness. Beyond the movement. Beyond the endless expanse of nothing that seemed to cloak the fall downward.

"Are you down there?" I exclaimed.

I heard someone calling my name. Someone off in the distance. I whipped my head up, surveying the world around me. All it did was fall into darkness. Slowly, the creeping nothingness swallowed up colors. Shapes. Sounds. My eyes widened as the road disappeared. I looked up, watching the stars get swallowed whole by the hellish expanse of Vantablack around me. I kept backing up until my legs touched the mangled guard rail. I felt the piercing, heated shards dig into my skin while the flames themselves were put out by the nothingness that surrounded me.

Then a piercing sound ricocheted through my ears.

I stumbled back, falling off the edge and into the darkness below. I reached up for the world above me, but it quickly fell away. Everything got swallowed up. I felt myself falling. Panicking. Breathing harder and harder. I flailed my arms, turning myself around until I was facing what I thought was the ground.

And it was then I saw it.

"No," I gasped.

I bolted upright in my bed, feeling sweat trickling

down the nape of my neck. I wiped at my brow, listening as my alarm for school went off. I licked my chapped lips, wincing at how dry they were as I tossed the covers off my bare legs. I closed my eyes as my feet touched down onto the dirty carpet of my floor, burying my face in my hands.

"Not again," I murmured.

That damn dream never ceased to haunt me. For as long as I could remember, it started off every fucking school year. Without fail. The night before my first day of school, I'd have that dream. It didn't matter what I did, what I ate before bed, whether or not I took something to help me sleep, or what I watched in order to fall asleep. For years, that same dream ushered in my years of school.

And it seemed as if my senior year of high school was no different.

"I need a shower," I murmured.

The cold sweats always made me feel gross. Especially when they soaked through the T-shirts I wore at night. I pulled it all off, even my soaked panties, before tossing them into the hamper. Even from beyond my bedroom door, I heard the snores of a man. Some man my mother had probably dragged home from the bar last night. I rolled my eyes as I walked into my bathroom. I turned the water on and let it run for five minutes before I sighed.

Apparently, I'd have to take a cold shower this morning.

"Great," I whispered.

It was the shortest shower of my life. But I did what I had to do. I washed my body, ran some shampoo through my hair, then decided to forgo conditioner so I could fucking get warm. I hopped out and reached for a towel, slipping and sliding everywhere in the process. I still didn't have my legs underneath me. This summer had been enough of a hell-binding, torturous state. What with my terrible ongoing job at the grocery store and Mom sucking down half of whatever I made at the bar every night. I got the job my freshman year to start helping out. I got the damn job in the first place so we wouldn't have to keep picking and choosing which bills to pay every month.

But when I went to turn on my bedroom light, I realized the only thing my money did was help my mother bring home more men.

Because our electricity had been shut off.

"Fucking great," I sighed.

I focused on getting ready for school, because the sooner I got out of the house the sooner I could let this entire summer fall from my mind. I tied my hair back into a low ponytail, then brushed my teeth. I pulled on the first outfit my hands found, since I couldn't see what the hell I was doing. And after rummaging around in the change jar for lunch money, I grabbed my backpack and an apple to have for breakfast. I even grabbed a water from the pantry, just to splurge on myself a little bit.

The relief I felt as I stepped out onto the porch almost knocked me off my feet.

I saw the foreign car in the driveway and shook my head. It sure as hell wasn't her boyfriend's car. Nor was it hers. I snickered as I walked up the driveway, making my way to school. My mother was notorious for bringing home random one-night stands. Even if she did have a steady boyfriend who gave her whatever the hell she wanted.

You know, in exchange for knocking her around a little.

"And yet, we still can't pay our bills," I muttered.

I took a large bite of my apple before cracking open the bottled water. I knew I'd catch hell for it after school, since my mother practically had a counter on the food in our home. But I didn't care. I was thirsty as hell after sweating through the night. After dealing with that stupid nightmare.

I shivered at the thought of it.

"There she is!" Michael exclaimed.

I smiled as I tossed my apple core down a drain pipe. Allison came barreling for me, her long blond hair billowing in the summer breeze behind her. I held my arms out, catching her as she ran into me, almost knocking me clear off my damn feet. I hugged her tightly as the collar of her Ralph Lauren shirt tickled my neck. And before I could even let go to take a look at her parents' traditional 'first day of school' outfit for her, Michael had his arms around both of us.

Squeezing the ever blessed-fuck out of our bodies.

"Michael, I can't breathe," Allison choked out.

"Mike. Are you high?" I croaked.

"Oh, I missed the two of you. I didn't see you guys at all this summer," Michael said.

"Stop. Please. I beg of you," Allison said breathlessly.

"I'll kill you in your sleep," I hissed.

Michael released us and we both dropped to our feet. Allison and I heaved for air, then I stood back and surveyed her outfit. Typical, for her parents. A bright pink collared shirt with a pale blue emblazoned Ralph Lauren logo against her chest. A khaki skirt with boat shoes that were, somehow, the same color as her khakis. I giggled at the laces matching the pink hue of her shirt and the pale blue earrings twinkling in her ears. I shook my head in fascination, never ceasing to be amazed at the outfits her parents could conjure.

I snickered. "Your parents single-handedly keep Ralph Lauren in business."

Allison held out her arms. "What? They're good clothes. You mean you don't like this outfit? I wore the blue just for you."

Michael grinned. "Well, by the looks of Rae, black and brown are in this year."

I rolled my eyes. "Says the boy wearing eggshell-colored shorts that come two inches above his knees."

Allison nodded. "I'm just impressed you know what shade 'eggshell' is."

Michael faked a tear. "Mom would be so proud of you."

I looked down at my outfit and shook my head. I looked like a maniac. My hair was frizzy from no conditioner. My black shirt had lint and dust all over it.

And my brown pants were so baggy my inner thighs rubbed together when I walked. None of which took into account my bright green flip-flops Mom had purchased for me this summer on a whim to apologize for some fight she had with her boyfriend.

A fight that wound up destroying my hand-me-down iPod because it got thrown against the wall.

"You guys ready for school?" I asked.

But my two best friends in the entire world were giving me 'the look.'

I sighed. "Guys, not now. Please."

Allison quirked an eyebrow. "Did you have that nightmare again?"

Michael narrowed his eyes. "Or did your mother do something?"

I shrugged. "Why can't it be both?"

Michael shook his head as Allison let out a string of curses under her breath.

I giggled. "Don't let your mom hear you talk like that."

Michael wrapped his arm around my shoulders. "Anything I can do?"

"Yeah. You can stop dwelling on it and help me get to school faster."

The three of us fell in line, abandoning my rundown neighborhood in exchange for perfectly-manicured lawns and sprawling homes. That was the Riverbend High area I knew. Not the rundown shacks in the shadows of the town I lived in, but the massive homes Allison and Michael lived in. They lived perfect lives. They had perfect families. Michael with his adoptive parents that loved him as if he were their own. And Allison with her biological parents that were still very much in love. It seemed that with the nicer suburbs came nicer lives. Nicer parents. Nicer homes to be raised in and nicer food to eat. I envied them for the lives they had. I envied the relationships they had with their parents.

I'd kill to have that relationship with my *one* parent.

Allison cleared her throat. "So what are you two doing this weekend?"

Michael smiled. "Please, oh please tell me this is leading into another weekend visit at your place. I love your basement, and girl talk is always fun to listen to."

I laughed. "You know I'm not doing anything. I only work every other weekend at the grocery store even though I beg for more hours. You know how it goes. Why?"

Allison linked her arm with mine. "Well, my parents are going to Palm Springs Thursday evening for a spa retreat. Won't be back until Monday afternoon."

Michael thrust his fist into the air. "Yes! Girl time! Nailed it!"

I threw my head back in laughter as Allison shook her head.

"Seriously, though. You guys should come over. The both of you. We can watch girly movies and eat shitty food," she said.

Michael smiled brightly. "And I can finally get you two to watch Top Gun."

I sighed. "Are you really still on that tangent? You

haven't gotten us to watch it for two years. What makes you think this weekend is gonna be any different?"

Allison snickered. "We'll watch Top Gun if you paint our toes."

Michael pointed at the two of us. "Deal."

My jaw dropped. "Wait, don't I get a say in this?"

Michael shook his head. "Already made the deal. Sorry, guys!"

Allison whispered, "I mean, he's going to paint our toenails. Make the most of it, okay?"

I shook my head, watching as Michael grinned. I knew there wasn't a damn thing that boy wouldn't do for Allison. He had it bad for her, and she knew it. It was cute, though. They'd been going back and forth for damn near two years with one another. Flirting, but neither of them making a move.

I mean, they'd make cute preppy little babies. With his above-the-knee shorts and her collared shirts.

The child would come out wearing boat shoes, if they had anything to do with it.

Allison furrowed her brow. "What's so funny?"

I giggled. "Nothing. Just thinking about this weekend."

Michael paused. "You better wash your feet. I'm not painting grody toenails."

I shrugged. "You already agreed. No toenails, no Top Gun."

He shook his head. "You're gross, you know that?"

Allison winked. "I'll wash mine, don't worry."

Michael stared down at me. "If you don't wash your feet, I'm painting your toenails purple."

I gasped. "You wouldn't dare."

Allison butted in. "Or pink!"

My eyes narrowed. "I'd kill you both in your sleep."

Allison moved from my arm to Michael's as the three of us stepped onto the school's sidewalk. We kept talking about our weekend, making plans for food and drinks and what time we'd be over. I knew it wouldn't be an issue, either. Mom never gave a shit what I was doing on the weekends. She was nowhere to be found, which gave me free rein of the house and whatever was in it.

Then the three of us came to a stop in front of the high school doors.

"You guys ready for our last year?" Michael asked.

Allison nodded. "I already know where I'm applying for college. Just gotta make the grades to get me there."

Michael looked down at me. "What about you, Rae?"

I shrugged. "Could be worse."

Allison peeked over. "Do you know where you're going to be applying for college?"

I didn't know how to answer her. I was a C-plus student, at best. Which meant my future included community college, a technical degree, and a prayer to somehow get the hell away from my mother for good.

Michael knocked against me. "Earth to Rae. You there?"

I shook my head. "Sorry. Allison's question dazed me there. Because for the life of me, I don't know how a sane person can be standing in front of school and be thinking about *more* school."

And as Allison playfully stormed away from us, Michael ran after her. Like he'd always done.

Leaving me to stand there and smile at them as dread slowly filled my gut.

2

CLINTON

I groaned and rolled over, burying my face into the pillow. It reeked of booze and regret, just how I liked it. My jeans rubbed against my legs and I groaned, then wiggled my toes. I felt my bike boots on my feet over the sweaty socks creating blisters against my heels. I rolled over, flopping onto my back as I sprawled out in my king-size bed.

And I lay there in the pitch black room, reliving the fantastic party the other night.

I grinned as the sun tried its hardest to stream around my blackout curtains. I cracked my neck, then toed off my boots. I needed to get these damn socks off. I needed to change my pants. I needed to get washed up for the first day of school.

Then again, I didn't really want to.

"Fuck school," I murmured.

I rolled back over, reaching for my cellphone. And

when I clicked the harsh white light on, I chuckled. Of course it was almost lunch time. I'd slept through my first two periods. What a great way to start my senior year. The smell of alcohol followed me as I sat up. I burped, and the taste was rancid. I was damn near the puking stage, but I refused to do that.

I refused to pussy out after the best party of the summer.

I slipped to the edge of my bed, groaning. I felt like utter shit. One too many beers, and it was hard to move. Hard to think straight. Hard to even fathom getting myself cleaned up so I could get to school. I mean, if my parents figured out I was late for my first day, all hell might break loose.

They might video chat me from their safari trip and really give me a good tongue lashing.

"Idiots," I said, snickering.

I pulled myself out of bed and stumbled into the wall. I caught myself with my hands, but the glaring rays of the sun made me cower away. Fuck, that sun was bright. Did it have a dimmer dial of some sort? I sighed as I stumbled my way around my darkened room, running my knees into furniture and jamming my pinky toe against my bed frame.

"Fuck!" I roared.

Why the hell did I need so much mahogany furniture in my fucking bedroom?

Oh, yeah. Because my parents had more money than sense.

"Fucking bullshit," I murmured.

I stripped my clothes off, leaving a trail from the foot of my bed all the way to the shower. I turned on the hot water and got in, allowing the burps to work their way up with ease. I refused to puke, though. And as I leaned my head against the tiles of the shower wall, I drew in a deep breath.

If I got to school right at lunch time, I could fill my stomach with enough bread to get me through the rest of the day.

"Or you could just not go," I whispered.

Nope. The last time I missed a day of school like this, my parents actually flew back from their vacation, taking the time out of their busy recreational flight schedule to be decent parents for once. And it ended up with them selling off my fucking bike. I wasn't losing another bike over this. That thing was my peace. My solace. It made me feel powerful and on top of the world.

Plus, it got me laid more times than I cared to count.

"Nope. Get your ass to school," I murmured.

The summer had been great, but it was time to get back to reality. I cleaned myself up, slowly sobering as my vision cleared. I sighed as I got out of the shower, feeling the steam wrap around me. It was nice waking up in an empty house, kicking around streamers and empty beer cans and wiping red Dixie cups off my bathroom counter.

Yeah. It felt nice to always fucking be alone.

"If someone fucked in my bathroom, they're never invited back," I said, sighing.

Getting ready for school was a pain in my ass. But it had to happen. I didn't give a damn, though. I'd show up for lunch break and find Roy. Screw chemistry and English class. I didn't need any of that shit in my life. I had no plans to go to college. I had no plans to continue education past high school. Despite my parents constantly nagging the fuck out of me for it, I had other plans. Other wants. Other wishes. I wanted to work on bikes and write my fucking books. I wanted people to leave me the fuck alone so I could indulge the only two things on this planet I loved.

Motorcycles and writing.

"Fuck my parents," I growled.

And as I reached for my toothbrush, I settled into my morning routine. A lonely routine I'd crafted over the years to deal with my parents never being around.

Hell, it wasn't my fucking fault they wanted to enjoy their money rather than their son.

The revving of my motorcycle engine was my second favorite thing about my damn bike. The first being how it vibrated underneath my ass. I pulled into the backyard parking lot of the school, where all the juniors and seniors were allowed to park their shit. I found myself a spot in back, next to the woods where I knew no one would fuck with my shit. Not that they dared do it anyway. The last person to touch my bike without permission ended up with a broken nose and blood on their shirt.

So what if I got suspended for the rest of the month for it?

Don't fucking touch my stuff.

I turned my bike off and put the kickstand down. And after sliding my helmet off, I hung it off the handlebars. No one had even come toward my bike since that incident last year, so I knew my shit was safe. I slipped my bike keys into the pocket of my jeans, then straightened out my leather coat. People stared at me. Those who ate lunch at their cars so they could listen to music followed me with their eyes. Girls giggled off in the distance, causing me to wink at them from beyond my sunglasses. I loved it when the girls swooned. There was no bigger turn-on to high school girls than a senior who rode a bike. I licked my lips as I walked by a gaggle of cheerleaders, their eyes sweeping over my body with lust.

I winked at the head cheerleader. By the end of the semester, I'd have her right where I wanted her.

On my lap, riding my cock, with my bike vibrating underneath her ass cheeks.

I pushed my way through the back doors of the school, making my way to the cafeteria. My eyes scanned the room as I slid off my sunglasses in search of Roy. My best bud. My closest friend. I mean, Roy was a fucking kiss-ass. He wanted nothing more than to be exactly like me. Which was outstanding, until he wore my same fucking outfits. I hated it when he did that shit. I couldn't stand it when we turned up in the same clothes. Thank God his parents had refused to let him get tattoos that matched mine. But he was a pushover. Someone to boss around and laugh at whenever he ended up doing the stupid shit I asked him to do.

Roy was good entertainment.

I spotted him from across the room.

"There's the big guy!" Roy exclaimed.

I grinned as I started across the cafeteria, feeling teachers and vice principals alike stare me down. I walked with my shoulders rolled back and confidence in my step. They hated me because they wanted to be like me. Carefree, with enough friends and money to run circles around the town of Riverbend twelve times over. That was how Roy and I knew one another. Our parents constantly competed with their wealth and ran in many of the same circles. Hell, Roy already had his college years planned out by his father. One well-timed donation to any Ivy League school of Roy's choosing, and he could coast through the damn place on his father's dime.

I didn't want anything from my parents, though.

I didn't want any reason for them to keep meddling in my fucking life after I graduated.

Roy grinned. "I was wondering when the hell you'd show up."

I sat down beside him and he passed me a tray of food. Pizza, two rolls, two massive cookies, and a soda.

I smiled. "Oh, hell yeah. Pizza day's the best around here."

"Figured you'd need it after keg-standing through half the damn party last night."

I snickered. "How much of it did I get down?"

"Looked to be about seven beers' worth, I'd say," Roy said.

"Eh, looks more like six to me."

"I thought it was ten."

"It was a smaller keg. Pretty sure he fucking chugged half of it."

Roy chuckled. "Either way, you were sloshed. And it was incredible. That sloppy makeout session with Honkers? Priceless."

I paused. "You mean the new head cheerleader?"

He raised his eyebrows. "Who the fuck else is Honkers? You seen the tits on that girl?"

I grinned to myself before I took a bite of my pizza. So that's why she had her eyes on me coming into the school. Already trying to claim something that wasn't hers.

That'll make fucking her easier.

I nodded. "Speaking of honkers, here comes your girl."

Marina walked up, all smiles. "Hey, guys. Clint. And hi there, handsome."

Roy scoffed. "The fuck am I last for? You got the hots for my friend over here?"

She giggled. "Never. But rumor has it our new lead cheerleader does."

"You better lock that shit down, Clint."

"Trust me, I have plans."

Roy swiveled himself around and she flopped right down into his lap. I grinned as he ground up into her, making all the teachers shake their heads at him. He didn't give a shit, though. Just like me. And as I wolfed down my slice of pizza, I snuck his off his tray while he sucked face with his current piece of ass.

Who had nothing to eat but a banana for lunch.

Girl's got an eating problem.

It sure as hell didn't affect her tits, though. Because Roy was definitely a tit kinda guy.

Not my thing, but whatever. Tits were just tits. Nothing special about them. Now, an ass on the other hand? Fucking hell. It was clear these guys hadn't gone near a decent one yet in their lives. Because if they had? They wouldn't give a second fucking thought to tits on a girl.

Ever.

Marina took a small bite of her banana. "So how was your summer, Roy? I didn't see as much of you as I'd like."

Roy smiled. "You saw plenty of me last night."

"Roy."

"What? Did you not like it? Because I can certainly give it another shot if you didn't."

She giggled. "You're something else, you know that?"

I swallowed hard. "Did he fuck you well enough?"

Roy grimaced. "The fuck, dude? I don't go around asking if you fucked your girls well enough."

Marina laughed. "You know damn good and well he did."

Roy paused. "Hey, now. I don't like dirty mouths on my women. Tone the language down, or you're gonna have problems."

"Sorry, handsome."

She kissed Roy's cheek and I rolled my eyes. I didn't get the point of having a girlfriend. I mean, why the hell would I only want to fuck one girl at a time? Sounded boring to me. Marina started gabbing Roy's ear off about shit I didn't care about, which caused me to practically inhale my lunch. Anything to get away from her tinny voice and her boisterous giggle. Roy needed to bring less annoying girlfriends around if they wanted to sit with us at lunch. Because I couldn't handle that shit one bit.

Then Marina snickered. "Speaking of losers."

Roy laughed. "Holy fuck. Look who it is."

"Is that Rae?"

"Holy shit, she filled out over the summer."

"The fuck's she wearing, though?"

Marina rolled her eyes. "Why can't someone teach that poor girl some decent fashion sense?"

I cracked open my soda and swiveled around in my chair. And when my eyes fell onto her, I grinned. Rae Cleaver. Loser extraordinaire. Came from the wrong side of the tracks, and her clothes boasted of it every single fucking day. She was the pet project of the school. Well, one of them. For some reason, the county felt the need to draw redistricting lines among the suburbs in order to get some of the city scum into better schools. And the only reason I knew that was because my parents rallied hard not to let that happen. I mean, why the fuck did our education have to be ruined simply because we had money and they didn't?

Sucked to be them, but life wasn't always fair.

Even I knew that much.

Marina sighed. "She looks pathetic. Can someone go over there and tell her brown doesn't go with black like that?"

Roy slapped her ass. "Why don't you do the honors, sexy?"

Marina yelped, then playfully swatted Roy's shoulder. Yet another gesture that made my eyes roll before they went back to sucking on one another's faces. I didn't know how the hell they breathed through all that. Or how he tolerated that girl's wide-ass tongue filling up his face.

To each their own, I guess.

And as I picked up my tray to carry over to the trash can, Rae brushed through my peripheral. I turned my head, watching her a little too long as she sat off in the corner. She was sitting there, waiting for those two dinky little friends of hers. The preppy, uptight bitch and the boy who probably sucked dick with his butthole. She had a pathetic excuse for a lunch, too. Soup and a bottled water. What the fuck was up with these girls and not eating? Did they think that shit was attractive? Because if Rae thought that was her selling point, then she obviously didn't understand the appeal of decent clothes. I mean, with her dirty black shirt and her faded brown pants, she looked like something out of a horror novel. Surrounded by us, she looked completely out of her league. Tease her hair out and she'd look like actual white trash. Like someone from an actual horror film. Like that creature underneath a child's bed that only came out to play if the child's foot slipped over the edge.

Looks like I found my fun for the semester.

Then again, Rae Cleaver was always entertaining. Especially because she didn't take jokes very well.

3

RAELYNN

I sighed as I sat down at the corner table where we always sat. The first couple days of school were always stupidly long and boring. We went over the syllabus for every class the first day, then the second day was used to recap things we learned last year. They were the only two days of school where I never felt bad for zoning out. Where I never worried about falling asleep or missing something the teacher was saying.

"Only three more periods to go," I murmured.

I looked down at my lunch and sighed. It was all I could afford until I got paid this weekend by the grocery store. Soup and a bottled water. Even though I was fucking starving. I slipped the top off the soup and picked up my spoon. Thankfully, it came with a mound of crackers. I crunched them up and poured them over the top of the soup, making the liquid mess a little more solid. It didn't look appealing to the eye, but it sure as hell would feel good once it got to my stomach.

I saw something move in my peripheral and was relieved to have my friends show up.

It wasn't until I looked over, however, that I saw it wasn't them at all.

"You know, we really should have coordinated our schedules more so we could've…"

I traced my eyes up those faded jeans. Up that worn leather jacket. The figure plopped down into the seat next to me, where Allison usually sat. I wrinkled my nose as his face came into view. Clinton Clarke. The high school asshole and overall 'pump and dump' station.

The boy was a regular manwhore, and he owned every bit of it.

Barf.

Clint grinned. "We really should have coordinated our schedules. I'm gonna miss having you in English."

I wrinkled my nose. "What do you want?"

I put my spoon down, refusing to eat in front of him. I watched his eyes follow my movements, and something crossed his face. Disgust? Confusion? Neither of those would've shocked me. If Clint wasn't absolutely freaked out by the way I ran my life on a daily basis, my general presence was probably confusing to him. I mean, really? A girl that didn't want to jump his bones at the drop of a hat?

It probably confused the hell out of him.

And the thought made me giggle.

"Got something you wanna share with the class?" he asked.

I shrugged. "Nope."

"You got another outfit you can change into so you don't keep hurting my eyes?"

I grinned. "Don't like it? Don't look."

"Kinda hard not to look."

"Is that a crack at my weight? Or a crack at the fact that you secretly think I'm sexy and don't want to admit it?"

He snickered. "You wish I saw you that way."

"Trust me, you're not my type."

His eyebrows rose. "Oh? And what is your type? The monster in the closet?"

"I feel like that's a joke that probably requires some explanation. And ever since I had English with you last year, we both know you're not the best at those."

His face fell. "Fuck you."

I sighed. "What do you want, Clint?"

I heard high-pitched laughter come from across the cafeteria and rolled my eyes. Marina Lancaster's laughter was the loudest, most piercing thing I'd ever heard. It was the most recognizable laugh, too. I saw Clint's eye flinch, but then a grin appeared on his face. I didn't like that grin, either. It made me shift in my seat, uncomfortable in his presence. That was the grin of Satan himself. Who had a plan to do something to destroy me in front of a cafeteria full of people.

Where the fuck are Allison and Michael?

"I just wanted to say hi," Clint said.

I licked my lips. "Yeah. Right."

He feigned shock. "What? Do you really not believe me, Miss Cleaver?"

"Not a fucking chance."

"You really should watch that little mouth of yours. Boys don't like women with dirty words in their vocabulary."

"I'm just shocked you know the word 'vocabulary.'"

Clint's eyes boiled with anger. "Unlike some fat-ass idiots in this school, I don't have to pay attention in class to pass mine."

"No. You just need Mommy and Daddy's money to help you do that."

He leaned his forearm against the table. "How's your mom doing, Rae? I heard she had quite a time this past weekend."

I rolled my eyes. "Clever, Clinton. A mom joke. We're all impressed. Such original material."

He narrowed his eyes. "It's Clint."

I started slow-clapping, which caused Marina to laugh even harder. And while her laugh was the most annoying thing on the face of this planet, it only served to piss Clint off more. Which was a marvelous sight.

I stopped clapping. "I don't care what you want to be called. If you're going to come over here and harass me with your idiotic tactics, at least be prepared to take your own damn medication, asshole."

Clint snarled. "At least my mother's not a filthy cum-dumpster like yours is."

"Nope. She's just an absent, rich, tottie little woman who's addicted to painkillers and plastic surgery. Which would be the reason why your father left her, right? Traded her in for a newer model. Also known as your stepmother?"

"At least she wants to look decent for my father. You don't even want to look decent for yourself. What, you hate yourself that much? Or do you just hate the attention you know I'd love to pay you if you wore decent clothes?"

I scoffed. "I'd never give a second thought to the likes of you."

He grinned. "Why? Scared I'd make you a sexaholic, like your mother?"

"No. I'd only be scared of the multiple STDs you'd pass on, seeing as you're nothing but a useless manwhore."

"The last thing I am is useless, sweet cheeks. You just don't like admitting that because it means I might just be better than you. When really, this entire school is better than you."

"Why? Because most everyone in this school has more money than me? Why don't you harp on something you haven't already beaten and shot out back?"

He smiled widely. "Maybe I'll just pay your mother some attention this coming weekend, then. What's the bar she likes to frequent? Bar None's?"

I tried not to let the comment get under my skin because I understood how boys like Clint worked. I had no patience for him, and I wanted to waste no more energy on this asshole or anything he had to say. He was only trying to look tough for his friends, to come into his senior year with a bang. Like he did every fucking school year. Only this time, he'd chosen me to sink his teeth into.

And he was about to get a very rude awakening.

I sighed. "Look, Clinton. I get it. Really, I do. You come over here and you tease me and push my buttons because you want a reaction. Because your parents are never around to pay you any attention. I understand, completely. My mother pays me no attention, so we're more alike than you think."

He snarled. "I'll never be like you."

"Why? Because you have money, or because you lack class?"

"You don't know the first fucking thing about having class."

"I do know the first fucking thing about ruffling your feathers, though, Mr. Peacock."

He narrowed his eyes. "Don't you dare."

I giggled. "What, Mr. Peacock? Don't like the name?"

"It's Clint, you useless little bitch."

"Mr. Peacock it is. I knew you'd come to enjoy it."

I watched his fists ball up, and for a split second I thought he was going to slug me. I braced myself. Prepared my body to fight its way out of this corner he'd backed me into. The cafeteria became eerily silent. I felt everyone watching us. I felt my hands trembling from a lack of nourishment. I felt the room tilting as my blood sugar plummeted. I had to eat. Despite what I knew was coming if I tried, I had to get something in my stomach.

I worked up the courage to pick up my spoon and dip it into my soup. As Clint's eyes became engulfed in rage at my words, I puckered my lips and blew a stream of cool air across the steaming hot soup before clearing my throat.

"Are you done? Because if you are, my friends are here and I'd like to eat in peace."

I saw Michael and Allison standing behind him holding their trays of food, ready to sit down with me. I put the spoonful of soup between my lips, and I could've sworn I saw his eyes follow the movement. But it was a fleeting motion and I wasn't sure if I'd caught it right. He turned around, surveying my friends, and it was then I saw it.

I watched his posture relax as that wild smile came back into view.

It was as if everything played out in slow motion. Michael's food tray fell from his hands as he lunged toward Clint. Allison jerked her tray up toward her own face, tossing food all over her chest as Clint quickly got up. He threw himself forward, his hand making its way underneath the table. I heard Allison squealing as food poured over her and I heard Michael yelling at Clint to get away from me. And as Clint's hand slammed underneath the table, I watched my only food for the rest of the day jostle. My water bottle turned over, flooding my brown pants as the piping hot soup tumbled against my chest. I felt it soaking my outfit as I stood up, my jaw dropped open as the spoon fell from my hand.

Clint's chuckle dawned on my ears, causing the world to move at regular speed as I snapped my face over toward his.

I licked my lips. "You're going to regret that."

His eyes fell down my body. "Trust me, I already do. No one wants to see those clothes clinging to a body like yours. You should probably go home and change."

Allison hissed. "You're a fucking loser, Clint."

Michael stepped in front of her. "Get the heck out of here."

Clint lunged at him, causing Michael and Allison to flinch. He laughed at the two of them, then turned back to me. I looked down at the mess my clothes had become. The soup that was on my stomach instead of in it. The searing hot pain forced tears to my eyes as he snickered, then walked away. I shook my hands off. I saw teachers rushing up to him and me. I saw the principal already pulling Clint aside, which only garnered him more respect from his bullshit friends.

And it was then I tuned in to the rest of the cafeteria.

It was then I tuned into the raucous laughter as everyone stared at me.

A teacher came over to talk to me, but I gathered up my things and raced out of the room, leaving the laughing behind. I felt Allison hot on my heels as I threw myself into the bathroom. I heard the door close and lock. And as I brushed tears away from my eyes, I clenched my teeth tight.

"He's just a dick, Rae. Don't let him get to you," Allison said.

I clenched my fists. "It's not him I'm angry at. It's the rest of those dickweeds."

Allison pulled at some paper towels and ran them

underneath some water. I didn't have a chance in hell of cleaning up these clothes enough to look respectable throughout the rest of the day. Not that I'd looked respectable beforehand. But at least I'd looked better than this. She handed me a soaked paper towel before getting one for herself. Together, we wiped the soup off my shirt.

She shrugged. "I mean, at least it's a black shirt. Sit in the right lighting and people won't even know it's there."

I sighed. "Yeah, well, they'll still smell it coming from a mile away."

"Good thing tomato soup smells good?"

Somehow—like she always did—Allison got me to laugh. My grimace became a grin, and soon we were gabbing while trying to clean off our clothes. I sighed as I racked my brain, trying to figure out what the hell I was going to do for the rest of the day.

Then it dawned on me.

"We need to go to my locker," I said.

Allison paused. "Do you have a change of clothes there?"

I nodded. "I mean, they're not the best clothes. But look at what I'm already wearing. I have P.E. this year because I skipped it my freshman year."

She smiled. "Your gym clothes are in your locker?"

"Will you come with me?"

"I'll do you one better. Give me your locker number and combination. I'll go get it for you."

"You're a lifesaver, you know that?"

She winked. "I have a tendency to have good ideas every once in a while."

And as I rattled off what she needed to know, she slipped out of the bathroom. Leaving me to stand in the mirror and take a good, hard look at myself.

Something I hated doing.

Especially if I was alone.

4

CLINTON

With my sunglasses sinking down the bridge of my nose, I tossed my jacket over my shoulder. History. I hated history class. Any history class, really. But especially world history. The fuck did I care what happened on the other side of the planet over a hundred years ago? Didn't affect me now. But, for some reason, it was required of me to know.

I didn't mind being late to class, though.

The teacher pursed her lips. "How nice of you to join us, Mr. Clarke."

I grinned. "Pleasure's all mine, Mrs. Christ."

"Take a seat, and know it's your spot for the rest of the semester."

I scanned the room, taking in the pathetic crowd of losers that had already been in class for damn near twenty minutes. And as my eyes gravitated toward the front corner desk, there she sat. Rae Cleaver. In a pair of bright orange shorts, a white tank top, and some random jacket tossed over her shoulders. My smile grew positively out of control. She'd changed into her gym clothes. And oh, was it a sight to behold. I didn't think I'd ever seen Rae in anything other than pants. I mean, did the idiot not take P.E. her freshman year to get it out of the way?

Figures. Stupid as hell, just like her mother.

I snorted as I made my way toward the back row. I sure as hell wasn't taking the seat behind Rae. I mean, I didn't want to smell the musty stench of her house all damn period. I flopped myself in the back corner desk, where I pushed my sunglasses up my face. And as that stuck up, preppy little Allison leaned in toward Rae, I saw the two of them whisper to one another. Exchanging secrets about me.

I mean, it was painfully obvious they were talking about me.

Thanks for making me the center of your world, ladies.

The teacher clapped her hands. "All right. Now that our daily distraction is over, let's get back to the syllabus."

I raised my hand. "Mrs. Christ?"

"You can get a syllabus at the end of class. Take notes while you're here, and don't be late to my class again."

I heard giggles rising up from the front corner of the classroom. Allison, with her bright blond hair, and Rae. With her plain brown hair, her annoying little freckles, and her dark eyes. Like blackened pits of despair that reeked of the desolate wasteland called 'her neighborhood.'

I watched her throughout class. I watched Rae tuck her foot up under her thigh, splaying it out more against her seat. The teacher rambled on about shit I didn't care about as Rae's frizzy ponytail swung against her back. That jacket slipped from her shoulders, revealing a softly-toned strength underneath them that called for a second glance.

Or a really fucking long stare.

Maybe she's not all pig fat, after all.

"Mr. Clarke?"

I whipped my head to the front of the classroom as Mrs. Christ called my name.

"Yep?"

The teacher sighed. "Can you answer for the class why world history is so important?"

I licked my lips. "Uh, because it's important to know thine enemy?"

Some of the class giggled, but all Rae did was stare at the whiteboard, studiously ignoring me, even though I knew she felt me staring. I knew she felt my presence. I knew she wanted to look back, too. Allison kept peeking. Snickering. Shaking her head at me, like some disapproving mother. I guessed she was preparing for her future role as a stay-at-home soccer mom, ready to punish her kids with a swift blow of her angry gaze.

If her future husband was lucky enough, she'd put out a decent blowjob every once in a while.

"Mr. Clarke," the teacher said curtly.

I sighed. "What?"

She narrowed her eyes. "Tuck in the attitude and

consider this a reflection of your daily grade. What's the importance of world history?"

"I take it my answer wasn't an acceptable one."

Allison scoffed. "Obviously, idiot."

The teacher frowned. "Miss Denver, let me handle it."

I grinned. "Then handle it a little better this time around."

The class oohed, and it caused me to smile widely. I loved getting underneath my teachers' skin. Why they kept promoting me up grades, I'd never understand. Why they kept giving me grades I never earned, I'd never get. Maybe they didn't want to put up with me anymore. Or maybe my parents had given so much money to this damn place that they felt they couldn't fail me. Either way, it wasn't as if my parents were in town to do anything about it.

I mean, they had at least a day's worth of flights ahead of them before they could even think about popping me upside my head.

Mrs. Christ nodded curtly. "Is there anyone else that wants to join Mr. Clarke in a daily failing grade?"

I shrugged. "Not my fault you don't care about your enemies."

"That's enough, Clinton."

Rae giggled. "Be careful, he doesn't like that name very much."

The class laughed along with her and I shot her a death glare. I wanted to wrap my hand up in that damn ponytail of hers and tug until she cried for me to stop. Who the fuck did she think she was, embarrassing me like that?

Oh, she'd get what was coming to her soon enough.

"Miss Cleaver, one more outburst from you and you'll be heading to the principal's office."

I snickered. "I don't think she's ever been there before. Might be a fun field trip."

Allison turned around. "Your parents around to sign your permission slip, Clint?"

I glared. "I don't know. Why don't you ask your mother when she's getting home from my father's bed later?"

"That's enough!" Mrs. Christ exclaimed.

And then Rae turned around. "Put a fucking sock in it, asshole."

Part of the class was dying with laughter, and the other part stared in horror. I smiled deviously at her as our history teacher walked over to her desk, tapping on it twice. I knew that signal all too well. It was practically my mantra during my high school years. One tap means a warning, two taps means the principal's office. And when Mrs. Christ leveled her eyes with me, I held up my hands.

"I'm going. I'm going. I know how this works," I said.

The teacher sighed. "And you'd do well to try and straighten yourself out. Because unlike the rest of your teachers, I'm not afraid of your parents. I've got no issues failing you right out of my class and holding you back a year if that's what it takes to straighten you out."

Rae scoffed. "Good luck with that."

I feigned shock. "Why, Miss Cleaver. You're already in hot water. Whatever did you say that for?"

"I'll put my fist through your face if you don't stop."

"I'd love to see you try."

Mrs. Christ raised her voice. "Principal's office. Now!"

Rae bit down on the inside of her cheek in frustration and I blew her a kiss. I slid my sunglasses down on my face, watching her boil over with anger as I tossed her a playful wink. Oh, having history together was going to be fun. Especially right after our lunch break. Back-to-back moments where I got to pick and poke and prod until she finally exploded.

And maybe, I could get her in the principal's office a few more times with me.

I walked over to the classroom door and held it open for her. I bowed deeply as she walked through, and I felt her bump my forehead with her hip. Hard. The motion made the class cackle with laughter again, but it stunned me for a split second. The softness of her skin. The warmth of her hip. The strength behind it as I stumbled back a bit.

Rae definitely had some secrets underneath those clothes.

And I want to uncover all of them.

I shot up at the thought and shook my head. I let the door bang closed as I trotted to catch up with Rae.

She was striding, trying to get away from me as we made our way for the stairs. I shoved the door open, forcing it to swing back before letting go. And as I turned around, I watched Rae hold out her hands. The door slammed back into her, knocking her clear off her feet as curses left her lips.

"Fucking hell, are you serious?"

I puckered my lips. "Oh, baby. You kiss your momma with that mouth?"

She bounced down the stairs. "Get the hell away from me."

I caught up to her, slinging my arm around her shoulders. "And here I thought we were becoming best buds."

Then, out of nowhere, she gripped my wrist. She wrangled me away from her body, twisting my arm around my back. She bent my wrist up, causing me to growl out as she shoved me into the wall. And as we stood there on the platform between the staircases, she shoved her knee into the back of my thigh.

"If you ever touch me again, be prepared to lose your hand. Understood?"

I snickered. "Feisty little one, aren't you?"

She shoved me one last time, then released my wrist. I turned around, rubbing at my shoulder as she made her way quickly down the steps. Well, well, well. Rae Cleaver was just full of surprises, wasn't she?

It only spurred me on, made me want to rush to her side. I got there just in time to open the bottom stairwell door for her, then ushered her through. She glared at me, causing me to chuckle as her face scrunched up. Those insane freckles on her face always moved at the slightest twitch of her muscles, causing her eyes to ignite. She reacted more than anyone I'd ever picked on. And I enjoyed the way she attempted to defend herself.

Especially when she put her hands on me.

I like them a little spicy.

I strode after her, shouldering her as we made our way for the principal's office. She scoffed and moved away from me, but I brushed against her again, trying to see how angry I could make her before we got to our final destination. And when she shoved me with her hands, the strength behind her push damn near knocked me off my feet.

I stumbled. "Wow. Got some power behind that push."

"And don't you forget it."

I grinned. "Never thought a goody-good like you would get sent to the principal's office. That's usually my forte."

And while she ignored me, I knew she couldn't for long.

"Those shorts look good on you. Though your legs could use a fresh shave."

"Do your bras always look this terrible on you?"

"Why the hell didn't you just take P.E. our freshman year? You look ridiculous in that getup."

"Whose jacket is that anyway? Let me see."

I pulled the jacket off her shoulders and that's when it happened. She spun around, ripped it clear from my hand, and pressed her fingertips against my chest. She backed me all the way into the wall as I held up my hands, playfully grinning at her as she glared up at me. Her brown eyes went from black tar pits of desolation to glowing amber gems. Lit up by an exploding sky and pulsating with the anger of a thousand rabid dogs.

I'd never seen this side of her before. And it was intriguing.

"Listen here, you waste of space. You're pathetic. You get underneath people's skin because you can't stand your own life, so you have to make everyone else miserable just like you are. I know how you operate, because my mother's the same way. The two of you are no different, which means I'll treat you no different. So keep being a manwhore and keep putting out and keep trying to deflect from the sadness you feel inside. And while I'm reaching for the stars, enjoying my life, you'll be struggling to climb out of the hell hole you've dug for yourself. Got it?"

Her nostrils flared. Her eyes grew wider. Her cheeks flushed with a deep red tint, accenting the freckles they backdropped. I almost couldn't take my eyes off her. I almost couldn't slip away from her grasp. But when she shoved my chest one last time, it shocked me back into reality.

"Did you just call your mother a whore?" I asked.

"Ugh!"

She stormed through the front foyer of the school, and I watched as she left. Just... left. She didn't pass go. She didn't collect her two hundred dollars. And she sure as hell didn't follow me to the principal's office.

Oh, that would get her detention. The goody-good who tried her best to be as rich as her best friends would sit her ass in some lonely room for the rest of the week. Which made me salivate with excitement. I mean, there was nothing more fun than ruining someone's day.

But when I watched those same people ruin their week just to get away from me?

I mean, it was practically a fucking Christmas gift.

5

RAELYNN

I sucked air through my teeth as my pencil doodled along the edges of my notebook. After completely bailing school a couple of days ago, I'd been called into the principal's office first thing yesterday morning. I mean, I didn't even get through the damn front doors with Michael and Allison before the principal beckoned me with his crooked finger. It made me irate that I was having to pay a price by simply standing up to Clinton Clarke. It was sickening to me that I was being punished after saying what I knew the *teacher* even wanted to say to him!

And now, here I sat, doodling in my notebook and waiting for the time to pass.

The principal gave me detention after school for an hour for the rest of the week. As recompense for my outburst, for shoving him into a wall—which was wonderfully caught on camera for people to behold— and for storming out of school without a note. Great.

Fucking grand. It was me, the nose picker, the born-again meth head, and the drug dealer.

The only good thing about detention was the fact that Clint hadn't actually showed up. He wasn't there after school yesterday, nor was he there today. And while I knew he'd pay a hefty price for it, it wasn't like he cared. Kids like him never cared about that kind of shit. The only thing he cared about was his image, the pussy he wanted to slay, and how he looked riding his bike.

Which was pretty pathetic, if someone asked me.

I sighed as I kept sketching in the margins of my notes from class. I drew little characters to act out scenes from world history we'd already learned about. I drew a bobblehead of Clint with his tongue hanging out and his eyes crossed. I smiled as I made a little speech bubble. I giggled as I wrote out all sorts of jokes that made him look like the knuckle-dragging, drooling idiot he was.

Then the detention teacher shushed me.

I peeked up at him, watching as he went back to reading his book. I rolled my eyes and propped my chin against my hand, continuing to sketch little bobbleheads. I had one of Clint with his ripped leather jacket tossed over his face. I had one of him bent over, with his ass crack showing. I had one of him drunk, with his eyes rolled back and vomit sliding down his chin. I quickly felt the therapeutic effects taking hold, and before I knew it there were four entire blank pages filled to the brim with comedic, insulting doodles of this asshole.

Soon, the bobbleheads became extensive drawings. I created an entire character around this guy. A character that went around trying to pick on people before getting his ass beat. The pages of my notebook became comic book blocks. And soon, dialogue flowed from my fingertips. I licked my lips, focusing on the way my pencil markings flowed across the paper. And I thanked my stars I had mechanical pencils. I got them for free at the grocery store, along with the lead. Which meant never having to get up and sharpen my pencil.

So my creative flow was never interrupted.

Serves him right.

I drew him in all sorts of scenarios. Falling into a volcano after being shoved out of a helicopter by Allison. Being tossed to the alligators by Michael after he made an unsavory joke about her. Me, shoving him off a cliff and watching as he plummeted to the water, crying like the gigantic baby he was as his arms flailed around in the air.

An image from my dream bombarded my mind. My own arms flailing as I fell, deeper and deeper into the darkness.

Not even Clint deserves to know what that feels like.

I ripped the page out of my notebook and crumpled it up. Which earned me a hearty shush from the teacher at the front of the classroom. I decided to draw me putting Clint into the wall instead. Shoving him so hard into the wall his nose bled. Pulling at his wrist so much it dislocated. I let my imagination run away with me, concocting all sorts of scenarios where Clint got exactly what was coming to him.

Then I closed my notebook with a sigh.

I looked up at the clock and saw I still had thirty more minutes. Great. Thirty fucking minutes to sit here and contemplate my life. I pulled my ponytail out of its holder and re-did it. Put it up higher on my head to get it off the nape of my neck. I wasn't sure why the room was so hot, but for some reason I kept sweating down my back. It made my shirt stick to my skin and caused the seat underneath me to grow damp.

And the only thing it made me think about was how relentlessly Clint would be teasing me right now if he were here.

Thank fuck, he isn't.

I gazed out the window and let my mind wander. I replayed one of the many conversations Allison had already spewed over lunch about her future plans. College, and all that. It didn't shock me that, miraculously, Michael wanted to go to the same college as her. He pretended that it was because their sports management program was the best in this part of the country. Allison, of course, was clueless about what he was doing. She was clueless about how Michael felt about her, and it was almost comedic. It was so juicy and delicious that I could've written an entire comic book series on their interactions. On the way Michael drooled over her and how absolutely brain dead she was to the entire thing.

It was sweet.

In a weird sort of way.

Allison's conversations had me thinking, though. I mean, regular college would never be for me. But I also didn't want to work at the grocery store for the rest of my life. If I wanted to really chase a dream, I'd chase character design. I'd apply for schools that cared more about artistic talent than grades, and I'd submit a portfolio. Granted, it wouldn't be a professional portfolio. Just shit I'd done in my art electives. But the thought made me smile.

Being able to do graphic and character design for the rest of my life genuinely made me smile.

Or maybe I could start my own comic book line.

I sighed as I slid down into my chair. Unlike Allison and Michael, however, I'd have to work full time in order to save up the money. I didn't have the grades for scholarships, and being poor only got someone like me so far with federal grants and shit like that. I sure as hell wasn't taking out loans, either. Not without some sort of guaranteed way to pay them back. Which meant me working in the grocery store full-time—or working another job full-time—until I saved up the money for my first few semesters.

Which meant Mom couldn't drink my money away.

Which meant I'd have to move out.

Which would cost money for rent and bills and shit like that.

Which I wouldn't be able to afford on an hourly paycheck of minimum wage.

Fuck.

I didn't want to let those things stop me, though. Because every time I walked into my house, it reminded me of the kind of life I didn't want. It reminded me of the kind of legacy I didn't want to leave behind. Every time I went over to Allison's house or Michael's place, the kind of life I wanted slapped me in the face. And not just the money, either. It was the happiness. Having a loving family that gave a damn about each other. Having mouth-watering food on the table for every meal. Having every kind of drink I could have ever possibly wanted spilling out of the fridge at any given moment.

I didn't want to just survive, like my mother.

I wanted to thrive, like Allison and Michael.

Shit takes money, though.

Why the fuck did good things always take money?

"Detention dismissed."

The teacher's voice caught my ear and I gathered up my things as quickly as I could. I had to work from seven to close at the grocery store tonight. But Michael said he was treating Allison and me to soup and sandwiches. I dashed out of the room, heading straight for the front doors of the high school. I shoved myself out of them, ready to race home to find my bike so I could get to the bistro quicker.

Until a horn honking caught my ear.

"Come on, Rae! Get in!" Allison exclaimed.

She waved her arm out the window to catch my attention and I smiled. I trotted over to the SUV Michael's parents had bought him and climbed in back, happy to be with my friends. He blazed a trail away from the school, heading into town as Allison craned her neck to look back at me.

"So, how's the time you're doing? What's it like? Does it remind you of prison?"

I rolled my eyes. "It's not jail time. It's just detention."

Michael snickered. "And we've never had detention. You have to fill us in on everything that's happening. What's it like? Does it smell? How's Clint been?"

I sighed. "You know damn good and well Clint Clarke doesn't show up to things like detention."

Allison paused. "Wait, he's not showing up?"

Michael chuckled. "Doesn't shock me one bit. What do you think they'll do to him if he doesn't go?"

Allison scoffed. "The nerve of that jerk. Sticking you in detention by ruffling your feathers, then skipping out on the punishment he deserves. Selfish little—"

I grinned. "Careful, now. You might ruin that pristine outfit of yours."

Michael sighed. "I mean, he'll probably get expelled. Which would give us all a nice break."

Allison fell back into her seat. "Well, I for one hope it happens. Everyone's tired of that knucklehead."

I smiled. "Allison, your insults give me life. You know that?"

Michael grumbled, "I can't stand that guy. Someone needs to beat some sense into him."

Allison gasped. "Michael. I've never known you to be a violent person."

I snickered. "He's not, until he is. I've seen him come close to punching someone in the face.

Remember that guy that kept teasing you sophomore year?"

Allison thought about it. "Oh, my gosh. I completely forgot about that. The foreign exchange student from Germany that we had. Timmy?"

Michael frowned. "Tommy."

Allison patted his shoulder. "That's right. Tommy. He was teasing me about my braces, and you stepped in to shut him down. What was it you said to him?"

I shook my head. "I can't believe you don't remember this. He said—"

"—If you ever decide to look her way again with anything but admiration in your eyes, be prepared to lose them," Michael supplied.

Allison giggled. "Aww, my hero. We can always count on you, can't we?"

The pride in Michael's face warmed my heart.

We rode in silence until he pulled the vehicle into the parking lot of the bistro. I looked across the road and sighed, already dreading my four or so hours of work. But it was necessary if I wanted to eat lunch. Or put away any money for my future. Or generally not piss my mother off with not having any money she could mooch off me.

Michael craned his head back. "You ready to go eat? It's on me."

I smiled. "I appreciate it, but you know I can—"

Allison cleared her throat. "Let the man pay, Rae. Sometimes, paying makes them feel powerful. Right?"

Michael smiled brightly. "Right."

I rolled my eyes and giggled as I got out of the car.

The three of us walked into the sandwich shop and I ordered as much food as I could without seeming self-ish. A full-size sandwich, since Michael got himself one. A bowl of soup, since Allison got herself one. A dessert, since all of us wanted one, and a large drink. Which I could refill and take with me to work.

"I'm proud of you, you know."

I whipped my head around, staring up into Michael's face.

"What was that?" I asked.

He grinned down at me. "For standing up to Clint. I'm proud of you. People don't do that with him, and they should. Someone needs to teach his arrogant ass a lesson one of these days. Maybe they'll be inspired by how you stand up to him and actually do it."

Allison slipped between the two of us. "Oh, yeah? And who do you think is going to put the school bully in his place?"

He shrugged. "Anyone, really."

I sighed. "He's not worth it, guys. Trust me. Bullies like him feed on the rise he gets out of people. For all we know, he'll go home and orgasm to it later."

Allison gasped. "Rae!"

Michael threw his head back, laughing. "She's got a point."

And as our food got handed to us, I debated whether or not to save half of my sandwich. After all, it would make a very good breakfast.

If Mom didn't steal it from the refrigerator first.

6

CLINTON

I smashed the buttons. "Come on, you can't go faster than that? He's getting away!"

Roy tilted to the side. "You're the one who decided to modify your car at the last second. I would've been fine had you not pulled some shady shit."

"Shady shit! It's not shady when I'm making last minute tweaks to my car. The fuck's wrong with you?"

"Well, how about we agree to disagree and smoke the asswipes?"

Our cars raced around the track on the projection screen television. I'd decided to have Roy over instead of going to detention. Playing Forza 4 sounded a hell of a lot better than sitting in some smelly, nasty, stinky room with Rae fucking Cleaver. And we had a good race going, too. I shot up from my chair, walking closer to the projector screen as we came upon our competition.

I pointed. "Go off the track. See that ditch? Fly over it and meet me on the other side."

Roy snickered. "The fuck? Are you trying to get me thrown—"

"Just do it, dickweed! I'm trying not to cost us our rank in this damn game!"

I kept pressing buttons and fiddling with the modifications I'd made to my car. This damn thing was my pride and joy. I'd been grinding until the early hours of the morning over the summer, winning races and getting enough in-game cash to buy what I wanted to for it. Its speed was unmatched. The engine horsepower was out of this world. The car fucking screamed around the track, smoking these newbies like it was a fish fry.

Then the front door slammed out.

"What the—?"

My eyes peeled away from the screen, and I watched in shock as my father walked through the front doors. He was followed by my stepmother, who looked like her head was about to explode with fury. The horrific sound of my car crashing into a tree caused Roy to groan.

Roy stood up quickly. "Mr. Clarke. Mrs. Clarke. How was the safari?"

My father leveled his eyes with me. "Roy. Go home."

"Right away, sir. See you tomorrow, Clint."

Pussy.

I tossed my controller onto the couch as the race came to a close. We almost had it. We almost had those idiots! And now our ranking would fall. We wouldn't have the money we needed to fix our cars. And I'd have to deal with my parents ranting and screaming for a while so they could make themselves feel like decent people.

It wasn't until Roy closed the front door behind him that my father spoke.

"What's this I hear about you getting into it with your teacher and a female student on Monday?"

My stepmother came and stood beside my father, trying to present some sort of bullshit united front, even though the two of us never talked. I wanted nothing to do with her—or my real mother, for that matter. I was glad that bitch came in and ruined my father's marriage. I was glad to be rid of my drug-addicted mother who wanted to do nothing more than spend my father's money until we were out on the fucking street.

But that didn't mean I had to be all buddy-buddy with his new, hot piece of ass.

I sighed. "They pissed me off. The hell was I supposed to do?"

Dad narrowed his eyes. "First of all, you watch that language in this house. And second of all, you man up. A man never allows his emotions to rage out of control like that. You need to learn how to keep it on a leash."

"Like you do Cecilia over there?"

"What did you say?"

Her eyes stayed pinned on me, but she didn't move. She didn't say a word, and she sure as hell didn't come to my defense. Figures, since she'd always been far removed from the situation. Just another plastic-surgery woman who simply knew how to take her place next to Dad. As my father came into the living room, I prepared myself to buck against it. It wouldn't be the first time I'd physically fought him. It would just be the first time he had the balls to start a fist fight like that in front of someone.

Dad gripped my leather jacket. "You'd do well to remember your manners and mind them in the presence of adults."

I grinned. "Do adults manhandle their children in their own home?"

"Take it easy, Howard. You're toeing a line."

My eyebrows rose at hearing Cecilia's voice. But it did nothing to harness my father's rage. His anger. It did nothing but remind me exactly where I got my anger issues from. Exactly why I'd always felt like a burden. Exactly why I'd always hated my fucking father, no matter what he felt he'd done for me.

Dad shoved me against a wall. "How many times am I going to have to bail your pathetic ass out of these situations?"

I shrugged. "I don't know. How much money you got on you nowadays?"

He growled. "I'm sick and tired of that school calling us, Clinton. Don't you know we have better things to do than worry about our fully-grown son who seems incapable of doing anything right? How the fuck do you expect to have any future?"

"Howard."

Hearing Cecilia's voice was so foreign to me. And

yet, it was nice. Actually having someone step up to my defense.

Sort of.

I licked my lips. "Fully grown because I just turned eighteen? Or fully grown because you started your first business at eighteen?"

Dad scoffed. "You're a fucking joke."

Cecilia cleared her throat. "Howard. That's enough."

I smiled at my father, wondering if he'd actually listen to the tits with a voice. My father didn't give a shit about anything but himself. And his new hot wife. He didn't give a damn when my mother first got addicted to painkillers because of her cesarean with me. He didn't give a shit when she slipped into post-partum depression and threw herself off the roof. He certainly didn't give a shit when she stopped taking care of the house and started spending all his money. Leaving me home alone to stew in my own waste and starve.

Oh, no. He only gave a shit when he couldn't keep up with the credit cards she kept taking out in his name. He only gave a shit when it impacted his finances. Not me, or my well-being. So it didn't shock me one bit when I felt his hand tighten against my leather jacket instead of releasing it.

Because my father never gave a shit about me for a fucking day in his pathetic life.

"You get your shit together, you hear me? Or you're out on your ass. Plain and simple."

I scoffed. "You gonna throw me out while you're in

Bora Bora? Or before you two jet off to Australia for Christmas?"

Dad chuckled. "You've got balls, I'll give you that."

"Howard. Cut it out!"

"Shut up, Cecilia!"

I chuckled. "Wow. You really know how to treat the ladies."

Dad shoved my chest. "You've got one last chance to keep your ass out of trouble until I can stick you somewhere after you graduate. One chance, you hear me?"

I glared at him. "Or what?"

Dad smiled. "Or you're really not going to like our next conversation."

I watched my stepmother stride over with her thin legs and her high heels. She grabbed my father's arm, yanking it away from my leather coat. I dusted off his touch as she forcefully pulled him away from me, giving me some space to slip away from the wall. I wasn't staying here another fucking second. Not with that asshole in the house. I walked into the kitchen and grabbed a beer from the fridge, sticking it in the inside pocket of my jacket.

"And don't you dare think about going anywhere tonight!" Dad roared.

I shrugged. "Too late."

I slipped into the garage and stormed for my bike. I jammed my fist into the garage door button on the wall, watching it roll up. I threw my leg over my motorcycle as Dad appeared in the doorway. I cranked the engine up too quickly to hear whatever the hell it was he was screaming at me.

"What was that? I can't hear you!"

I pointed to my ears, watching as my father's face reddened with frustration. Cecilia appeared behind him, rubbing his back and trying to calm him down. Fucking hell, that woman was too good for him. They were all too good for him, including my mother. I knew, deep down, my father was the reason why my mother got ruined. Putting up with his bullshit and always bending to his ways and dealing with his anger all the fucking time. It made me sick. And soon enough, he'd destroy Cecilia, too. Cast her out into the backyard like a piece of used furniture to burn before finding another trophy wife to stand at his side.

Another woman to burn with the rest of them.

I backed my bike out of the garage and swung it around. I heard my father rushing after me, but I took off down the driveway. I looked in my rearview mirror, watching him run until he had to bend over to catch his breath. That's what he got, with all the traveling and car riding and not enough time spent in the gym.

"Fat ass," I murmured.

I drove into town, setting my sights on the park. It was the one place where I could always go, get cheap food, and sit. Possibly write. I always kept my notebooks and pens in the back compartment of my bike, just in case inspiration hit me.

I also kept it hidden as much as I could. I never wrote when people were around. Because holy fuck, if my friends knew I wrote poetry and short stories as a hobby? My reputation would be shot. I'd be just like every other asshole I gave swirlies to on a regular basis.

And the idea of Roy stepping into my position practically made me cackle.

Because he'd only ever be half the man I was.

7

RAELYNN

I shoved some things into a backpack on Friday morning, readying myself for this fun little weekend. I was ready to get out of here. Especially since I wasn't working. Ready to get through the last hour of detention so I could be on my way to my best friend's house for another wonderful sleepover. But, for once, I came downstairs to my mother already down there. I walked into the living room, skirting their makeout session while I waited in the wings. The lip-smacking made my stomach turn, and I breathed a sigh of relief when D.J. finally left. The smell of coffee filled the foyer as I tried to erase those sights and sounds from my mind, silently feeling sorry for the asshole she was cheating on.

Then again, there was a big chance he knew it. Why he continued to pay some of her bills and keep her around if she was, I'd never understand.

Then again, I also didn't want to understand.

With my clothes and my phone charger in a bag, I made my way into the kitchen. I heard D.J. race out of our driveway, peeling out like he thought he was hot shit. I knew announcing to my mother I was going away for the weekend could go one of two ways. She'd either wave me out the door while she nursed her hangover with another beer, or she'd chew me out until I got fed up enough to slip out the door myself.

But after an entire week of detention, I didn't care if the woman tried strapping me down to keep me home. I was fucking going to this sleepover.

I peeked around the corner. "I'm going to spend the weekend at Allison's."

Mom sighed. "That's fine, honey. You'll be home Sunday?"

"Yep."

"All right. Well, maybe next week you and I can have an old-fashioned girls' night? Like how we used to?"

I studied my mother and how rough she looked. The hickeys on her neck. Her knotted, disheveled hair. The way her shoulders slouched as she sat at the kitchen table, pouring beer into her fucking coffee. I came around the corner and went to sit beside her. Something was off. Something didn't feel right. And while I wanted to turn down the invite to her version of a girls' night, I also didn't want to leave her like this.

"Mom?"

She slowly looked over at me and I saw how tired she looked. The bags underneath her eyes. The pallor of her skin. Her trembling hand brought her mug of coffee to her lips, where she chugged a little too hard and a little too long. I placed my hand on her shoulder and she flinched, which told me everything I needed to know.

And when she finally faced me, I saw the blackened expanse of her right eye.

I sighed. "Oh, Mom."

She patted my hand. "Yeah, an old-fashioned girls' night soon. Okay?"

"Promise you won't invite D.J.?"

And even though she nodded, I knew she was lying. It didn't matter how many times her boyfriend smacked her around. Or made her cry. Or made her feel worthless. Whenever she wanted to spend time with me, he inevitably showed up. She always broke down and called him back. Begged for him to come over so she could 'make things right.'

Which was the reason I always kept earplugs on my bedside table.

I stood up, kissing her cheek as a shudder left her lips. She was holding back tears, and it broke my heart. Because no matter what kind of shit my mother got herself into, she was still my mother. And she'd been through hell all her life. Starting with her own parents, who'd routinely slapped her around. Followed by my father, who proposed when they got pregnant with me, only to jump ship when I was only three years old. The string of boyfriends she'd had over the years were varying degrees of the same. A cokehead that got her addicted before she finally let him go. A rehab facility coordinator who ended up being the reason she got clean. And who ended up being married. A string of one-night stands that introduced me to so many sexual things a teenager should never have been exposed to.

And now? D.J.

The man who paid some of our bills in exchange for my mother's soul.

"Please take care of yourself," I whispered against her ear.

She nodded. "You know I always do. No matter what, I'll always do my best to take care of you."

"You're important too, Mom. Always remember that."

"I miss you, you know."

"Well, then maybe we'll have that girls' night soon."

Mom smiled softly. "You know, D.J.'s not really that bad."

I sighed. "I'm sure he isn't, Mom."

"And he takes care of us. He's the reason why we only have to choose one bill to ignore a month. Not the multiple ones, like we used to do."

I nodded. "I know, Mom. I know. And I miss you, too. But I have to go. I'm going to be late for school."

I rubbed her back as I tried to process everything. I never could tell my mother how much I missed her without getting angry with her. And I felt myself growing very upset very quickly. Without trying to hold her accountable for her actions throughout the years. While the rational part of me knew she kept trying her hardest, the other part of me wondered why the fuck she always had to try it with guys. Why not get a job on her own? It wasn't like I couldn't fend for myself. Why not take out some loans? Get a technical degree? Make something of herself instead of hopping from man to man, hoping he'd swoop in and free us from this bondage?

I mean, I was familiar with the books my mother read. Books that were passed down to her through trash cans and bags dropped all around our street. Our neighborhood was practically a rich person's dump, and I'd caught my mother many times opening up trash bags to dig around and see what was inside.

Mom cleared her throat. "You need any lunch money, beautiful?"

I shook my head. "Nope. I've got my own."

"Good girl. Make sure to always do that. Provide for yourself."

I bit my tongue on what I wanted to say. Because no matter what I wanted to do, I'd never kick a person when they were down.

Unlike D.J.

Even though my heart didn't want to, my gut told me to leave. So I did. I left my mother to chug back her beer-laced coffee and I headed straight for school. With every step I took, I grew infuriated with D.J. With every step I took, comics unfolded in my mind. Graphic novels with curt colors, dripping with blood from D.J.'s veins. I shook with fury as I walked out of the neighborhood, trying to focus on where I was going.

Why the hell did men like D.J. and Clint have to exist in this world?

That was exactly who my mother's boyfriend reminded me of, too. Clinton fucking Clarke. The two of them were cocky. Arrogant. Angry. Entitled. Rude.

Flat-out mean.

As the mouth of my neighborhood dumped me onto the curb, I made my way for Allison and Michael. They flagged me down with their arms, and I gave them both a thumbs-up, letting them know I was cleared to come over this weekend. The two of them high-fived as I picked up the pace, letting my dark, dank neighborhood fall into the background as the green grass and rolling white picket fences of our quaint area in Riverbend fill my view.

Then something whooshed by me.

The roaring of the motorcycle engine caught me off-guard, and I flinched. I knew it was Clint, and my only hope was that he hadn't seen me. I picked up the pace, jogging down the sidewalk to try and get to Allison and Michael. But when I saw his brake lights flash, I grumbled to myself.

Especially when it pulled over to the curb. Blocking my path to my friends.

Great. Just great.

He pulled off his helmet. "Well, well, well. Good morning, detention rat."

I ignored him and kept walking, watching as Michael bolted for me. Allison trailed behind him, trying to get to me before Clint could do any sort of damage to my morning.

Then I heard him whistle. "Nice ass, Cleaver."

Michael linked his arm with mine. "Put a sock in it, Clinton."

Allison snickered. "Yeah. Go terrorize someone your own size."

Clint chuckled. "Trust me, that ass is big enough for me."

Allison scoffed. "Disgusting pig."

"I like watching you walk away, Cleaver! You should wear skinny jeans more often!"

I went to swirl around, but Michael tightened his grip on me. Allison's hand fell to the small of my back as the two of them escorted me across the street. I wanted to smack that fucking grin right off Clint's face. I wanted to ball-stomp him into the curb until he was crying out for his drug-addled mommy. Yes, Clint was D.J. The younger, more pompous version. What I wouldn't give to put the two of them in a room and give Clint the rude awakening that was coming to him.

Maybe he'd turn into a decent human being if he knew being a womanizing, abusive asshole was his future.

We got across the road and I heard Clint rev the engine of his bike. I spun around, ripping away from my two best friends as I glared hotly at him. He puckered his lips, blowing me a kiss before he wiggled his tongue around in the air. And as he slid his helmet back onto his head, I stuck my middle finger up. Just for him. For his eyes only to take in.

And as he rushed by us on his bike, I heard him laughing at me.

"Come on, let's get you inside," Allison said softly.

The burning sensation on the backs of my eyes made me feel weak, frustrated, incompetent. I was tired of that asshole, and I didn't know why he wouldn't stop torturing me. I'd watched my mother bend to these men her entire life. And I knew if I simply stood up to them as they came into my life, I'd be fine. They'd go away. They'd find some other woman to torture and I'd be free of them.

But I was standing up to Clint. And he kept coming back. If I ignored Clint, he'd only come at me harder. Why couldn't he leave me alone? Why couldn't he go pick on someone else?

I didn't understand it anymore.

"So what color do you want your toes painted tonight?" Michael asked.

I cleared my throat. "Red sounds nice."

Allison opened the doors. "Oh, spicy. I like it. Matches your personality."

Michael smiled. "You know, you could rock a head full of red hair, too. I mean, with those freckles and this beautiful skin you've got."

Allison gasped. "That's it! We should dye your hair, too!"

I shook my head. "Oh, no."

She pouted. "Oh, come on. It'll be fun. Your hair can match your toes, and you can take some of my shirts that probably match, too."

I grinned. "You mean you have shirts that aren't pastel colors?"

Allison's face fell. "Ha. Ha. Ha. Jerk."

Michael chuckled. "Maybe just some under-the-hair highlights, then? You know, so when you wear it down, you can't see them. But when you wear your ponytails, you can?"

I furrowed my brow. "How do you know so much about all this shit?"

He groaned. "Mom."

Allison giggled. "Well, if you don't want to you don't have to. But you'd look hot with them."

I sighed. "Why don't we dye your hair, then?"

Allison's eyes widened. "And deal with the wrath of my mother? Not a chance. You know how she feels about hair dye. Ever since she had that reaction a few years back, she's been on that all-natural healthy-everything kick. If she came back to me with dyed hair, she'd probably disown me."

Michael scoffed. "I hate to admit I even know this, but there are all-natural hair dyes out there."

I threw my head back, laughing. "Your mom is fantastic, you know that?"

He smiled. "I was adopted by some good ones, yes."

Allison took my hand. "So you'll think about it?"

And as I sighed, I ended up nodding my head.

"Okay. I'll think about it."

8

CLINTON

I swung my bike into the parking stall in front of the school. It was open, for once, and I wanted to make sure I took full advantage of it. All the best girls in this high school hung out in front. And it was those same girls that took to the back parking lot during lunch. Oh, the mischief they got into. It practically made me salivate. I felt their eyes on me as I revved my engine. I turned it off and put the kickstand down. I felt them scanning my long legs and the breadth of my shoulders as I kicked my leg over my bike. I slipped my helmet off, then slipped my sunglasses on quickly. They all watched the powerful man on campus with googly eyes, hoping to get a slice of me.

And I enjoyed putting on a show for them.

"Ladies," I said, grinning.

The head cheerleader walked up. "Hi there, Clint."

I licked my lips. "Hello there, beautiful."

"Nice ride you've got. Been meaning to let you know. It's much better than the one you had last year."

"That'll teach my father to sell it out from underneath me. Bought and paid for with my own money, too."

She smiled. "Your own money, huh? So, uh, when you taking me out, then? With that money of yours?"

I grinned. "Whenever you let me take a peek underneath that skirt of yours. You know you can't do that to my heart, beautiful. High-kicking those legs at practice without letting me get a close-up look."

"Oh, you're bad, Clint."

I winked from beyond my sunglasses. "And you love it, gorgeous."

She giggled as she turned on her heels in her pristine white tennis shoes. Her barely-there hips sauntered back over to her friends, where I knew she'd boast about talking to the bad boy on campus. They always did. The girls around here thought cozying up to me would boost their status in this school. That they could somehow unravel the mysterious bad boy that didn't give a fuck what anyone else thought.

And I most certainly used that to my advantage.

"I see you're already locking things down with tits over there."

I chuckled as Roy walked up to me, his arm slung around Marina's shoulders. She swayed those thin hips of hers in the skirt she wore, chewing on her bubblegum like her fucking life depended on it. I still didn't know what he saw in those women. Girls with bony arms, gangly legs, and horse faces. But he didn't understand why I enjoyed my women with a little more meat on their bones. It evened out.

Gave us more to gawk at without getting jealous, too.

I shrugged. "She's nice enough."

Roy quirked an eyebrow. "Nice enough? A few days ago, you were ready to get it on with her. You feelin' okay?"

I snickered. "You might want to envision me getting it on with her, but I haven't even started that rat race."

Marina giggled. "And here I thought leather jacket over here was the kinky one of the group."

Roy rolled his eyes. "What the fuck have we talked about with that mouth of yours?"

"Sorry, Roy."

"You're so nasty. All the time. That talk is meant for only me, when we're alone. Got it?"

I chuckled as Roy gripped Marina's chin. But, once they started sucking face again, I turned away. I didn't want to watch that shit. Gross as fuck. The way they swapped that chewing gum around like it was a shared snack made my stomach turn. Roy was a nasty one, though. He enjoyed things with women I'd never indulge in a million years. Like passing them around and jerking off on their faces with other men surrounding her, too.

I mean, come on. I had some fucking standards.

And I sure as hell wasn't jerking off in front of a crowd of dudes.

A small crowd gathered and I pushed off my bike. I

hung my helmet off the handlebars of my bike, like I did every morning. We all started shooting the shit while those of us taken within the group practically dry-humped one another in front of the school. Roy pinned Marina to the front wall, kissing down her neck while she made sounds that would haunt me in my damn nightmares.

Then the main show arrived.

I saw Rae walking up with Michael and Allison. And I knew they were giving her a pep talk. She looked on the verge of tears, and it was priceless. Oh, if I made Rae cry this semester, it would be the icing on the cake. She prided herself in being tough. Strong. Different than the rest of us. But she wouldn't be so different if the big, bad Clint made her cry.

I made everyone cry.

Even my own damn mother.

"I hate to see her go, boys," I said, chuckling.

Rae scoffed. "Do you ever know when to stop?"

Michael piped up. "Don't pay him any mind, Rae. Keep walking."

And as her friend Allison started rubbing her back, I found my 'in.'

"Hey, Allison," I called out.

She shook her head. "Whatever it is, I don't care about it. Come on, Rae. Let's get to homeroom."

The crowd parted for me. "Have you and Michael fucked yet? Or is the jury still out on whether or not he'd rather partner up with me?"

The three of them stopped and that brightly-colored twat whipped around. Allison clung to Rae as he stormed me, taking long strides with those chicken legs of his. I shot up, rolling my shoulders back as he approached me. There wasn't a damn kid in this school that towered over me. Not when I stood at over six fucking feet tall. Michael craned his neck back to keep my eyes in view. His nostrils flared with anger as a grin spread like wildfire across my face.

"Oh look," I said, "I poked the bear."

Michael's eye twitched. "You leave them out of this. You wanna pick on me? That's fine. But, only a pussy little prick like you picks on girls."

I circled around him. "Oh, yeah? Trying to be the big, tough guy so we don't figure out you suck dicks with your butthole?"

He grimaced. "Could you be any more crass? I mean, really. Come on."

I shrugged. "All I'm saying is own up to who you are and what you like. If dudes are your thing, why hide it? Only embarrasses you more."

I blew against his ear, causing my friends to laugh when he jumped. Michael's eyes bubbled with rage and I heard Rae calling out for me. Telling me to stop. Her friend held her back, though. Kept her from storming over. And as Michael stood toe-to-toe with me, I smiled.

"Let me guess. Her pussy's not tight enough for you."

Michael growled. "That's it."

The beast snapped, and I saw his fist coming

around from the corner of my vision. I heard Rae and Allison shriek, calling out for him as I wrapped my hand around his wrist. I brought my knee into his stomach, buckling him as he gasped for air. And as the girls came charging for me, my friends closed the circle. They pumped their fists in the air. They pushed Rae and Allison away as I watched Michael gasp on his hands and knees.

"I mean, really. If you're going to be a man's man, at least man up a little bit. You of all people should know gay dudes don't like pussies."

He lunged off the concrete and wrapped his arms around me. He barreled through the crowd behind me, knocking me clear over my bike. I heard him cursing. I heard him shouting. I heard the pitter patter of footsteps as my bike went tumbling to the ground. The second I heard metal and paint scraping against the concrete, my vision dripped red. I lost all sense of time and space, of what I was doing.

Because no one fucked with my bike.

"You're dead meat," I grunted.

I brought my elbow down into Michael's back and he pulled away from me. He kicked my shins, then reached down and grabbed my ankles. He flipped me clear over my fucking bike before stepping over it as a crowd of kids gathered. They chanted, "Fight! Fight! Fight!" And as I scrambled to my feet, I saw him coming for me again.

Only this time, I was ready.

I hit him with a right hook that sent him stumbling back. I heard the girls crying out, but it was no use.

Their voices faded into the background. Michael's face slowly morphed into my father's. I hit him with a blow to his gut, taking him back down again. And as my knee came up to connect with his chin, I felt anger swelling my veins, blood rushing through my ears. I heard nothing but the sound of my own racing heart as steam came barreling out of my ears.

I had some anger to dispel. And Michael's face always irritated the fuck out of me.

Time to make a statement.

I reached down and grabbed Michael's shirt. I pulled him off the ground, holding him in midair before I dropped him to his feet. I threw a few punches he dodged while he tried to get his bearings. Then he came for me again. He ran straight into my stomach, taking me to the fucking ground again. But as I wrapped my legs around him, I rolled him over. I forced him to look up at the sky before my face came into view. I smiled broadly down at him as I saw my father, pinned underneath my legs.

"You're gonna regret that move, asshole," I glowered.

His arms came up in defense of his face as blow after blow landed on his arms. I heard sirens wailing off in the distance and I knew I had to wrap it up. But not before I broke this fucker's nose. I felt him bucking underneath me. I felt him trying to get away. And just as I went to pry his arms away from his face like the coward he was, I felt someone tugging at my leather jacket.

"Get. The fuck. Off him!"

Rae's voice took me back. I felt her hands wrapping into my leather jacket, pulling me away from her friend. And for a second, it stunned me. Her knuckles dragged across the nape of my neck, shooting electricity down my spine. I heard teachers calling out in the distance, rushing toward us as she pried me off her friend.

Then she tossed me to the side. Like I was a fucking rag doll.

I wiped at my mouth as Michael scrambled off the ground. His eyes bulged with anger as he tried coming at me again. Rae placed her hands against his chest, and for some reason I didn't like that. I didn't like her touching him like that. Fuck, I didn't like her touching me like that.

I spat. "Get the hell out of my way."

Rae whipped around. "Not a chance in hell, you womanizing, abusive dickwad."

Everyone cheered as the three of them scampered off. But her words cut deep. I watched them rush off as someone tugged at my arm, trying to get me inside the school. Girls kept looking on, smiling and cheering my victory. I shook myself away from whoever the hell had a grip on my elbow before I scurried into school. The last fucking thing I needed to be caught doing after seeing my father yesterday was fighting. Because I knew damn good and well that selfish asshole would toss me out on my ass the second he got the chance. The second he found any reason to deem me a threat to his new wife, or to him, or to that bullshit prison I called home.

But I couldn't shake the way Rae handled herself. The way she handled me. It was reminiscent of her putting me into that damn stairwell wall.

And for a split second, I wondered where she learned how to handle herself like that.

9

RAELYNN

The second I heard Clint's words, I saw Michael snap. I saw it in his eyes, and his fist flew like wildfire. I didn't even know Michael knew how to throw a punch like that. But when I saw Clint wrap his hand around Michael's wrist, I knew he was in trouble.

I shrieked. "Michael, no!"

Allison kept screaming as the fight continued. Clint's fucking goonies closed in the fight, and I struggled to get through the crowd. I heard them tussling around, punches being landed and grunts filling the air. Someone gasped and I heard something drop to the ground. And as Roy physically shoved me back, I jammed the heel of my hand directly into his ballsack.

Marina gawked. "What the fuck?"

I shook my hand out as I stepped around Roy. He could die, as far as I was concerned. I started charging Clint, with Allison hot on my heels before the sea of people closed again. I leapt into the air, feeling them catch me and hold me back. And that was when I realized Michael was the one gasping for air.

Shit. Shit shit shit shit shit.

"I mean, really. If you're going to be a man's man, at least man up a little bit. You of all people should know gay dudes don't like pussies."

Clint's words fired me up like nothing I'd ever experienced before. And I found a renewed sense of vigor to tear through that damn crowd. I saw Michael practically toss him over his bike and I heard Allison cheering him on from behind me. I scrapped with a few people in front of me, trying to get them out of my way. And the more people I tossed to the side, the more adrenaline I felt rushing through my system. My vision bounced between Clint and Michael and D.J. and my mother. It was hard to focus. Hard to see straight. Hard to keep things in line as faces morphed and changed right before my eyes.

Then Allison's voice pierced my hazy thoughts.

"No! Stop it! You're going to kill him!"

I looked up, only to see Clint hoisting Michael in the air. I gawked at the scene as kids cheered and clapped, chanting for Clint to slam him into the ground. Michael had his hands around Clint's forearm, and fear gripped my chest. And the second Michael went plummeting to the ground, I knew I had to get to him.

Otherwise, we'd be in a hospital later.

Everything happened so quickly after that. First, Michael was in the air. Then he was punching Clint. Then Clint was somehow on top of him on the ground. I took one last charge through the crowd, physically shoving girls and guys alike to the concrete. Sirens wailed in the distance as teachers rushed over to see what was going on. The last thing Michael needed was to get caught fighting, and the last thing any of us needed was to be seen as cohorts in the matter.

"Get. The fuck. Off him!"

My hands came down on to Clint's leather jacket and I tugged. I wrapped my hands up in the worn material and felt something akin to a god take over my body. I tugged at him once. Twice. Three times, before I felt his body move. I tightened my grip into his jacket so tightly I felt my knuckles dragging across his skin. I gnashed my teeth together as Allison rushed around us. I growled out like a wild animal as I felt his body budge. I pried him off Michael, watching as Allison helped the poor boy to his feet.

Then I tossed Clint to the side.

Like some discarded paper plate of useless food.

I rushed to Michael, who was foaming at the mouth with anger. His eyes bulged and his nose was bleeding, but overall, he looked good for going a few rounds with Clint Clarke. Which always a bad idea, given how massive Clint was in the first place. I placed my hands against his chest while Allison tugged at his wrist, trying to pull him away from the fight as I tapped my hands against him.

"Come on. Let's get out of here. We need to get you cleaned up."

Clint growled, "Get the hell out of my way."

And when I whipped around, I leveled my eyes directly with his.

"Not a chance in hell, you womanizing, abusive dickwad."

Allison grunted. "Come. On. Michael. It's done. Enough is enough. Walk away. Just walk away from him."

I turned around and kept pushing at his chest, trying to get him away from all this chaos. Fighting Clint Clarke was a bad fucking idea because the boy was practically made for scrapping. Built for school-yard fights and drawing blood from his enemies. The kids around us booed as Allison and I physically dragged Michael away from that fucking fight. Clint kept yelling after us, but I wasn't paying attention to what he was saying. Michael kept hollering back, too. And the only thing I did was reach up and place my hand over his mouth.

"Stop it. He's not worth the energy, I promise you that," I said.

Some of Clint's friends followed us, trying to block us in again. But Allison kept stepping on their toes. She jammed her heel into their feet, causing them to buckle and cry out. I was very proud of her. It made me smile as she backed up, clearing a pathway for us to get away from the chaos. The teachers were on their way, and I had a sneaking suspicion that siren call off in the distance was for us. And if Michael got caught fighting in any way, that blemish on his record might override his good grades and keep him from getting into college.

Michael grumbled, "I'm gonna bury that fucker."

Allison sighed. "You're making me break a sweat. Can't you tuck it in?"

I giggled. "You're going to be in deep shit if you're caught. Why don't we get this sleepover started early?"

With our backpacks practically hanging off our bodies, we dashed across the front lawn of the school-yard. Michael had Allison's hand tightly in his, and I brought up the rear. Just in case anyone else tried coming after us. The last thing we needed was to deal with the fallout from this bullshit drama. Because as far as I was concerned? Clint could take the brunt of it all. By himself. Since he was the asshole that started it in the first place.

But I had to work not to give him the satisfaction of looking back.

I don't know why I wanted to look back and check on him, but I fought that urge. He didn't deserve someone making sure he was all right like that. We rushed across the street just before the schoolyard bell tolled, signaling the beginning of the day.

The day we'd all skip in order to get this party started.

We didn't stop running until we got to Allison's house. She pulled out her keys, and Michael's hand instinctively fell to the small of her back. I smiled at their connection. At how this had somehow bonded them. And since Allison wasn't brushing him off, I figured that was as good a sign as any.

That Allison returned Michael's affections.

We all walked inside and I stood there, marveling

at the grandeur of Allison's home. It never ceased to amaze me. I slowly closed the front door behind me, taking in the beautiful staircase. The wooden banisters that glistened in the sunlight streaming through the multiple windows of the home. The hardwood floors that matched those banisters, covered intricately with plush rugs that sat underneath cushioned, comfy furniture. No matter how many times I went over to Allison's or Michael's homes, I was always amazed at how they looked. Large, with vaulted ceilings. Beautiful stainless steel appliances that always looked brand new every time I came over. Massive flatscreen televisions mounted on walls and expansive decorations that added a classy sort of flair to the entire place.

I sighed. "Wow."

"I'm going to grab some things to bring down into the basement. Rae, can you take Michael down there?"

Allison's voice ripped me from my trance and I nodded.

"Yep. Come on, Michael. Let's go get you cleaned up. You look like hell."

He snickered. "I feel like it."

I shrugged. "That's what you get for trying to take on Clint Clarke first thing in the morning."

While Allison rummaged around in the kitchen, I took Michael's hand. I led him down into the basement, where I clicked the light on, illuminating the beautiful expanse of one of the most perfect spaces I'd ever seen. It was practically its own apartment down here, complete with a little kitchenette area, a mounted flatscreen television, every single streaming service known to man loaded on the smart television, and bedrooms as far as the eye could see. There were bookshelves lining the walls, filled with books I wanted to read. The plush microfiber furniture was broken up with bean bags we always flopped onto when coming downstairs. The soft carpet underneath my feet caused me to toe off my shoes, just so I could feel the material tickle my toes.

But, when Michael sat down with a grunt, it pulled me back to reality again.

"I'll be right back. We need to get you cleaned up," I said.

Michael sighed. "I don't plan on moving until lunch."

I giggled as I walked into the bathroom. I fished out the first aid kit from underneath the sink, then walked back into the main room. I sat down by Michael before I opened the kit, preparing myself to clean him up. He had caked blood on his nose and a scrape just above his left eye. Not to mention the massive amount of spit he had dripping down his neck. I ripped open an alcohol wipe and gripped his chin softly. I turned his face toward me, tilting his head in order to clean him a little better.

Then I gave him a knowing smile. "For the record, I'm never going to forget that you leapt to defend Allison's honor instead of mine."

Michael's eyes widened. "Rae, I'm so sorry. I didn't mean t—"

I shook my head. "It's fine, Michael. It's all right. I know you like her."

He paused. "Is it that obvious?"

"Oh, yeah. Very. But she's doing a good job hiding the fact that she likes that you went to bat for her. Against Clint, of all people."

"You don't think she's upset with me?"

"Did you see the way she let you take her hand? The way she let you usher her into her own house? Come on, Michael. You're not that dumb."

He hissed. "That hurt. Ah."

I shrugged. "Don't go up against Clint again and it won't hurt."

"I'd do it again in a heartbeat for her, though."

I nodded. "I know you would. Just know I see things you don't. She feels the same way. But you know how Allison is."

"She's perfect the way she is."

His words warmed my heart. "Bravo to you, by the way."

"For what?"

I winked. "For taking on hell itself to defend your woman. We like those kinds of gestures."

10

CLINTON

I sat there during after-school detention, wrapping yet another cold washcloth around my fucking split knuckles. They hurt like hell, but they didn't hurt as much as my pride. I wanted to beat that fucker into the ground. I wanted to split his damn face open and let people see Michael for the hoity-toity bullshit of a human being he really was. I licked my lips as I gazed out the window. My entire body hurt, if I was being honest. He put up a damn good fight, though I'd never admit it to anyone.

But Rae? She fucking threw me off him like it was nothing.

Why are you still thinking about her?

The question was a good one. And one that overtook my mind as I sat there after school in the dank, sweaty, smelly classroom. I dabbed at my knuckles, which had been bleeding on and off all day. The school nurse literally did the bare minimum needed to get me cleaned up before sending me back to class. She couldn't have given less of a shit about me if she'd actively tried. Then again, she'd cleaned up a lot of my messes over the years.

She was probably just as tired of me as I was of her.

Why the hell was Rae on my mind so much lately? I mean, she was a pain in the ass. Nothing more than that, either. She came from a shitty family. From a shitty part of town. She was nothing more than mere entertainment during these boring-ass school days. And her snark made me want to spit in her general direction. Her snarky remarks every time I said something to her got underneath my skin.

Who the hell did she think she was anyway?

While she might be the only chick in this school who didn't turn red in the cheeks and get all tongue-tied around me, that didn't make her special. It only made me work harder to make sure she understood she really wasn't all that different after all. She wasn't as strong as she thought she was. She wasn't as 'neat-o' as her mother probably told her she was. In the end, she was exactly like us. Exactly like the rich bitches she snubbed her nose at every time she walked into the damn school.

I mean, we even let her walk into this school. With her ratty clothes and her on-time homework and her hard-earned money for lunch. Did she think she was better than us? Because that wasn't the truth. Not by a longshot. She should've been praising us for letting her walk through those doors. She should've been thanking her lucky stars she didn't get it any worse around here, coming from the part of town she did.

The fuck's her problem?

I scoffed as I sat back in my chair. I was done wondering about her. I was done with the unanswered questions I had regarding this stupid little girl. By the time this semester was over, I'd know what her deal was. I'd know what made her tick. I'd know why she felt she could waltz around here, buck up to me, and pull me out of my own damn fights.

You fucked up this time, povo.

"Mr. Clarke?"

The teacher's voice pulled me from my trance and I slowly looked over at him.

"Yep?"

"The nurse wants to see you one last time. Then you're free to go."

I snickered. "She miss me already?"

The teacher rolled his eyes. "Keep up that attitude and I'll make you stay here another hour for shits and giggles."

"Ah, cursing. Such a bigshot move."

He glared at me as I stood up. I picked up my things and winked at him, then headed out the door. I unwrapped my knuckles and tossed the bloodied rag into the nearest trash can, then headed for the front doors. I sure as hell wasn't seeing that fat-ass nurse again, nor was I going to walk anywhere near the principal's office.

Because I had plans for my weekend.

"Not so fast, Clint."

I paused just beyond the front doors as I held them open. The nurse's voice caught me off-guard, and I sighed as I closed my eyes. I turned around, watching as she beckoned for me to come inside. I snickered as I moved toward her, watching her point to the front office door.

"My office. Now."

I rolled my eyes as she took my backpack off my arm. I sauntered through the door, puffing my chest out for the receptionist still at the desk. She shook her head at me, but all it did was make me grin. If these people thought they could put a damper on my parade, they had another thing coming. I had plans with Roy this weekend. There was a massive party I was going to, whether they liked it or not.

But when I rounded the corner into the nurse's office, I groaned.

"Seriously?" I asked.

The nurse closed the door behind us. "Seriously. Sit."

"I'm fine, Mrs. Abernathy."

"Get up there, or I'm calling your father to come down here and deal with you his way."

"Pretty sure he's on a plane somewhere else."

She snickered. "And I'm sure telling him his son has a possible concussion would get him to turn around in a heartbeat."

I hopped up onto the paper-covered seat and the nurse began her evaluation. She shined lights in my eyes and made me open my mouth. She checked my knuckles before covering them in this goopy substance. She wrapped them up with gauze and poked around in places an overweight married woman shouldn't have been touching on a high school student. She felt along my ribcage and squeezed my shoulders. She shoved some sort of wooden implement down my throat, causing me to gag. I smacked her hand away, watching as she leveled her eyes with me.

Then she slid her fingertips around my neck. Causing me to wince.

"And there it is," she said.

I paused. "What?"

She sighed. "Well, you don't have a concussion. But you've given yourself whiplash."

"How the fuck did I get—"

"Language."

I rolled my eyes. "How does one get whiplash without a car accident?"

"Whiplash is just a term for when the neck snaps back and forth too quickly. I guess when you were pushed over your bike this morning, you tensed. Right?"

I shrugged. "So?"

"When you tense, it makes it worse. You have whiplash, which means you'll have to take it easy. No riding fast. No more fights. Because if you injure your neck further, you'll be in the hospital with an actual concussion."

"Sounds better than this place."

She sighed. "All you need to do is keep it in line this year. Then you can graduate and go fight other adults on your own time. But, so long as you're fighting on this campus you're my responsibility."

I chuckled. "If I didn't know any better, I'd say it sounds like you care, Mrs. Abernathy."

"You make it hard to care, Clint. But I do."

Her words disarmed me, and the only thing I could do was laugh. I brushed off her comment as I slipped off the paper-covered table or whatever the hell I was on. But her words stuck with me as I grabbed my backpack.

"Not too fast on that bike, Clarke!"

I grinned. "I'll go as slow as possible. Promise!"

"Yeah, yeah, yeah."

I finally made it out of the school and walked over to my bike. Seeing how scratched up it had become made me seethe all over again. That fucker had no right to throw me over my bike. He had no right to ruin the paint job that took me painstaking hours over the summer to perfect. I grumbled to myself as I shoved my backpack into the compartment on the back of my bike. I slipped my helmet over my head, wincing as it clamped down around my neck. I'd have to watch that. Because it definitely didn't feel pretty.

And as I tossed my leg over my bike, I saw Mrs. Abernathy standing at the front doors of the school.

Really?

I shook my head as I cranked up my bike. I put on a nice show for her, inching my way out of there as slowly as I could. Going the speed limit, and nothing more than that. But once the school was out of view, I cranked it up. I blazed a trail down the main stretch of our little slice of Riverbend, weaving my way through town. I pulled over for a snack, running my ass through my favorite fast food place, then pulled over to eat. I took a long bike ride, trying to clear my thoughts. Trying to prepare myself for the bomb-ass pool party that didn't start until tonight.

Courtesy of Marina's parents' empty house.

After stuffing my face full of greasy food, I cranked up my bike. I sped back to my place, charging through the front doors of my empty house. I snickered as I turned on lights. A massive mansion my father owned, and I was the only one that occupied it on a regular basis. While he and my fake-titted stepmother were jetting off to beautiful places, I was here. Being parented over Skype and only seeing them whenever I really got my ass into trouble.

Not like I give a shit about them, either.

After changing into my swimsuit, I pulled my jeans back over my legs. I grabbed my stuff for the night, including a towel, then made my way back out to my bike. I sped over to Marina's place, where Roy stood out front to greet me. I parked my bike in the driveway, inching it off to the side. Because I sure as hell wasn't keeping it on the road after the scrapes and bumps it had taken that morning.

Fucking Michael.

"Figured you could use a drink."

I smiled at Roy. "Please tell me that's—"

"Jungle juice? Hell yeah, it is. You know Marina makes the good stuff."

I hung up my helmet and grabbed my towel.

Taking the drink from Roy's hand, I sloshed it back. I mean, I chugged it down. I felt the alcohol working its way through my veins as girls giggled off in the distance and water splashed around the corners of the house. I clapped Roy's hand, bringing him in for a shoulder tap before we made our way around the house. I handed my empty glass off to a girl by the jugs of jungle juice, flashing her a devious smile. One well-timed smile and the silent promise of a kiss goodnight and my drink was full as the line continued to grow beside me.

I winked. "Thanks, hot stuff. Love the suit, by the way."

She giggled. "Thanks, Clint."

Roy held out his arms. "Welcome to the party. I think it's the biggest one yet."

I grinned. "Which means the girls are in their smallest bikinis yet."

"Hell yeah, they are."

"Good. Now, where's that damn hot tub?"

Roy pointed, and I saw a gaggle of beautiful girls in it. Their string bikinis barely clung to their bodies as I made my way over. I tossed my towel off to the side, chugging back my second drink before ridding myself of my clothes. I felt their eyes on me, gazing over my muscles and marveling at my tall form. Ladies love the tall ones, and I was the tallest guy out of all these fuckers at this party.

Which gave me a very unfair advantage.

"Ready to make way, ladies?" I asked.

They all giggled as I stepped into the tub, sinking

into the hot water. Bubbles raged around us as I swam between a couple of them, allowing my arms to settle on the outside rim. A beautifully-tanned girl swam over, sitting directly onto my lap. And as she wrapped her arms around my neck, I tried my best not to wince.

"I heard you were in a fight this morning," she purred. "Are you okay, Clint?"

I grinned. "A few bumps and bruises. But you should see the other guy."

"Is there anything I can do?"

I smiled. "Why don't you kiss me and make it all better, beautiful?"

And the pain in my neck quickly dissipated as her pillowy soft lips inched closer to mine.

11

RAELYNN

"Are you sure you have to cancel? I mean, I'm sure Dad's work will understand."

Michael and I sat on the couch, listening as Allison bartered with her parents. We looked at one another with knowing looks. Our weekend was about to be flushed down the toilet.

"I get it. I understand. No, no, no, I'm not disappointed. I just know how much you were looking forward to this. Are you okay?"

I sighed as I pushed myself off the couch. I gathered up the snacks Allison had handed to me earlier and pressed them into my backpack. No use sitting on the couch if we had to get out of here before her parents got back.

"An hour out? Gotcha. Want me to order a pizza or something? I know that always makes you feel better."

Michael grumbled. "Better get a move on."

The two of us began packing ourselves up as Allison hung up the call. She came back into the room with a sorrowful look on her face. I held up my hand. I didn't want her feeling bad for this. It wasn't her fault. I mean, her mother was a stay-at-home mom, sure. But her father owned his own business. A few of them, in fact. And that always made for a very volatile schedule. This wasn't the first weekend extravaganza his work had impeded, and it wouldn't be the last.

Allison sighed. "Well, I guess this is as good a time as any to tell you guys."

I paused. "What do you mean?"

She shrugged. "I was hoping to celebrate this weekend. But since my parents are on their way back from the airport…"

Michael paused. "You got in somewhere, didn't you?"

Allison smiled softly. "I got into UCLA. My first pick. I just got the acceptance letter a couple days ago. I'm officially in their architecture program."

"Oh. My. Gosh!"

I squealed with delight as I rushed toward my best friend. I picked her up, swinging her around as laughter fell from her lips. Michael pulled her away from me and hugged her close. The two of them shared a long embrace as I watched, smiling from ear to ear. I walked up behind Allison and rubbed her back. Michael tucked her head underneath his chin while he held her close.

And for a split second, I was jealous of the relationship blooming between them.

Michael murmured. "I'm so proud of you."

I smiled. "So am I, Allison. Really."

She sighed. "That really takes a load off my shoulders, you know?"

"So what does that mean for your senior year? Can you coast it now?"

He chuckled. "She'll have to submit her final report cards at the end of every semester. Just to make sure she keeps her grades up."

"Well, that's bullshit."

Allison giggled. "I'm just so glad I got in, you know? I didn't want to leave California in order to study, and now I don't have to."

"Which means we can see each other all we want."

She turned around, facing me. "Exactly."

I embraced her again, hugging her close and swinging her from side to side. Michael wrapped his arms around both of us, trying to get back in on the action. I looked up at him, giving him a knowing wink. And after he was done blushing furiously, we all stepped away from one another.

"Ice cream. Sunday afternoon. That's what we'll do to celebrate," I said.

Michael nodded. "And it's on me."

Allison rolled her eyes. "Not everything has to be on you."

Michael scoffed. "Why don't you two let me spoil you every now and again? I don't get it."

I laughed. "Because you're always doing it."

He rolled his eyes. "Fine. But I'm picking you up. Be ready by three? That sound good?"

And after Allison and I nodded, the three of us headed upstairs.

It was almost painful, walking away from our planned weekend. But I understood why we had to do it. I walked myself home, watching the sun set over the horizon as the smell of garbage and darkness filled my nostrils. I thought back on the conversation I'd had with my mother this morning. Maybe this would be a good time for our girls' night in. I mean, with it being so last-minute and all that, she wouldn't have enough time to invite her bullshit boyfriend over.

Or so I thought.

"Hey, Mom. You here?"

She poked her head down the stairs. "Rae? I thought you were at Allison's for the weekend."

I set my bag down. "Her parents' spa retreat or whatever had to be canceled because of her father's work. So I'm home."

"Oh, that's nice."

"Want to do our girls' night tonight? I've even got some snacks in my bag. Some chips, some cookies. There's a sandwich or two, too."

Instead of seeing my mother smile, I saw her wince.

"What?" I asked.

She sighed. "I didn't think you were going to be home until Sunday. So I invited D.J. over for the night."

"Ah."

"I'm sorry, honey. It's just that—"

I waved it off. "It's fine. Don't worry about it. It was a last-minute thing anyway."

"You can have dinner with us. He's picking up something nice from that Italian place up the road. I could give him a call really quickly. You want some lasagna?"

I shook my head. "No, it's fine. I've got plenty of food in my bag."

"We could throw a movie in after dinner?"

"Mom, it's fine. I promise. I have some homework I need to get done anyway if I have any chance of actually enjoying my weekend. You two have fun, okay?"

I carried my things up the stairs, brushing quickly by my mother. Of course she'd take this time to invite D.J. over. What the hell else did I expect? I made my way into my bedroom and closed the door, ready to tear into my reading for English while I munched on some cookies. I flopped onto my bed and pulled out my books. I spread out my snacks as my mouth began salivating. I didn't know what it was about the on-brand cookies that tasted so good. But they were always better than the off-brand ones my mother bought.

However, I didn't even get halfway through my reading before the fighting started.

"I'm sorry, D.J. I didn't realize you wanted me to get wine."

He sighed. "Beer doesn't go with Italian food. Are you that thick-headed?"

Mom scoffed. "Well, I'm not a wine connoisseur. I

wouldn't even know what kind to get with noodles and shit."

"No, you just know how to open your throat and chug it back so you can get drunk all the time. Right?"

"You're the one always dragging me off to parties when I'm completely content hanging around here with you. Just you. In your arms."

"Well, maybe if you weren't such a boring little fuck, I wouldn't always have to drag you to parties to get you to loosen up!"

I rolled my eyes as I reached for my headphones. Then I remembered that D.J. had thrown my iPod full of music against a fucking wall. Great. I hunkered down in my bed, pulling the covers over my ears. I tried blocking out their fighting as I struggled to get through my reading. But finally I couldn't take it any longer. It had taken me two hours to do what should have only taken forty-five minutes, and I couldn't take their arguing any longer.

Homework can wait.

Mom cursed. "Fuck, D.J.! I just wanted to have a nice night with you. Why did you have to come in here and blow a gasket first thing?"

D.J. snarled. "You cuss at me one more time and I'm going to show you exactly what dirty mouths like yours deserve."

"Oh, really. A threat to hit me? Like you don't do that enough as it is. You keep slapping me around enough and I just might hit back!'

"I'd like to see you try, you pathetic excuse for a woman."

I shook my head as I slipped out of bed. I stored my snacks underneath my bed for a rainy day, then changed my clothes. I put myself in the only sundress I had. I wanted to feel the cool summer air on my legs as I walked around. Because being anywhere right now was better than being here. D.J. was hot, then cold. Good, then bad. One week, he brought over flowers and money and gifts. And the next week, they were fighting downstairs until he decided to beat on my mom. I felt it coming, too. The beatdown. The cold to his hot.

And if I was here for it, I wasn't too sure I wouldn't try to kill him.

"Just get out!" Mom yelled.

Something crashed against the wall before D.J.'s voice sounded.

"You're lucky that didn't land, you little bitch."

I heard my mother on the verge of tears as I slipped into my tennis shoes. I pried open my window, feeling the cool summer breeze against my legs as I slipped out onto the roof. I shimmied down the drain pipe, dropping to my feet. And after smoothing my dress down over my knees, I took off for the road.

I couldn't stand it any longer.

I had to get the hell away from this place.

12

CLINTON

I pulled into the driveway of my father's mansion and sighed. Ten o'clock at night, with the party just getting started, and Marina's parents had to ruin the whole fucking thing. I mean, come on. Women were practically fighting over me. I was teasing them to the high heavens, too. Acting like I'd kiss them, only to turn my head and start flirting with another. Chicks loved that shit. Loved working hard for a man they wanted. And I was working them in the hot tub like magic.

Until Marina's parents busted the damn thing up.

Roy got to stay, though. I watched the way he sucked up to her parents. The way he started rattling on about trying to keep everyone safe and keep Marina away from the 'ruckus.' Oh, he sucked up well to them. Kissed their asses so much they actually let him stay. Roy! Of all fucking people! The boy who was fucking their daughter in the middle of the damn football field after school, and they let him stay. All because he knew how to put on a good show. All because he knew how to appear like the good boy before seducing his girlfriend.

I wish I had a girl to have some quality time with.

I shook the thought from my head. I got laid enough as it was. Quality time with a girl would only dampen shit like that. Once a guy started cuddling with a chick, that's all she wanted to do. Cuddle. I'd have to start begging for blowjobs after that. And fuck that nonsense. Clint Clarke didn't beg. If anything, women got down on their knees and begged to give me one. Just to say they had the pleasure of tasting my cock in their mouth.

The thought made me grin as I swung my leg over my bike.

Nope, there was no point in going steady with a girl. I hadn't done it before now, and I had no intention of doing it later on in life. I didn't see the point in it. Fucking around with one girl and her getting pissed off if I saw a nice ass walking by me. What was the point in that? Why spend my time begging to get fucked when I could go out any night and be guaranteed a fuck? Relationships were pointless. They destroyed people. Turned them into shadows of their former selves.

I should know, too.

I watched it happen with my mother.

I opened the garage door to get inside and paused. Seeing my father's cherry red convertible in the garage made me groan. What the fuck now? Why the hell was he home? What the fuck did he want to shove up my ass this time?

I braced myself for whatever I was walking into as I approached the side garage door.

"About damn time you showed up."

His voice hit my ears as I walked through the door. I stood in the sprawling kitchen, seeing him and Cecilia sitting at the table. There was food out. A plate set for me. Their plates were clear of any food they might have been eating and everything had grown cold. I snickered as I closed the door behind me. I shrugged as I slid my bike keys into my pocket.

Then I licked my lips. "Didn't know family dinners were our thing."

Dad narrowed his eyes. "Where have you been?"

"Marina's. Hanging out with Roy."

"Why the fuck did I get a call from the school saying you'd been in a fight this morning?"

You're dead, Mrs. Abernathy.

I shook my head. "It was nothing. Some pathetic boy came at me and I defended myself."

Dad stood up. "Not what I heard."

"Well, I don't care what you heard. That's not what happened. He crossed a line, so I defended myself."

"Does that crossed line happen to be something he did to that bike of yours? Because I've got every intention of taking that away from you right now."

"You aren't taking that from me again."

Dad charged from around the kitchen table and I puffed out my chest. Cecilia stood up, hollering for him to stop as he barreled directly into me. I winced as the pain in my neck grew. He shoved me against the wall, then pinned me with his hands wrapped up in my shirt. Apparently, all he heard was I'd been in a fight. He didn't give a shit about the injuries I'd suffered during the event.

Typical, for my father.

Cecilia slammed her hand on the table. "You know that nurse said he's only a few steps away from a concussion. Let him go."

Dad growled. "You're so full of shit. Thinking you can walk around here like you own the place. Don't forget who bought you that bike."

I grinned. "You bought my first bike. I dipped into my trust fund with your permission to buy the second one."

"And don't you dare forget who can take that away from you."

I snickered. "If you did, you'd be stuck with me. Which is something I know you don't want."

"Not when you're a piece of trash."

"Like father, like son."

I gnashed my teeth at him before I saw his hand come into view. And before I could even blink, I felt his knuckles crack against my cheekbone. My neck felt as if it were on fire, and I stumbled on my feet. I felt my father grip my shirt again and bring me back into the wall, only to come down against my face again.

He hit me three solid times before Cecilia's shrieks caused him to pause.

"Howard! Stop it! You're going to put him in the hospital!"

I felt my father release my shirt and I slipped back down to my feet. But my father spun around and I heard him yelling at her. I knew he was probably spitting on her. I watched him stick his finger in her face, but she stood her ground, her small frame enveloped in the most expensive of fabrics. The two of them yelled back and forth at one another, but I had no idea what they were saying. I didn't care, either. All I knew was I had to get out.

I had to get away from this place.

I reached for the garage door and ripped it open. I stumbled out, my vision slowly coming into focus. I saw the garage door closing and I made a break for it. I heard my father screaming my name as I ducked underneath the moving metal door. I dug my keys out and slung my leg over my bike. My father's voice approached me from behind as I quickly struck up my engine.

"Get back here, you son of a bitch. That bike is mine!"

And just as I felt his hands on the back of my leather jacket, I tore off.

Cecilia's cries faded into the background. My father's cursing fell away from my ears. The engine of my bike roared underneath me, vibrating as it carried me away from that fucking hellhole. The wind rushed through my hair. I sped out of the neighborhood, making my way for the high school. I didn't know where the fuck I was going, but I sure as hell wasn't going home.

Ever, if I could swing it.

I hope you rot in hell, Dad.

I drove around town, feeling my wallet burning a hole against my ass cheek. I stopped off at a diner, where my stomach started growling at the smells of food. I walked inside and slid my helmet off, watching as people gave me strange looks. I made my way for the bathroom and scoffed when I saw myself, finally realizing why people kept giving me awkward glances.

One of my father's slaps had actually bruised my face.

"Just great."

I sighed as I splashed some water on it. I ran some through my hair, watching as it glistened. The bruise was faint. But with the pale skin I'd inherited from the fucker himself, it was easy to see. I licked my lips and dried off my hands, then ran the paper towel over my face. I winced at the pain. My neck felt stiff. My cheeks were on fire. My ears were ringing from how loud my father had been yelling at me.

Then my stomach kicked in again.

"I need some food."

I tossed the paper towel away and slammed out of the bathroom. I took a seat in a corner booth, where the biggest waiter in the diner came up to me. I peeked over at the girls, watching as they cowered away. Fucking figured. I'd gone from the man every woman wanted to flock around, to the man people feared. And all because of some fucking bruise that wasn't even my damn fault.

Note to self, girlfriends and bruises from my father ruin my mojo.

The waiter sighed. "Can I get you anything?"

I leaned back. "Got anything on special?"

"Ten percent off our chicken and waffles."

I wrinkled my nose. "Odd combination."

"Drench it all in syrup and it's fantastic."

I sighed. "Sure. That's fine, then. An order of that, a slice of German chocolate cake, and coffee."

"Cream and sugar?"

"Yep."

He paused. "It might not be my place, but you need to talk to someone?"

I snickered. "Nah, I'm good."

"You sure? That's a pretty decent shiner."

"It only looks bad because I'm pale as fuck in the middle of California."

And even though the two of us shared a small moment of laughter, I still saw the nervousness in his eyes.

"That's all. Thanks," I said.

He left to place my order while everyone continued to stare at me. The freak in the leather jacket with the blackened cheek.

13

RAELYNN

I stared off into the darkness as I sat on the park bench. A ratty park, on the outskirts of the suburb where our small little area was stashed. The metal monkey bars were rusted through. Half of the swings were broken. The plastic of the slides had been cracked for years. Even the sandbox had been infested with bugs and fleas and all sorts of things, driving the families around here to abandon it. But I found solace in this place. In the crispy grass that had been fried by the sun. In the dead trees that surrounded this little patch of land. I sipped my green tea, reveling in its taste. Just another thing that separated me from the coffee-guzzling masses of those that surrounded me.

I sighed as I dwelled in my moment of turmoil.

I'd never been good at brushing things off. I had to pick through it. Tear it apart before piecing it back together. If I didn't, I'd be stuck in a never-ending cycle of untapped emotion and swirling memories. I had to delve deep into it so I understood how to talk about it intelligently. Or, at the very least, build a fucking bridge and get over it.

I needed to pick through the chaos of my home. The insanity of my mother. The decrepit state of her good-for-nothing boyfriend. I closed my eyes, listening as her shrieks filled my mind. Sipping on my tea as the sound of D.J.'s hand cracking against her jaw made me wince. Grimace.

Wish I was anywhere other than here.

"Deep breaths," I whispered to myself.

I continued sipping my tea until there was nothing left. I felt my mind slowing down. And, for once, I relaxed. A cool summer breeze kicked up, pulling the last of my hair out of its ponytail. I reached for the band before it fell to the ground. I ran my fingers through my hair, trying to work out the knots. I smoothed it over my shoulders, fluffing it in the wind. My dress kicked up around my shins, cooling off my thighs as I sat on the wooden park bench that still held the heat of the day within its bones.

Then I heard it.

The rumble of a motorcycle.

I can't be that unlucky. Please tell me I'm not that unlucky.

I sighed as I opened my eyes and set my empty tea container on the ground. I drew in a deep breath, listening as the bike crept closer, rumbling up the road behind me and finally turning off.

And moments later, I found myself staring at Clint Clarke's torso.

I sighed. "What do you want?"

"Is anyone sitting here?"

I snickered. "Nope. And neither are you."

I glared up at him, but all I saw was that snarky little grin of his. That stupid smirk I wanted to slap right off his fucking face. Only it didn't reach his eyes like it normally did in school. There was a sadness to his features that I knew all too well. I watched him carefully as he moved off to the side. Despite what I'd told him, he sat down beside me, hissing as the heat of the bench came into contact with his ass. I stared at him, watching as his eyes connected with something off in the distance. And as his guard came down, so did his grin.

It sank into a frown that had become the physical mantra of my life. A frown that constantly looked back at me in the mirror every morning.

Clint cleared his throat. "Sorry I kicked your friend's ass."

I shook my head. "He got in a few punches, too."

"Doesn't mean he didn't get his ass beat."

"And you deserved every punch he landed."

He shrugged. "Maybe so."

"Really? You're trying to be the good guy now?"

"I'll never be the good guy. Not my thing."

I turned my eyes out toward the playground. "Why are you such a dick all the time? Isn't it enough that we can't stand you?"

I saw Clint turn his head as he stared at me. And even though I felt him burning a hole in the side of my face, I refused to look over at him. I refused to give him the satisfaction of gazing into my eyes. He stared at me for a long time, and I wondered what he was thinking. I found myself wanting to have a peek inside his mind, just to know why the hell he was staring for so long.

Then his voice filled the space around us.

"I don't know. I guess 'cause it's easy. And it's something I'm actually good at."

I rolled my eyes. "The pity card won't get you far with me."

"Not looking for any."

"Good."

He shrugged. "It's true. I'm good at making people hate me. I'm good at being a dick. That's what I do."

I arched an eyebrow. "Wow. Deep motivations, bro."

"Hey, you're the one that asked a dumb question."

"Just didn't expect the answer to be dumber."

"Why do you always do that?"

I snickered. "Do what?"

"Fire back with such animosity?"

I whipped my eyes over to him. "You're asking me —the boy who's bullied me on and off for years—why I address you with a burning hatred? Are you fucking kidding me right now?"

He shrugged. "Maybe if you were nicer, like your friend Allison, people wouldn't be so standoffish to you."

"Is that before or after you made overt sexual jokes about her to Michael?"

"I mean, at least they weren't directed at her."

"Oh. Yeah. Right. Because that makes it all better."

I scoffed and shook my head. I leaned back against the park bench, wishing and praying and hoping he'd go away. I just wanted some peace. Some quiet. Some fucking clarity. I didn't want to deal with his bullshit.

I didn't want to deal with Clint.

"So what are you doing out on a night like this?"

I closed my eyes. "You aren't going to leave me alone, are you?"

He scoffed. "I mean, I figured you'd be with goody two shoes Allison or some shit like that."

"I was, until our plans got canceled."

"Ah, she busy kissing Michael's booboos?"

I bit down on the inside of my cheek. "If you don't leave, I'm leaving."

"Have a safe trip home."

I crossed my arms over my chest, irate at his ability to completely spoil whatever moment of happiness I found for myself. But I wasn't leaving. I had been here first, and he was the one that wasn't wanted in this scenario. If he wanted to be rid of me, then he could leave the same way he came. And if he didn't want to leave, then I'd annoy the hell out of him until he did.

Clint chuckled. "Stubborn, I see."

I shrugged. "You're the one making this more difficult than it needs to be."

"Not really. You don't want to be around me, then leave."

"I'm not the one who obliterated the moment with my presence in the first place."

"Big word for a small girl."

"Well, if you paid attention in English class at all, you might have a few to throw around yourself."

"Kind of a non-sequitur, if you think about it."

I furrowed my brow. "What?"

"A non-sequitur. A phrase that doesn't—"

I held up my hand. "I know what a non-sequitur is, you dick. I'm just not sure how—"

I looked over at him and found him smiling at me. And not the kind of smile I was used to seeing on his face. It wasn't malicious. It didn't shiver me to my core. It was… just a smile. A genuine, eye-reaching, illuminating smile. I'd never seen Clint smile like that before. Hell, I'd never seen him smile at all. But something like this?

It made him look almost boyish.

"Shocked I know the term? Or shocked that I used it correctly?"

I drew in a sharp breath. "What I said was only partially—I mean, if you twist it—I—you know what that word means?"

He chuckled. "English is my strong suit. That's why I don't pay attention in class."

"Didn't you almost fail, though?"

He shrugged. "C-minus. Not bad for never turning in homework."

"That means you would've had to ace all your tests, though. Read the material?"

"What? You think I can't read?"

"Not that you can't. Just that you don't."

He grinned. "Maybe I have a few tricks up my sleeve every now and again."

I quickly turned away from him and tightened my arms across my chest. I wasn't going to let him disarm me. I wasn't going to let him in. I wasn't going to let him closer, or talk to him about anything, or even tell him why the hell I was out here. I wasn't going to indulge my personal life with the school bully. No matter how he tried to woo me into it.

But, I had to admit, he'd officially shocked me.

He snickered. "Still not gonna talk?"

I shook my head. "Nope."

"Even though you now know I'm not just a bully?"

"No one is ever 'just' anything. Being a bully is your dominating trait. So it is what it is."

"But, if it wasn't, you'd talk to me. Wouldn't you?"

"Doesn't matter now, does it?"

He chuckled. "Answering a question with a question is never a good thing, Cleaver."

And even though I tried keeping my guard up, I felt it slowly slipping down with him.

Something I didn't even think to be possible.

14

CLINTON

I mean, I got it. I understood why Rae didn't want
to talk with me. I just found it crazy that we both
ended up here at the same time. I mean, fuck. She was
sitting on my bench! A bench I'd practically claimed
back in eighth grade. I came to this damn park whenever I needed to clear my head. Whenever I needed to
fuck some shit up without getting into trouble with the
town of Riverbend. Most of the cracks in these slides
were from me. The broken, rusted-through metal
monkey bars had been broken through in the first
place because of me terrorizing this damn place. I
mean, parents and families alike had abandoned it
years and years ago. The second the sandbox became
infested and sent kids to the hospital, they shunned this
place. Making it the perfect park for angsty teenagers
and homeless people alike to find whatever fucking
piece of solace they could in this decrepit park. And
with Rae sitting on my damn bench?

I didn't believe in coincidences that much.

Especially since you can't stop thinking about the girl, asshole.

I licked my lips. "I come here sometimes, too."

I heard Rae snicker to herself, but she didn't say anything.

"It's true. I've come here regularly ever since eighth grade. I sit on this exact bench, right where you're sitting, and I stare between those two dying trees."

I pointed off into the distance as she drew in a deep breath.

"It's not going to work. I know you're making this shit up."

I shrugged. "Think what you want, but it's true. I come here at night, sit where you are so I can look between those trees, and I get the perfect view of the north star."

I looked over at her, watching as her eyes lifted. I saw her gazing through the trees before they widened a bit. She looked over at me, shock pouring over her features. Then she went back to staring at the ground. She scooted over a bit, closer to the edge of the bench. Away from me, like I was the plague. Like I was some sort of virus. Like I was a piece of trash she wanted nothing to do with.

And I don't know what the fuck spurred my mouth to start running. But once it started, I couldn't stop it.

"I came here the first time my father ever hit me. I had a teacher threatening to hold me back in eighth grade because I never turned in my homework, of all things. And the fight that ensued with my father was rough. It was the first time I'd ever yelled at him. The first time I'd ever stood up to him. And when he saw I wasn't backing down, he hit me. He hit me so hard it threw me clean across the damn room. I ran out of the house, got on my pedal bike, and didn't stop until I collapsed with exhaustion in this park. Slept on this bench until morning, before Roy's parents found me laying out on this thing."

I felt Rae's eyes slowly panning over to me as I sighed heavily.

"At school, it's easy to forget about all that shit. It's easy to forget about home. About my mother. About my father and how aggressive he is. I get to be a different version of me there. A stronger version of me."

Rae scoffed. "You think you're stronger because people are afraid of you?"

I shrugged. "I guess."

She paused. "You know, that's actually pretty typical. Guys like you don't have power at home, so you take it out on others in a place where you feel powerful."

"I take it you have a point here?"

"I do. It means your sob story isn't so special. Or sob-worthy."

The laughter that bubbled up my throat spewed out of my mouth before I could catch it. I tucked my arms over my chest, letting my head fall back. My eyes closed as laughter took over me. My shoulders shook and my stomach jumped, and for the first time in a long time I felt free of the chains of my home. Without having to be at school.

Which was a miracle in and of itself.

"What's wrong with you, Clint?"

I sighed, trying to rein in my laughter. "Oh, ho ho. Holy fuck. So much, Rae. So much is wrong with me. But let's be real for a second. You're just as screwed up as I am, at the end of the day."

She didn't answer, and that caused me to look over at her. I saw her curl even more into herself, and something inside me wanted to reach out to her. Physically. I forced it back, though. I tucked my arms tighter underneath my arm pits, trying my best to make her feel comfortable.

Because I wanted her to be comfortable around me, for some reason.

I sighed. "Look, I get it. You don't have a good home life. You look at all those big houses we have and the fancy clothes Michael and Allison wear, and you think it's a better life. But it isn't. We all have our issues. My dad slaps me around more than I care to admit. I'm sure your mom has some equally fucked-up shit she does to you."

Rae spat. "Which is none of your business."

"Maybe. Maybe not. But it does you no good not to talk about it."

"Oh, like you talk about it with everyone?"

"I just did, didn't I?"

And then, as if the heavens decided to actually play in my favor, Rae sighed.

"Mom's got this boyfriend. D.J. And he's such a shitbag of a guy, you know? I mean, I know it broke my mother down when my dad left. I was only three, so I don't remember shit about him or anything. But, she just filtered through so many stupid men before landing on, what? D.J.? Some dude that pays some of her bills sometimes and slaps her around a bit? Fucking hell, I can't stand it when they start arguing. One minute, he's bringing over Italian dinner for a nice meal, bringing her flowers. Bringing me gifts. And the next minute? Mom's got a black eye and she's out drinking at bars all weekend before dragging nameless men home to try and make herself feel less alone. I don't get it. Why can't she just… survive without them? Why can't she just put in the effort to thrive? Why does some guy have to be the miraculous answer to all her problems? It's exhausting after a while. Trying to keep up and deal with it all in the background." Then, after a pause, "But not as exhausting as being around you. You really do me in. I'd take D.J. over you any day."

I chuckled and shook my head. Ever the strong one. Trying to keep up that icy demeanor when all she wanted to do was drop her guard. Nevertheless, the need to reach out and hug her was so great I felt myself shaking. I wanted to punch whoever this D.J. guy was until his eyes fucking bulged. How dare he treat a woman like that? How dare he think he could put his hands on a woman and get away with it? I watched Rae's cheeks blush deeply. Even in the darkness, I saw her skin redden. And as she flickered her eyes toward mine, she scoffed.

"What?" I asked.

She shook her head. "I can't believe I just told you all that."

"Why?"

"You mean, other than the fact that you're the biggest asshole at our school?"

I sighed. "Don't be like that, Rae."

"Be like what?"

"So moody."

She leered. "I'm not moody."

"So that bubbling rage in your eye is a reaction to something else? Maybe the pollen? Possibly the fleas infesting the sandbox over there? Did you get bit by a raccoon? I hear the Riverbend raccoons have rabies."

She scoffed and shook her head. But soon, that scoff turned to a giggle. Which morphed into laughter that tilted her head off to the side. The beautiful sound wrapped around us, and I couldn't help but smile. Her arms fell away from her chest and she placed her face in her hands, shaking her head as more laughter fell from her lips.

"What is even happening, Clint?"

I smiled. "You're growing weak for me. Just like all girls do."

Her laughter paused. "Don't do that."

"Do what?"

"If I'm not going to be moody, then you're not going to be a pompous windbag manwhore."

My eyebrows rose. "How long have you had that one tucked away?"

"Not as long as you'd think. I'm quick-witted in some moments."

"I see that."

She looked over at me and her eyes fell to my lips. My smile made her smile, and for the first time I saw her eyes ignite. With the moon above reflecting in her amber pools, it reminded me of the strength of a tree. The rungs of a redwood covered in sappy bark, cloaked in the effervescent darkness California had to offer. I found myself swimming in them. Falling into them and never wanting to return.

The writer in me wanted to pen a poem devoted to the swirling rungs of her brown eyes.

Rae cleared her throat. "What are you looking at?"

I cocked my head. "You."

"What about me?"

"I like this side of you."

She blushed. "Oh, come on. Cut the shit and get to the punch line."

"What punch line?"

"Whatever it is that made you come over and sit down on this bench."

"Is it really so hard to imagine that you're the reason I felt compelled to sit down?"

She snickered. "Felt compelled? Who are you again?"

I turned my body toward her. "I'm the Clint you've always seen."

"I've never seen this side of you."

"Do you want to see more?"

My hand gravitated to her cheek and I cupped her soft skin. My thumb brushed against it as her eyes searched mine. Wild, and curious, and a bit mysterious. And as a grin settled across my face, she smiled up at me. I felt her nod against my hand before she nuzzled my palm. I felt myself being pulled into her atmospheric orbit. Stanzas of poems not yet penned regarding her beauty rushed through my mind. I felt her face getting closer as her body heat encompassed me. And when our lips touched, fireworks went off in my mind.

This was the kind of girl wars were started over.

My elbows tingled. My toes curled. I felt electricity sizzle down my spine. Her tongue pressed against my lips and I was all too eager to let her inside. All too eager to wrap her up in my arms. I pulled her close, heaving her into my lap, and she straddled me with effortless perfection. An entire epic poem spilled forth in my mind, encompassing the whole of Rae. From the soft touch of her fingertips against my jaw to the searing heat of her lips against my own.

Even the way her body fell against me constituted its own story of praise.

I pulled back softly. "Ever been on a bike?"

Rae shook her head. "No. I haven't."

"Want to ride on one?"

When she didn't answer me, I stood up. I picked her up in my arms with ease as she squealed and clung to me. I set her down on her feet, taking her hand and tugging her toward my motorcycle. She resisted at first.

But then she gave way to me. Gave way to my silent command as we headed for our escape.

"Come on. I'll take you for a ride," I said.

And without a second thought, I handed off my helmet to her.

15

RAELYNN

Clinging to Clint around his waist as we zoomed through the streets of our hometown wasn't something I ever thought I'd be doing. And yet, I found myself holding tighter to him with every passing mile. He took the long way around town, pointing out toward the ocean and slowing down so I could gawk at it. We stopped at a bakery that was in its closing hour and he picked us up some pastries at half price. We even stopped to get me one last green tea, while he chugged back a black coffee.

It was a side of him I would have never imagined existed in my wildest dreams.

I stopped questioning where we were going after a while. But once we pulled into the driveway of his home, I grew nervous. What the hell were we doing back here? I figured he'd take me home. Or back to the park. Or drop me off at the high school.

"Uh, Clint?"

He turned off his bike. "What?"

I slipped the helmet off. "What are we doing at your house?"

He put his kickstand down. "Well, you said you didn't wanna go home. But everything else around here's closed. We got these pastries. Figured you'd wanna go somewhere, drink something, and eat."

"So we're at your house? Where your father is right now?"

"Nah. Dad goes to the casino to blow off steam after we fight. He won't be back until tomorrow night at the earliest."

"And your stepmom?"

He scoffed. "She's always at his side. If he's not here, she's not either."

He helped me off the bike, catching me as I stumbled. I felt myself blushing underneath the strength of his arms, but I tried not to show it. I tried not to give in to it. This was madness. This was Clint Clarke, for fuck's sake. The boy that had swung on Michael this morning! There was no way the butterflies in my gut were for him. There was no way on God's green earth I felt the way I did because of him.

And yet, when he took my hand to lead me inside, I felt my stomach jump.

Turn around. Go home while you still can.

I watched Clint type in a password on a keypad that opened the garage. And with the bag of pastries in one hand, he led me straight through a door and into his kitchen. I gawked as I walked inside, too. His kitchen alone was bigger than Allison's entire fucking living room. Holy shit, if I thought Allison's and Michael's parents had massive homes, then I'd really been an ignorant little girl.

Because Clint's father didn't own a home.

He owned a damn mansion.

"You want the cinnamon or cheese danish?" Clint's voice pierced my shock.

"Um, cheese."

He nodded. "Cinnamon for me, then. Which is great, because I'm a cinnamon fanatic."

"Good to know."

"What do you want to drink?"

I didn't hear his question. I kept scanning the room with my eyes, wondering how big this place was.

"Rae."

I heard the chuckle in his voice and my eyes whipped over to his.

"What's up?"

He grinned. "Wanna see the rest of the house?"

I nodded with delight and he dropped the pastries. He scooped my hand into his, and together we started through the house. He showed me the living room, with a massive projection screen on an entire wall. He showed me something called a sitting room, which was literally just a room with a bar and some chairs. He took me into a library. A legitimate library with floor-to-ceiling bookshelves that lined every square inch of wall in the damn place.

Then he led me upstairs. To the middle of the three levels the house had.

"Who the hell needs this much house?"

Clint chuckled. "Dad, apparently. He bought this place before Mom even got pregnant with me. Only three people live here, but it's got six bedrooms. And all of them have their own bathrooms."

I scoffed. "Seems a bit like overkill."

He shrugged. "That's my father for you. Here, this is my room."

He reached through a doorway and turned on the light. And when his bedroom came into view, I stopped in my tracks. It was the size of mine and my mother's put together. And then some. I slowly walked into the room, taking in the blackout curtains over his windows. The beautiful wooden frame of his massive king-size bed. The carpet underneath my feet made me feel as if I were walking on memory foam pillows.

And yet, there was such a sinister presence within all of it.

"I'm so sorry," I whispered.

I slowly turned around, watching as Clint closed the door behind him.

"For what?"

I shook my head. "For… everything, I guess."

He nodded. "It's fine. I don't make it easy for people to see me."

I snickered. "This is the part where you apologize, too."

"I'm getting there."

He made his way to me. I felt his hands against my waist, and I didn't hate it. His green eyes sparkled as they danced with mine, and I felt him peering into my soul. His black hair fell into his face, prompting me to raise my fingertips in order to brush it away. Our skin touched. I felt my breath hitch in my throat. And even though I wanted to pull away from him, something inside me rooted me there. Grounded me, forcing me to stare into the eyes of a boy who understood me more than most.

More than anyone, really.

"I like this side of you," I whispered. I cupped his cheek, and he nuzzled into my palm.

"I'm sorry for always being a dick. It's just easier than anything else."

"Trust me, I get it."

He nodded. "I know."

Our foreheads fell together and his hands slipped to my hips. I felt him gathering up the fabric of my dress as our lips slowly moved together. Our eyes met. My heart slammed against my chest. And as the backs of my legs met the edge of his mattress, his hands slid my dress up to my thighs.

Just as our lips collided.

His tongue met mine and stars erupted behind my eyes. I felt my body pucker for him and places on me tingle I'd never paid attention to in my life. Like the slats between my toes as I wrapped my legs around him. Or the crooks of my knees as his hands slid down my legs. With every stroke of his tongue, my skin prickled. With every groan of his I swallowed down, my hairs stood on end. I felt electrified. I felt myself sizzling into a puddle of nothingness. And as his hands gravitated to my panties, I felt the rest of my walls crashing down.

Are you really about to do this?

I slid his leather jacket away from his shoulders and quickly gathered his shirt over his head. He wrapped his arm around me, hoisting me higher on the bed before he knelt against the mattress. His muscles came into view and I licked my lips, staring at the ink that adorned his arms and torso. He was beautiful. Every part of him. Angrily beautiful in ways I understood. My fingers slid through his hair as his lips came down against my neck. I felt my thighs warming and my panties wetting. He pushed my dress up as he kissed down my neck, exploring me with a kindness and a gentleness I would have never associated with him.

With every press of his lips against my skin, he rewrote what it meant to be Clint Clarke.

"Oh, yes," I whispered.

He groaned as his lips fell to my thighs. I toed my tennis shoes off, feeling him slip my panties down my legs. He rose up long enough to pull the fabric away from my body. And when my feet got tangled up in the fabric, he smiled down at me. He chuckled along with my giggles, making me feel comfortable in my own skin, even with the thick thighs and broad hips that didn't look very much like the girls he usually stared at.

Then I watched him unbuckle his jeans.

It happened so quickly, I almost didn't catch it. He crashed back down to me, our lips colliding as my legs spread for him. He reached down for something as his jeans fell to his knees and soon, something hard fell between my thighs. I felt him pulsing and dripping, his kisses becoming sloppy as his fingers explored my depths. I moaned for him, buckling underneath his touch. He nibbled at my neck as his fingers filled me, stroking my swollen walls.

Before his girth replaced those dexterous fingers.

"Clint," I gasped.

"Holy fuck, Rae."

"Yes. Oh, my—just yes."

He chuckled before his lips captured mine again. I felt his forearms press against the mattress on either side of my head. I wrapped myself around him, feeling his thickening length stroke against my walls with every thrust of his hips. I gasped for more. His bed bucked as he picked up the pace. I raked my nails down his back, listening to him growl into the crook of my neck. My toes ran down the backs of his legs. I locked onto him, feeling him growing thicker inside me. My eyes rolled back, my body shook and I quivered around him as my body began to tense.

"That's it. Come on, Rae. I feel you. Just let it go."

"Clint! Yes! Oh, Cli—"

My jaw unhinged and my back bowed so deeply I figured it would snap. My body shook for him. Quaked for him. And a darkness overcame me. I chanted his name like a shattered prayer, a choked, wanton sound falling from my lips. I felt him pumping into me, thrusting faster and faster. Harder and harder. Begging my body to hang on just a second longer.

Before he, too, burst.

"Rae," he growled.

When he collapsed against me, I felt full. With every thread of his arousal that touched my body, I felt blanketed in him. His sloppy kisses turned to soft nuzzles of his nose as his face found the crook of my neck again. He rested against me, his muscles cradling the curves of my body. And as my arms fell away from his back, I sighed with relief.

I smiled up at the ceiling.

All because of the bully from Riverbend High.

16

CLINTON

My eyes fell open and I groaned. The smell of her still lingered in the room with me, and it made me smile. I rolled over, half expecting to see her next to me, lying there with her dress bunched up over her hips and her legs spread. Ready to go another round as the two of us woke up together.

But when I rolled over, there was nothing but my bed to greet me.

"Figures," I murmured.

As I lay there, staring up at the ceiling, my mind fell back to last night. What had gone down between me and Rae. How good it felt. How right it seemed. I'd never experienced something that calm and collected with a girl before. Usually, they were eager to suck me off for a bit before poking their pretty little asses out for me. But this was something else, with Rae. Something slower. Deeper. More sensual than I'd experienced before.

"Fucking hell," I said, sighing.

I rolled over one last time, placing my face where her head had been. I drew her scent in deep as my mind pulled me back to those moments. How nice she had felt in my arms as I fell asleep. How soft her skin felt against mine. How much her body had enveloped me as we grew to fevered heights.

"I gotta write something," I said, groaning.

I sat up in bed and reached for my bedside table. I pulled out another notebook and pen I kept stashed there, and my muse ran wild. I scratched down rudimentary poems and premises for short stories. I cranked them out, one after another, until the sun pierced through my blackout curtains. I ran my hand through my hair, flipping through the pages of nonsense I'd written down simply because Rae had refueled something inside me.

"What the fuck?" I asked breathlessly.

My cell phone vibrating on my bedside table pulled me from my trance. And for a good reason, because I didn't want to think about shit like this anymore. I tossed my notebook and pen back into the bedside table, then reached for my phone. But my muse still hadn't calmed down. Words rattled through my mind that I hoped I'd be able to recall later. Words that could have only described the beauty and the appeal that had been Rae last night.

I opened up the text message I had and saw it was from Roy. And as I read it, a cold bucket of ice water got tossed onto my muse.

Roy: Get your ass over to my place. I had a great

time with Marina last night. And you'll never guess what we did in her parents' bed.

For some reason, I felt the need to roll my eyes. I tossed my phone onto the mattress and slid out of bed, resolving myself to a shower. Though I was hesitant to wash Rae's scent off my body. I took an extra-long hot shower, allowing my mind to wander a little more one last time.

Then I got out and got ready to head to Roy's.

Dad still wasn't home when I got downstairs. Which didn't shock me one bit. He and Cecilia had probably gotten a hotel room somewhere, where he could bang out his anger toward me with her body. I shook my head. That poor fucking woman. What girls like her wouldn't do for money astounded me. Money was useless. Money was almost nothing, despite what people wanted to believe. I grabbed a banana from the fruit bowl and peeled it open, eating it as I walked out to my bike.

I tossed the peel off to the side, threw my leg over my bike, and started for Roy's.

With thoughts of Rae bombarding my mind.

Oh, Clint.

The way she said my name so sweetly made my skin tingle. Unlike the squeals and the whimpers from most girls, hers were soft sighs. Guttural groans. Less of a porn video and more of a religious experience. I didn't believe in God and all that shit. But I did believe in angels.

And Rae was one of them.

I need to write that down later.

I rode over to Roy's and found him on the porch, waiting for me. And the second I took a look at his neck, I knew I was in for a long story. He had hickeys everywhere. Bite marks. Nail marks down his arms. I mean, he was fucking covered in evidence of her. And while I usually would've been interested in a story like this, I found myself not caring about the topic at all.

"So after you assholes left, her parents stayed downstairs," Roy said.

I parked my bike in front of his porch and turned off the engine.

"Uh huh. I take it you two had sex in their bed?" I asked.

"Oh, not just their bed. Their shower. Their bathroom. Bent over their fucking dresser. It was hot, man. Marina was all like, 'Mom, my television isn't working. Can we watch a movie in your bedroom?' And the second she looked at me with those 'fuck me' eyes, I knew it was on. We didn't even get five minutes into the damn credits before she hopped on this dick."

"Sounds like you had a good time," I said, grinning.

"Oh, hell yeah. You know what she let me do?"

"I take it you convinced her to try anal."

"Fuck yeah, I did! She gripped those bedsheets like such a good girl for me, too. I'll never fucking go back. That was the tightest hole I'd ever experienced. I don't even want her pussy anymore."

I snickered. "Told you it was a great experience."

"Great? This was a miraculous experience. I've never come that hard in my life, dude."

While this would've been the part where I inter-
jected with my nightly escapades, I found myself
playing my cards close to my chest. I didn't want to tell
Roy what I'd gotten up to last night. I didn't want to
confide in him all the dirty, nasty secrets of the night.
Usually, I did. The two of us went back and forth, until
one of us outdid the other for the day. But I didn't feel
like I could confide in him with what happened
between me and Rae.

It felt wrong, for some reason.

"So, please tell me you left some marks behind on
her body, too. Because that's a pretty bitch-ass thing for
you to be marked up and for her to not be," I said.

He snickered. "She was all over me, dude. I got my
marks in, but make no mistake. She couldn't keep her
paws and her lips off me. She gobbled my cock down
with ease before we even got started. I didn't even have
to warm her up."

"Hell yeah, Roy. That's the way to do it."

"Marina sure is a giver. And I think I'm gonna
keep her around for a little while."

I grinned. "Sex really that good?"

"Have you been listening to me at all? The sex is
fantastic. I mean, yeah, she's a bit thin. But I like 'em
thin. Less to push away to get to the holes I really
want."

I shook my head. "Nope. After I'm done, I want to
fall against my girl and feel her catch me with her
softness."

"You've always been attracted to fatties. I don't get
that."

"Not fatties, Roy. Just those girls with a little more to give is all. Trust me, if you ever feel a pair of soft thighs wrapped around your waist, you'll never go back."

"No, thanks. If her thighs rub together, you can count me out. You know how badly pussy smells after thighs have been rubbing against it all damn day? Fucking hell, no thank you."

I chuckled. "Pussy stinks anyway. Get over it, or don't eat it."

He shrugged. "Marina's don't stink. I don't know what the fuck she does to it, but it smells like fucking candy and roses, man. Keeps it bare for me, too. I mean, every inch of her is just smooth as ice cream. When I do feel like going down on her, I'm there for a while. Especially since she lets me do practically whatever I want if I can make her come a few times with my tongue."

"A few times? Let's not overstate now."

"What? Okay, okay. Three times with my tongue. The most I've ever done."

"On Marina? Or in general?"

He grinned. "Not enough detail for you yet?"

As Roy launched into yet more stories about his girlfriend, my mind drifted back to Rae. I wondered if she'd gotten home okay last night. If I'd see her again, privately. I thought forward to Monday, and whether or not things might be weird at school. Would she acknowledge me? Would it be business as usual? Was she embarrassed that she'd slept with me?

I found myself hoping she wasn't embarrassed at

all. In fact, I found myself hoping we could actually be civil.

Maybe even kind to one another.

"Earth to Clint, you there?"

I shook my head. "Sorry. I was drowning in the boring stories of your sexual escapades."

He gawked. "Boring? Boring!? You call fucking my girlfriend in her parents' bed four times boring?"

"No, I call it nasty. Because that's their marital bed. All they do is fuck in it. So now, technically, you've fucked Marina, her mother, and her father. Because you know their shit's all over that mattress."

He paused. "Holy fuck, I need to shower again."

And as I threw my head back with laughter, Roy scampered off into his house. Readying himself for the scrub-down of the century.

Which gave my mind more time to drift back to Rae.

17

RAELYNN

I drew in a deep breath before knocking on Allison's front door. I'd barely gotten any sleep last night, and I needed to talk with my best friend. But not Michael. Holy shit, Michael would kill me if he knew what had happened.

"Hey there, Rae! Come in, come in. You hungry? There's still some leftover breakfast."

Allison's mother was an absolute ray of sunshine. I smiled at her as I walked through the door she held open for me, feeling the cool air conditioning of their home envelop me. I had to hold back tears. I was more emotional than I'd ever felt in my life, and I sure as hell didn't want to be explaining to Mrs. Denver why I had come to her house crying.

"We've got biscuits, some eggs that are still warm, sausage I can reheat—"

"I'm actually not hungry. But thank you, Mrs. Denver," I said.

She quirked an eyebrow. "You? Not hungry? You feeling okay, Rae?"

I snickered. "Just had a big breakfast at my house is all."

She looked at me for a long time and I prayed she bought the lie. And even though I figured she knew I was lying, she didn't call me out on it. She simply nodded her head and walked off, calling for Allison as she got to the bottom of the staircase.

I shoved my hands into my pockets, hoping to conceal their trembling.

"Allison! Rae's here, honey!"

"Coming, Mom!"

"Thanks, Mrs. Denver. I appreciate it," I said.

She smiled. "Anytime. You know you're always welcome."

I nodded. "I know."

"And if there's anything you ever want to talk about, just know it stays between us. Okay?"

I smiled softly. "I really appreciate that. Thank you."

Allison came bounding down the steps with her blond hair up in a bun. She grabbed my hand and tugged me back upstairs, dragging me. Step by step. We stumbled into her room and she closed the door, and the smell of nail polish remover wafted heavily under my nose.

"I figured since we couldn't paint our nails last night, we could do it now. I mean, Michael isn't here. But we can still do it. Right?"

I furrowed my brow. "Did you set all this out before

you came down?"

She snickered. "Not a chance. I just started to change out my own nail polish when Mom yelled that you were here. I figured it was a nice coincidence."

She flopped down onto the floor, then reached for my wrists. She dragged me with her, and together, we picked out our next nail color. She dropped her feet into my lap before she handed me the pale pink color she wanted on her toes. She'd already cleaned the nail polish off them once, leaving me a dry and alcohol-soaked canvas for which to do my shoddy work.

Which gave me some time to gather my thoughts.

"Did something happen with your mother?"

I shook my head. "No. Not at all. I mean, yes. But that's not why I came over."

Allison sighed. "D.J. again?"

I rolled my eyes. "When is it ever not D.J.?"

"What did he do?"

"The usual. Fighting. Mom threw something against the wall at him. Things got heated. I ended up sneaking out of my window and heading to the park last night."

"Why in the world didn't you come here? You could've stayed overnight instead of going back home after all that mess."

I paused. "I didn't go home until this morning."

"Oh?"

I bit my bottom lip. "I stayed with Clint last night."

Allison yanked her foot away. "You did what now?"

"It's not—"

"How in the world did you end up there?"

I sighed. "He found me at the park. Did you know his father slaps him around?"

"Who in the world cares what his father does? How did you end up at his house overnight? Wait a second. Did you—?"

I slowly looked up at her and her eyes bulged.

"You didn't."

"It just sort of happened, Allison. I'm still not completely sure what happened."

She scoffed. "An alien took over your body. That's what happened. Are you serious? You slept with Clint Clarke?"

My face fell. "Let's say that a little louder. I don't think the rest of the block heard."

"Does Michael know?"

"Hell no! Michael doesn't know, and he won't know."

Allison nodded. "Good. Because after that fight, he'd kill you if he found out."

"Yeah. I know."

I screwed the cap back onto the nail polish and tossed it to the ground. I put my head in my hands, trying to steady my breathing as tears rushed my eyes. Allison's hand came down against my back, drawing small circles with her palms. I drew in a deep breaths as my heartrate skyrocketed. Every time I thought back to last night, my hands trembled. My heart stuttered.

And I still didn't know if it was a good or bad thing.

Allison kissed the side of my head. "Tell me what happened."

I shrugged. "I don't know what happened. That's the issue. We talked for a little bit. I found out why he's such a dick all the time. He was kind enough to try and get my mind off D.J. and all that shit. And then, we were in his bedroom and I lost control of myself."

"There's gotta be more to this, Rae."

I shook my head. "There really isn't. One minute we were talking about our shitty parents, then the next minute he was kissing me and I didn't want him to stop. It was just—"

"Are you sure we're talking about the same Clint Clarke here? I mean, the boy who slugged away at our best friend?"

I nodded slowly, feeling so many emotions flood my stomach. Shock. Awe. Happiness. Confusion. But none of it was guilt.

Which confused me even more.

I looked up from my hands. "I really want to tell Michael about it."

Allison scoffed. "You can't. After taking the beating he did and stepping up for us—"

"For you."

I looked over and saw Allison blushing.

"Well, at any rate, after what happened Friday morning, Michael wouldn't speak to you for a while. He's awesome and all, but the boy can hold a grudge."

I groaned. "I don't like the idea of keeping secrets from my best friends, though."

She shook her head. "Trust me, it won't do him any good to know. Plus, you've got me. You've told me, and you can keep telling me until you come to terms with what's happened. Because I feel you shaking. I know you regret what happened."

"That's the thing. I don't. I'm not shaking because I regret it. I'm shaking because—"

I flopped down onto my back, staring up at her ceiling fan. How the hell did I explain any of this to her when I couldn't even explain it to myself?

Allison lay down next to me. "You don't need all the answers now. Just talk about what you can."

My hands covered my face. "What the actual fuck is happening with my life right now?"

She giggled. "I know one thing we have to figure out, though. And that's what to do about Clinton come Monday."

"I... I don't know, Allison."

"Well, let's start with what you want to do. What do you hope happens Monday?"

I shrugged. "I don't know that either."

"We should figure it out, then. Because something tells me he's not going to leave you alone. Nothing is ever that easy with him."

"I didn't fuck him so he'd leave me alone."

She paused. "Then why did you?"

I closed my eyes. "Because it felt like he understood me. And I liked that."

Allison took my hand as the two of us stared at the ceiling. The smell of nail polish remover slowly faded away, but the memories of last night didn't. I squeezed her hand, trying not to think about it. Trying not to root myself in last night. But I couldn't help it. The way I'd fallen asleep against Clint. The way his muscles felt cradling me last night. How I woke up at four in the morning only to realize I'd fallen asleep right beside him. Wrapped up in him. With my leg pressed between his and my head tucked underneath his chin.

It was so unlike the Clint Clarke I knew.

And yet, it made all the sense in the world.

Allison cleared her throat. "Penny for your thoughts."

I squeezed her hand again. "I fell asleep with him last night."

"What time did you get home?"

"About four-thirty in the morning."

"Did he take you home?"

I shook my head. "I didn't want to wake him up."

"Why not?"

Because I knew if he asked me to stay, I would have.

I sighed. "I don't know. I don't know much of anything right now. I just—needed to tell someone. And you were the only person I could think of that wouldn't completely alienate me for it."

The room fell silent as butterflies ignited in my gut. The same kind of butterflies I'd had last night. Why the fuck did I feel this way? It felt like I had a crush on the school's biggest asshole. Which was wrong on so many accounts I couldn't even begin to explain all of it to myself. I closed my eyes, trying to push all the memories away. It was a one-time moment I had the chance to write off as me being completely vulnerable. Not right in the head, what with everything going on between my mother and her bullshit boyfriend. And I knew people would believe me, too. If I told them it was a moment of absolute insanity due to my home life, they wouldn't question things.

But I'd know it wasn't the truth.

And Clint might pay a hefty price for it.

Why the fuck do I care what kind of price he pays for it? He beat up my best friend!

"Shit," I whispered.

Allison snickered. "Sounds like we need to find a distraction for you today."

"You mean we can't just lie here and debate on ways to erase my memory?"

She giggled. "I mean, it sounds fun in theory. But I wouldn't appreciate it if you forgot all about me."

"Not my entire life. Just the past forty-eight hours."

"How does getting lunch out somewhere sound? We can take the mind-erasing from there."

And as my stomach growled out, betraying my actual hunger, a smile crossed my face.

"Soup and sandwiches?" I asked.

Allison sat up. "Soup and sandwiches it is."

18

CLINTON

I heard my father storm through the door Sunday evening, much later than I figured he'd come back from that damn casino. He was muttering to himself, something about bananas and shoving them down someone's throat. I grinned to myself as I heard the trash can lid bang against the wall.

Good. He found it.

I heard Cecilia's soft voice cooing at him. Treating him like some damn child as she tried soothing away his worries and his anger. It was pathetic, really. Listening to a grown-ass woman coddle a grown-ass man like that. I didn't want to be in the house. Not with her, not with him, and not with the tension they brought with them.

If I was lucky, they'd be on another airplane in the morning. Heading off on yet another trip.

And out of my damn hair.

I picked up my cell phone and shoved it into my

pocket. It was late, but I didn't care. I grabbed the keys to my bike and snuck down the stairs, bypassing the living room altogether. Stepmommy dearest and my bullshit father were curled up, watching a movie. And still, I heard him grumbling to himself. He was the most miserable asshole on the face of this planet, and I couldn't wait until I graduated.

Because I had all sorts of plans on how to get out from underneath him.

I opened the side garage door without a sound and rummaged around for the second bike helmet I knew I had stashed away somewhere. And just as I tucked it under my arm, I heard my father's voice.

"Clint? You out there? You know damn good and well what your curfew is on the weekends."

I threw my leg over my bike and cranked up the engine. I slipped my helmet over my head, then pinned the other one between myself and the bike. I zoomed out of the garage, leaving my house in the shadows as I tore out of the neighborhood. I didn't give a shit about my father or his rules. If he wanted to be a decent parent, he could stay home, stay away from the casino, and stop beating up on me whenever he didn't like something I was doing.

I cruised down the road until I came to the opening of the neighborhood. And instead of taking a right to head on into town, I took a left. I found myself at the mouth of Rae's neighborhood, and I slowed down to see if I could find her house. I only had a general idea of which one it was. It wasn't hard to spot once I came upon it.

I recognized that rusted-out bright green bike of hers she used to ride back in middle school.

I looked through the living room window and saw her mother watching television. She was leaned up against someone. Some dude that was snoring away with his head lobbed back. I shook my head as I walked the bike into the driveway. My eyes scanned the front of the house, coming upon one lone light that was on upstairs.

Hopefully that's Rae's bedroom.

I put the kickstand down, though I didn't turn off the engine. I set the extra helmet on the bike, then started picking up gravel rocks from her driveway. I tossed them at the window, missing the first couple of times. But, the third rock landed directly against the glass. Making a much louder sound than I had anticipated.

But it did draw Rae to the window.

"What the—Clint?"

I waved. "Come on down. I have a helmet for you."

She shook her head. "I can't. I'm about to go to bed."

I shrugged. "So?"

"Mom's downstairs with some guy, Clint."

"And I'm pretty sure they're both knocked out. Or in a trance. She hasn't looked out the window at me yet."

I watched her bite her lower lip, and the motion tugged at my gut. She looked so cute like that, with her hair in a bun. I preferred it down, like it had been the other night. I saw a smile creep across her face before she closed her window, then the light to her bedroom went off.

At first, I thought she was turning me down.

Until the front door opened.

"Come on. We have to hurry."

I smiled as I tossed her the helmet. She slid it over her head and I chuckled at her pajamas. She had on these flimsy pajama bottoms that had all sorts of stars and hearts and sparkles all over it. And the tank top she wore barely stayed on her body. She whipped some sort of woven jacket or whatever around her shoulders, then leapt onto the back of my bike.

And when I felt her arms wrap around me, my world slowly settled into place.

"I hope you're hungry. Because there's a diner I've got my eye on tonight."

Rae giggled. "And here I thought you had your eye on me tonight."

I grinned. "I have my eye on you tonight for dessert, that's for sure."

"You're so bad. But you better hurry. If there's a promise of food, I can't hold my stomach off for long."

"A girl that eats. I love it."

I backed out of her driveway and we tore off down the road. She squealed, clinging to me as I raced us into town. I adored the feeling of her wrapped around me. The way she fisted my jacket and buried her helmeted head against my back. I smiled brightly as we cruised through town. I took the long way to the diner, just so I had more time to savor the moment with her.

Eventually, though, we pulled into the parking lot. And I was all too eager to escort her inside with our hands tangled up together.

"You know, my mother would have a heart attack if she knew I got on the back of some guy's bike."

I slid into the booth. "Some guy?"

Rae nodded. "Well, you. But yes. To her? Some guy."

I chuckled. "I'm not just some guy, Rae."

"Oh, yeah? And what are you, then?"

I winked. "I'm *the* guy. You really should know this by now."

"Idiot."

The waitress brought us menus, but I was too busy staring at the flush in Rae's cheeks. Oh, she was so easily flustered. And I loved it. Her nose wrinkled up as she put the menu in front of her face. I reached out and slowly slid it down. She was too cute to cover up, with her freckles and her tinted cheeks and her wild hair.

Since when the hell did girls become 'cute'?

Rae cleared her throat. "Whatcha thinking about getting?"

I shrugged. "The usual."

"Care to fill me in on what that is?"

"A double cheeseburger with everything, a chocolate shake with extra cherries, and extra crispy fries. Two orders of them."

The waitress walked back up. "Well, now that I have his order, are you ready, hun?"

I grinned. "Yeah, hun. You ready?"

Rae shook her head. "His order actually sounds nice. Can you make two of those?"

My eyebrows rose. "That's a lot of food."

"And you apparently underestimate how much of it I can put away."

The waitress scribbled on her pad. "All right. Two double cheeseburgers with everything, two chocolate shakes with extra cherries, and two double orders of extra crispy fries. Anything else?"

A hotel room to properly work this meal off with the cutest girl alive.

Rae shook her head. "I'm good."

"Me, too. That'll be it, thanks."

The waitress gathered the menus. "I'll be back with your shakes in a few minutes, guys."

I sighed. "So is that guy I saw with your mother D.J.?"

Rae paused. "No, actually."

I leaned back. "That happen often?"

She nodded. "Every time they get into a fight. She rebounds with some guy, they fight again, D.J. showers her with gifts so she'll come back, then the cycle starts all over again."

"I'm sorry, Rae."

She shrugged. "Shit happens."

"Do you remember anything about your dad?"

"Wow. You really just wanna dive in there, don't you?"

"I mean, do you have anyone else to talk about it with?"

"Allison and Michael."

"Have you ever talked with them about it?"

She shrugged. "Doesn't mean I won't."

I quirked an eyebrow, listening to her sigh. "You know I'll understand."

"Why don't we start with what happened to your mother?"

I nodded. "All right. What do you want to know?"

"What really happened, Clint?"

I sighed. "I wish I knew. One day she was okay. And the next, she wasn't. Painkillers are a bitch, but when you put it together with postpartum depression, it becomes a big issue."

"Your mother struggled after having you?"

"My mother struggled all the time. I think the reason why Dad put up with it, too, was because of her looks. He's into the whole 'trophy wife' thing. And Mom didn't mind pumping out kids so long as she could shop and keep up with her plastic surgery addiction."

"I'm sorry, Clint."

I shook my head. "I truly do believe Dad ruined her. I mean, there are pictures I've come across of her from time to time, and the smile on her face is just—"

I got lost in my memories for a second. And I didn't get pulled from them until our milkshakes touched down. I nodded at the waitress and she left us be, then I felt something warm against my foot under the table.

And when I looked underneath, I found Rae wrapping her legs around mine. Trying to comfort me. Trying to cradle me. Trying to be there for me.

No one had ever done that for me before. I felt my heart leap to life.

"No, I don't have any memories of my dad. According to Mom, he wasn't even around much when they were together. I mean, they got engaged. Got married. Had me. But, for some reason, he jumped ship when I was three and that was that."

I sighed. "Did your mother ever tell you what happened?"

Rae shook her head. "I can't get her to talk about it. Like, ever. I don't know that I'll ever know what really happened. Why Dad really left us. Why he really didn't want us."

"I'm sure it wasn't that."

"Are you, though? I mean, it's possible. Mom's not easy to deal with. My grandparents disowned us, practically, because of her erratic behavior. For all I know, Dad got fed up with it and was worried I'd turn out the same way. So he left to avoid all that."

I reached out, taking her hand. "You don't seem erratic to me."

She snickered. "Oh, yeah? And sleeping with the high school bully on a whim after he got into a fight with my best friend isn't erratic?"

"You make it sound like that's a bad thing. Was it really that bad of a thing?"

And as our plates of food settled in front of us, Rae shook her head.

"No. It really wasn't."

19

RAELYNN

C lint grinned at me from across the table before he let go of my hand. We dove into the food, sinking our teeth into fabulous, greasy burgers that made me moan with delight. There was an extravagant amount of food. But I knew I'd eat it all. In some ways, I forgot Clint was sitting there. Watching me. Staring at me. Taking in the way ketchup slid across my cheeks and how the lettuce slid away from my burger, dropping onto the plate.

"If you cut it in half, the vegetables will stay better."

I slowly looked over at him as I found myself midbite into my glorious burger.

"Oh, yeah?" I asked with my mouth full.

He chuckled. "Yep."

He held up half of his burger and I put mine down. I wiped off my face as his eyes danced along me, watching my every move. I wasn't sure what the hell he was staring at, but I didn't like it. I'd never been underneath someone's gaze so intently, and it made me squirm in my seat. I picked up my knife, cutting the burger in half before I picked up the part of it I had already been chewing on.

And I found that the vegetables didn't slip out as easily.

I smiled. "Genius."

"I've eaten many burgers in my lifetime. I've perfected the art."

I shook my head. "There's no art to eating them. There's only the art of cleaning yourself up after them."

"That an art you've perfected?"

"You making fun of the way I eat, Clarke?"

He winked. "Maybe just a bit."

I rolled my eyes. "A teaser, even on a date. How romantic."

"I mean, we could share our milkshakes if you wanted. Get two straws. Nuzzle our noses together and feed each other cherries."

"I'm not eating anything from your fingertips. I don't know where those things have been."

He grinned. "I could tell you where they will be later."

"You sound pretty sure of yourself there. I wouldn't get too cocky."

"But maybe just a little cocky. Right?"

I felt myself blushing as I shook my head. We went back and forth like that over our food, but it wasn't the kind of dickish banter I'd known him to have. It was playful. Flirtatious. Nice, even. He had a great sense of humor, and I found myself laughing and partially choking on my food every time he slid a joke in at the right time. Who would've thought Clint Clarke had a decent sense of humor?

Certainly not me.

Clint pointed to my shake. "You got enough room for that?"

I leaned back. "I have to admit, this was a lot more food than I realized."

He grinned. "Maybe try not to keep up with me next time."

"If you challenge me, I'll make myself sick proving you wrong."

"And that would be one of the many reasons why you're not like your mother."

The comment caught me off-guard, and it settled itself deep in the pit of my soul. It affected me in so many ways that it brought tears to my eyes. I looked down into my lap, playing with the loose fabric of my cardigan. I blinked rapidly, trying to keep myself together. Except the tears fell anyway.

And I felt my body being slid across the booth seat.

"Come here," he murmured.

He wrapped his arm around me and I leaned against him. I felt his strength as he comforted me. As he slid his hand up and down my arm. I tucked my head underneath his chin, feeling him lean back with me. And as I rested against him, I allowed the full force of that complimented truth barrel over me.

"You really think I'm not like her?" I whispered.

He shook his head. "Not one damn bit."

I sniffled. "Thank you."

"You have nothing to thank me for. You're not like your mother. End of story. You're strong. You're vibrant. You're resilient. And one of these days, you'll get out of this place. Just like me."

I paused. "You want to get out, too?"

"More than anything on this planet."

"What will you do once you leave?"

He shrugged. "Not go to school, if I can help it. Maybe I'll open up my own bike shop. Or become an apprentice somewhere and get some certs. Work on some writing or some bullshit like that while I'm at it. Anything's better than what I'm doing now, that's for sure."

I nodded. "I know what you mean."

He pulled me closer. "What about you? Any plans after high school?"

"I'd love to move out with Allison and get a place together. Maybe with Michael moving in with us or something. She's been accepted to UCLA's architecture program, and I imagine Michael will apply to go there just to be around her more."

"That boy's got it bad for her."

I giggled. "He does, and it's adorable. I love it. And I'm totally for it."

The two of us sat in silence for a little while before he reached for his milkshake. He held the straw up to my lips and I took a small sip. Then he followed it up with a sip of his own. He went back and forth like that for a while. Until we'd drained the first of two milkshakes.

But when he offered me a sip of the second one, I had to wave it away.

"I cave. I concede. You win. Holy shit, I'm so full I hurt."

Clint kissed the top of my head. "We'll sit here for a few minutes then, before we head out."

I nuzzled against him. "Are we headed anywhere specific? Or you just taking me back home?"

He shrugged. "I figured we could do whatever you wanted. Go to the park. Go on a ride. Go to the beach. Go back to my place…"

I gazed up into his face, watching him peer down at me. There was a hint of darkness in his eyes. A wanton, knowing flicker that made my heart slam against my chest. I nodded softly, silently answering the question he refused to put out there. And as a grin settled across his face, he raised his hand in the air.

Prompting the waitress to deliver our check.

Our exit was a blur. We moved so quickly as laughter fell from our lips that I had a hard time taking in the scenery. I rested my head against Clint's back as we rode back to his house, with it being well past one in the morning. We pulled silently into his driveway, parked his bike, and stowed our helmets away.

Before we stumbled up the steps.

"Mm, you taste like chocolate," he said, chuckling.

I slid his jacket off his shoulders as he pinned me against the wall.

"And you taste like french fries," I said, whispering.

He winked. "Wanna see what that combination tastes like?"

I reached up, gripping his hair as I tugged him back down to me. Our lips collided, and he picked me up effortlessly, with an ease and a grace that made my stomach flutter with a million different butterflies. He was good at giving me that reaction. That feeling of effortlessly floating. He walked us into his room and closed the door behind him with his foot. And when the door thudded, I giggled against his lips.

"Ssshhh, we're gonna wake up the house."

He chuckled. "You'd like that, wouldn't you?"

He tossed me to the bed and I squealed. I held myself up, watching him strip himself bare for me. His muscles came into view, causing me to lick my lips. I scrambled, kneeling against the mattress as I followed his motions, sliding my clothes off my body until my bare nakedness matched his.

And the way he ran his eyes over me made me shiver.

"Fucking hell, you're gorgeous."

He crashed against me and we fell to his bed. His lips kissed every inch of my skin as I bucked and rolled for him. He kissed down my neck. He raked his teeth along my shoulder. He even nibbled against the crook of my arms. My arms, of all places! I tingled in areas I'd never paid attention to before. Like the small of my back and the tip of my nose. I gasped and moaned. I fisted the sheets as he slid my legs over his shoulders. I leaned up, watching him disappear between my legs.

And as the moonlight streamed around his blackout curtains, his tongue pierced my folds.

"Oh, shit," I choked out.

My head fell to the pillow and the room spun. My hands twisted wildly in his hair as I lost control of my movements. I bucked ravenously against him. I pressed my heels into his back. His tongue slid along my slit, making me wetter by the second. I trembled against his lips as I felt him fill me with his fingers. My toes curled and my eyes rolled back, giving way to guttural sounds that forced their way up the back of my throat.

"That's it. That's it. That's it. Clint."

I spiraled, falling into an endless sea of pleasure as his tongue pressed heavily between my legs. I felt my arousal trickling down my skin as I locked out against him. His hands pinned my hips to the bed. I felt him licking me clean as I fell, weak against the mattress. I gasped for air, the room spinning around me as he kissed softly up my body, leaving behind a trail of wet-lipped outlines that made me smile.

That made me hungrier for him.

"You're fucking perfect," he growled.

He captured my lips with his and I tasted myself on him. It filled me with a desire I'd never experienced, and soon I lifted my hips to him in sacrifice. He guided his thick girth against my walls, filling me. Shaking me. Causing me to cling to him. My nails dug into his skin. I felt his muscles rolling underneath his taut skin, working desperately for my pleasure. His movements were stark. Our hips snapped together. His bed moved with our rocking as I gasped against his ear. Bit down into his shoulder. Marked him in any way I could so any girl at school would see and realize he was taken.

Taken by me.

"Clint. Yes. Yes. Yes. Don't stop."

"Never. I'm not fucking stopping, and neither are you."

His words gave me shivers. My skin prickled everywhere, from my toes to my nose. My gut tightened as the sounds of skin slapping skin ricocheted around his room. I kissed the shell of his ear and whispered how amazing he made me feel with every broken breath. Fire raged through my veins, spurring the electrical shocks that pulsed against my spine.

I felt him everywhere. In the crook of my waist. Behind my knees. In the nape of my neck as he growled against my skin.

"So close. So close. So fucking close, Rae. Come with me."

My back bowed into him and my body unleashed. I clamped down around his length, pulling him deeper as my body begged for his nourishment. I wrapped my arms and legs around him, curling into him as he took what he wanted. And as his hands dug into the mattress, I felt the beast within him finally unleash, rutting against me as he poured into me, marking me as his own. Sinking his teeth into my breasts. Growling how perfect I was as he pinned me to the bed, breathing raggedly through his nose.

I committed every sound to memory. Every smell. Every touch. Every kiss. Every stroke. And when he collapsed against me, I slid my hands up and down his back. I danced my fingertips against his muscles. I kissed his neck and his shoulder and his ear softly, feeling him quivering against me.

"Stay with me," he murmured.

And as a smile crossed my face, I nodded my head.

"Fine by me."

20

RAELYNN

My eyes fell open before I shot up in bed. The room smelled different. It looked different. The layout wasn't what I was used to.

"Shit."

I threw the covers off me as Clint groaned next to me. I had to practically tumble myself out of bed, since the damn thing was so big. I fell to the floor, scrambling up before I ran straight into the wall. And as I stumbled along, trying to find the damn bathroom, Clint chuckled.

"Need a light?"

The room filled with a blinding light and I shielded my eyes. I grumbled underneath my breath as I reached for the door handle. I threw the door open, ready to relieve myself and try to get ready for school. Because fuck only knew what time it really was.

Instead of the bathroom, though, I was met with Clint's fucking closet.

He chuckled. "On the other side of the room."

"I hate you," I murmured.

I rushed through the bedroom, trying the door on the other side of the room. And when it gave way to a toilet, I sighed with relief. I closed the door behind me, rushing for it. Rushing for the relief it would provide me. However, the light outside made me nervous. It was much too bright for first thing in the morning. I'd most certainly missed my first period. How much of second period I'd missed, I wasn't sure.

A knock came at the door. "Need anything in there?"

I swallowed. "Just some privacy would be nice."

"I mean, you did hit the wall pretty hard. You okay?"

"I'm not bleeding, if that's what you're asking."

I drowned out his voice with the sound of the toilet flushing. I splashed some water on my face, trying to remove the sleep from my eyes. I took the liberty of using what I had around me. Hand soap on my face. Toothpaste on my finger. I used a generous amount of mouthwash, gargling before spitting it out. I picked up the hair-filled brush and said a small prayer, then ran it underneath the water. And as Clint knocked softly on the door again, I groaned.

"Can you give a girl a second?"

"You aren't the only one that has to pee, sweet cheeks."

I murmured, "Call me that again and see what happens."

"You know, you could just skip class."

I ran the wet hairbrush through my hair. "Not a chance."

"You could spend some more time with me."

"Yeah, like that's a smart decision."

He snickered. "Your words would hurt if I thought for even a second you believed them."

I finished brushing my hair before piling it on top of my head. I secured it with my rubber band, then stormed over to the door. I ripped it open, taking stock of Clint's towering form and raven hair, mussed and hanging over his eyes. I watched as those green orbs peeked out from underneath that thick head of hair. I watched as his grin grew into a salacious smile. He slipped beside me, inching me out of the bathroom before he closed the door.

Then he called out to me again.

"We could go back to the diner for some lunch."

I scoffed. "In your dreams, Clint. I have to get to school. I'm not like you."

He chuckled. "We could go to the park. Walk around. Spend a day on the beach!"

"You're crazy. This has got to stop. And it stops now. I can't keep doing this."

The door ripped open. "Doing what?"

"Don't you take that innocent tone with me, Clinton Clarke. This has to be done between us. Me, doing you."

He grinned. "Come on. You don't really want to do that. Why deny yourself such a good thing?"

"You're trouble. That's why."

"Hell yeah, I am."

I felt his eyes on me as I walked around his bedroom. I scooped my clothes off the floor, trying to quickly pull them on. I slid my brastraps up my shoulders, only for him to remove them again. I batted him away before I finally got it on, only for him to steal my pants. I shook my head at his tactics. At how he held my tank top over his head. I'd look like an idiot going to school in pajama pants and my cardigan, but it was the only choice I had.

I scoffed. "Clint. Cut it out. Give me my shirt."

He shook his head. "I really don't know why you want to cover up such a beautiful body."

"Because I don't do trouble. I have plans. I have school, and you're a distraction from that."

He handed my shirt back. "I'll take that as a compliment."

I rolled my eyes. "Of course you would."

"Why are you so bent out of shape over this? It's just one day. We can head to school at lunch time."

"Like the fun little entrance you made on the first day of school? No thank you. All I need to do is get through our senior year, then I can focus on work."

"You sound so boring. Where's the fun Rae I had last night?"

I shook my head. "She's gone. Dead. You fucked her into the mattress then suffocated her with your muscles."

His eyebrows wiggled. "Will some CPR bring her back to life?"

I felt his hands fall against my waist and I batted

him away. I slipped my cardigan over my shoulders, then looked around for my shoes.

"Aren't you going to get dressed?" I asked.

"Oh, I'm not going to class."

I paused. "Yes you are."

He snickered. "No, I'm really not."

I reached for his shirt, tossing it to him. "Yeah, you are. And you're going to get ready now, because you're my ride."

He stood tall. "Tell you what. I'll make you a deal."

"I'm not sucking your cock so you can take me to school, if that's what you're about to ask."

"If that didn't sound so tempting, I'd say your words wound me."

I sighed. "What is it, Clint? We don't have long before we have to leave."

He wrapped his arms around me and spun me around. I groaned with frustration before his fingertips started dancing along my sides. Giggles fell from my lips. I wiggled around, trying desperately to get away from his grasp. He picked me up, threw me over his shoulder, then spanked me on my ass. When I yelped, he did it again. And as I continued to yelp, he continued to do it.

"Clint, put me—ah!—down. What are you—ah!—doing?"

He laughed. "You're just adorable, you know that?"

He tossed me against the mattress and I felt myself jump. He pounced on my body, his lips falling hotly against my neck. I moaned as I pushed him away. I groaned as I tried to knock him off me. But I felt his girth growing, his body heating, his hands venturing along my body, pushing up my tank top. Pulling off my cardigan. Stripping me of the fabric I'd just gotten onto my body.

"Clint, I can't."

His lips found my ear. "A ride for a ride. That's my deal. Take it or leave it."

I snickered. "You're intolerable."

"Is that a yes?"

I grinned as I wrapped my legs around his naked waist. I rolled him over, feeling his cock settling hard against my thigh. My hands planted into his chest, and he looked at me with deviousness in his eyes. He licked his lips as his hands slid my cardigan off. I ripped my tank top over my head, bringing my clothed breasts into view. He slipped me back over, sliding my pants off with one motion of his hands. As he slid down my body, he rid me of the only barrier between us.

Then his eyes flickered up to mine.

"Ready to ride me off into the sunset, beautiful?"

And as I pulled him back up to my lips, I rolled him onto his back, straddling him as I kissed him and prepared myself to be filled with him.

21

RAELYNN

I panted for breath as I gazed up at the ceiling fan. Around and around it went, causing the room to tilt before I closed my eyes. I felt something flexing under my head. Something warm. Something strong. A heat rolled into me before something pressed against my ear. And the sounds it made sent chills down my entire body.

"It was worth it, wasn't it?"

I snickered and shook my head. I'd never give him the satisfaction of inflating that ego any more than it already was. But he was right. Missing second period had been worth that moment with him. Worth the torrential lust that poured over the two of us as he held me steady, rocking deep within me. I smiled thinking about it. I snuggled into him as he crooked himself against me, holding me with his arms. Cradling me with his legs. Allowing me to bury myself into the crook of his neck and hide away from the world.

"Hey there," he said, chuckling.

I smiled. "Hi."

He kissed the top of my head. "You doing okay down there?"

"I don't know. Depends. Does my hair look rough?"

"Are you asking me if you have sex hair? Really, Rae?"

I shrugged. "Don't have long to get to school now. We practically gotta get up and roll out."

He groaned as he rolled over and it made me laugh. I climbed on top of him, peppering his face with kisses. I settled my chin against his chest, watching as his eyes closed. Every movement he made entranced me. Every blink of his eye was a mystery I wanted to unravel. Every tick of his lips was a grin I wanted to question. Every stretch of his limbs was an opportunity I wanted to take to climb him like a fucking tree. And as his arms wrapped around me, I felt myself melting into him.

He sighed. "You're really thinking about school after all that? Because I can hardly see straight."

I snickered. "You didn't do your job as well as I did, then. Because my vision's just fine."

"Oh, you're gonna pay for that."

He rolled me over quickly as giggles fell from my lips. He muted them with his mouth, kissing me with a passion that sent my heart fluttering wildly. I slid my fingers through his hair, feeling him trying to wiggle between my legs. I moved my head side to side, and he tried to stop me as he deepened the kiss.

"Don't leave. Stay here with me," he whispered.

I giggled. "You can't keep distracting me with sex. It won't work after a while."

"I can spice it up enough to keep you here all day."

I winked. "Doubt it."

He scoffed and rolled over, gripping his chest, feigning a heart attack. It made me laugh. I slid out of bed, making my way for his bathroom. I needed one last check of my neck and my hair before I had any chance of covering shit up in school today. We were twenty minutes away from our lunch period. And us walking in together wasn't an option. He'd have to drop me off on the curb or something so the two of us could walk into the school at separate points.

Because I sure as hell wasn't ready for that firefight.

I pulled my hair out of its bun. "Are you sure my hair doesn't look bad?"

"It looks great, Rae."

"Are you just saying that to get me to shut up?"

"If I wanted to do that, I'd tell you what I really thought of your hair."

I grinned. "Now I'm intrigued."

I looked over at him, watching as he leaned against the bathroom doorway. He'd already gotten his pants on, but he still stood there shirtless. I let my eyes travel over the soft rings of his abs, my gaze lingering on the steady rise and fall of his chest. He crossed his arms over his body, flexing his biceps at me and causing me to lick my lips as he drew in a deep breath.

"If I wanted to get you to shut up, I'd tell you your hair doesn't mean shit to me. Because telling you that your hair is beautiful is like telling someone the sun's bright. It's obvious, trite, and overdone. If I really wanted to compliment you, I'd say how taken I am with the way your eyes match your hair. With the way your freckles undulate when you laugh. With the way your mind betrays an intelligence and maturity far beyond the high schoolers I have the privilege of spending time with. And if I really wanted to leave you speechless, I'd punctuate it with something like this."

He pushed off the doorway, crossing the threshold of the bathroom. His hand cupped my cheek, and as his thumb slid across my skin I felt my heart stop in my chest.

"I'd tell you the sun is jealous of the light you emit simply by being yourself. And that your hair has shit-all to do with it."

I drew in a ragged breath. "Stop it."

"I'm serious."

"I know you are, and I need you to stop it."

"Why?"

I blinked rapidly. "Because."

"Give me one damn good reason, and I'll stop."

Because you're not supposed to steal my heart.

"Because your long-winded compliments are going to make us late for lunch."

His eyes fell to my lips before his thumb ran along my skin. I shivered at his touch just before his lips pressed against mine. My head tilted back. He cradled the nape of my neck as he stepped forward, closing the gap between us. And as he slid his fingers through my hair, I whimpered against his lips.

"Your hair looks fine," he whispered.

I nodded quickly, then turned away from him. I cleared my throat and pulled my hair back into the traditional ponytail people were used to. I felt Clint's eyes on me, but I refused to look at him, because if I did I might just give in. I might just stay with him for the rest of the day instead of going to school and doing what I needed to do in order to get out of this hellhole.

He really does know how to own the English language.

The two of us got dressed, then he ushered me out of his room. With his hand on the small of my back, he guided me down the stairs, making a beeline straight for the front door. I knew why, too. Neither of us were sure whether or not his father was home. I mean, surely he'd be at work so close to lunch on a Monday. But things were always unpredictable. Schedules changed at the drop of a hat. Vacations got canceled at the last minute due to work. And sometimes, parents came home for lunch instead of eating out.

Clint reached for the doorknob. "I'll drop you off at the front curb on the road before I park behind the school."

I paused. "So we aren't walking in together?"

"Do you want to?"

"Does it matter?"

The two of us froze as his father's heavy voice sounded behind us. I slowly turned around, watching as Clint stepped in front of me. He reached behind me, slowly backing me toward the door. And as he opened it, I felt the heat of the day beat against my back.

I didn't let go of his leather jacket, though. He had to come with me. He was my ride.

Clint cleared his throat. "Morning, Dad."

"Who the fuck is that?" he asked gruffly.

"Hi. I'm—"

Clint cut me off. "None of your damn business."

His father narrowed his eyes. "You wanna try that again?"

"No. I really don't."

I drew in a sharp breath. "Clint, come on. We're gonna be late."

"Did she just come down from upstairs?"

Clint nodded. "Yes, sir."

"And is that fucking allowed in this house?"

"Probably not, sir."

His father charged him and I cried out. Clint shoved his ass out, knocking me outside before his father gripped his leather jacket. I reached out for him, watching as his father picked him up onto his tippy toes. And as his father barreled him back into the wall, I cupped my hands over my cheeks.

"I'm sick and tired of you thinking you run this house. Shut the damn door," he glowered.

I whimpered. "Clint."

He peeked back at me with nothing but sadness in his eyes. And as his hand reached out for the door, he nodded his head.

"Get outta here, Rae. Sorry for making you late and not being able to give you a ride."

"Mr. Clarke, this is all my fault. We just need to get to school. This won't happen again, I swear it. Please, Mr. Clarke."

His father gnashed his teeth at me. "Shut the hell up and get off my property."

Clint growled. "You talk to her like that again and you'll have to deal with me."

His father chuckled. "And you think you're what? Hot stuff? Because you can screw some poor girl from your high school in your own bed? You think that makes you hot stuff?"

And as Clint slammed the front door closed, I heard a resounding smack.

"No!" I exclaimed.

I heard his father yelling from behind the door, and it scared the living shit out of me. Holy fuck, his father made Clint's mean side look like Mary Poppins. I heard them fighting behind the door. It kept rattling with fury as I backed away from it. I stumbled down the porch steps, trying to get my feet underneath me as tears rushed down my face.

And as a woman's voice started yelling above all the ruckus, I made a mad dash for the road. I kept running and running. I ran until the yelling faded behind me and the sound of Clint's voice was but a distant memory. My lungs heaved for air. I felt my legs giving out as I got to the entrance of his neighborhood. I tore across the street, hearing horns honking as my cardigan wafted behind me. Sweat trickled down the nape of my neck. It grew hard to draw in air as I stumbled my way for the front doors of the school. I had to tell someone. I had to let them know what the hell was happening to Clint.

But, when I ripped the doors to the high school open, Allison appeared at my side.

"Girl. Holy mackerel. I've been looking for you all day. Michael! I found her!"

The sound of footsteps rushed beside me before someone else took my arm.

"She looks like hell. Come on. Bathroom time."

I shook my head. "No, no. I need to talk to someone. I need to—"

Michael rubbed my back. "We'll talk in a second. Right now, you need a brush to your hair, a wet paper towel to the back of your neck, and some water."

Allison sighed. "Did you oversleep?"

He scoffed. "The girl never oversleeps. You know damn good and well her mother did something."

I kept shaking my head, trying to get a word in edgewise. They dragged me down a hallway and into one of the unisex bathrooms our high school had. A new installment after our school system passed some law that required two of them to be in every school now. They tugged me in there and closed the door. I put my hands on my knees to try and catch my breath. A cool paper towel came down against my neck, and the temperature change made me heave.

Causing me to throw myself at the toilet.

"That's it. That's right. Get it all out," Allison said softly.

Michael sighed. "What should we do?"

"Is there anything we can do? Just be here for her?"

I couldn't speak. Couldn't talk. Between catching my breath and gagging into the toilet, I didn't have a chance in hell of telling them what had actually happened. Not that I could say anything in front of Michael without starting some sort of third world war between us all. No, I had to keep it to myself. Just until I could pull away from them long enough to talk to a counselor of some sort. Tell them what I'd witnessed. Tell them what was going on.

Maybe then, Clint could get the fucking help he'd needed all this time.

22

CLINTON

I punched mindlessly at the buttons on my controller. Roy kept yelling out, jumping out of his seat and trying to direct what I did with my car. But I didn't give a shit. I hadn't gone to school since my father blew his fucking cap through the roof and beat me to a bloody pulp. Well, practically. It felt like that for the past couple of days. My face ached. My nose kept bleeding at random times and my eye was swollen shut. The bruise on my jaw kept growing, and the more it grew the harder it got to eat.

Thank fuck, I like bananas.

Roy scoffed. "Come on, Clint. You mean to tell me that other eye still isn't good? You completely missed the guy on the left."

I snickered. "You put more mods on your car, didn't you?"

"Yeah. Cost me a shit ton, too. Trying to make

back some of the money so I can get to modding this other car I won last night in a race. It's a sweet one, too."

"Well, get us ready for another one. I'm gonna go get something to drink."

I set the controller down and walked out as Roy continued cursing under his breath. I shook my head as I walked into the kitchen, then sighed as I opened the fridge. The only good thing about this school week was that Dad had jetted off with Cecilia again. She'd convinced him to whisk her away to the Philippines. Why the fuck she wanted to go there I had no idea. But the promise of beaches, cocktails, and landing tail for my father was too much for him to pass up.

Which got him the fuck away from me.

That man had knocked me around for a good half hour after I shoved Rae out the door. And my only hope was that she hadn't stuck around long enough to hear any of it. It was brutal. I felt myself fighting for my life as I dodged some of my father's punches. Even when Cecilia intervened, he knocked her to the ground with his elbow. My father didn't give a shit about anyone other than himself. And after that moment, I knew he wouldn't think twice before burning me to the ground if it benefited him.

I wrote him off completely, telling myself that once I got out, I sure as hell wasn't coming back.

Ever.

"Hey, can you grab me a soda?" Roy called out.

"Coke, Mountain Dew, or Dr. Pepper?" I asked.

"Whichever one you haven't held up to your face yet. Which makes you look badass, by the way. I don't know why you aren't coming to school. The ladies would be all over you with those bruises."

I rolled my eyes as I reached for the exact Coke I'd pressed against my eye the other day. I carried the food back out to the living room, tossing it right at Roy's fucking chest. He stumbled with it, dropping his controller and crashing his car into a ditch. I chuckled as he cursed under his breath. But there were more important things than fucking Forza 4.

Like figuring out what the hell I was going to do about Rae.

"So, how long's the dad gone now?" Roy asked as he cracked open his drink.

"For the next couple weeks, I hope. At the very least, the rest of this one," I said.

"I smell a party coming on."

I shook my head. "Maybe once I'm healed a little. But not this weekend. Marina's place is fine."

"Why the hell don't you wanna show off those bruises? You always did before."

I shrugged. "Just don't feel like it this time. The fuck you care about it so much for?"

"Damn. Fine. I'll put a sock in it."

"Thanks."

I flopped back down into my seat, refusing to talk about what happened with Roy. He'd poked and prodded when he first came over after lunch, skipping his last two periods in favor of hanging out here. He did it often, too. Just randomly came over, knocked on the door, and took up space in this house. My father couldn't stand Roy. And sometimes, neither could I. But he was my only friend that didn't pry about my bruises beyond making a few bullshit comments.

Some worse than others.

We continued our racing game in silence, stacking up the winnings and racing around the tracks. Forza was getting boring, though. We had plowed through all the car racing games over the years, and it was the most mindless game on the damn market. Around and around a racing track, racking up money to modify cars we'd never have. Playing the same racing game as some defunct twelve-year-old somewhere whose mother wanted to pawn him off on games so she could fuck her boyfriend in peace.

If only they knew the life that was headed straight for them, full speed ahead.

"Earth to Clint. You there, man?"

Roy's voice ripped me from my trance and my eyes fell against the projection screen. Shit, the race had started and I was still hanging out at the starting line. I sighed as I peeled away from the flashing lights, racing around some random city with some random obstacles and some random cars chasing after us. I cut through the town, running some cars over trying to get into first place. I lost myself in the mindless momentum of it all. I sank myself into the tens of thousands of dollars we racked up in this game.

"Just twenty grand more," I murmured to myself.

A knock came at the door.

I jumped at the sound. It shocked me so badly that

Roy gave me a quizzical look. We finished up the race while the knocking continued, and I knew exactly who it was. I looked at my watch, clocking the time. School had gotten out thirty minutes ago. And not just anyone stood at someone's door, knocking for ten damn minutes.

Roy furrowed his brow. "Who the fuck isn't leaving you alone?"

I set my controller down after the race came to a close. Roy cursed the game, muttering under his breath about how we deserved more money from that win. I rolled my eyes as I made my way for the door, wondering if I should open it. Did she know I was here? Was my bike parked out front? I hadn't gotten on the damn thing in a couple days. For all I knew, Dad had sold this bike off as well.

But when she knocked at the door again, I opened it up just to get her to stop.

"You should go," I said.

Rae looked up at me, but she didn't say anything. Her jaw fell open in shock and her hand reached out to touch my bruises. I backed away from her touch. If Roy saw her out here, it'd be the end of both of us. He'd never let me live this down, and he'd tease her relentlessly about it in school.

Which meant I wasn't liable for the condition I left him in.

Rae gasped. "I've, uh… I've been worried about you."

I shrugged. "Well, here I am. Still alive and kicking."

"What did he do to you?"

"Who the hell's at the door, Clint?"

I rolled my eyes. "None of your damn business, Roy."

Rae tried reaching up for my bruises again, but I backed away. I closed the door a little more, trying to block her view of the inside of the house. It was a wreck. Shit was strewn everywhere, and I hadn't showered since Monday morning. But she didn't take the fucking hint.

"Let me come in. Let me help you clean up a bit."

I scoffed. "I'm fine. Get out of here, Rae."

"You need a doctor, Clint. Someone has to know what's going on."

I paused. "Did you tell anyone?"

"Tell anyone what?"

"Rae, don't you dare tell me you told someone at that fucking school what's happening."

"And what if I did?"

She tried reaching for my eye again, but I snatched her wrist. If she told anyone at that damn school what was going on and they started poking around, I wasn't sure I'd survive my father's assault. I'd kept it hidden from the school this long. And the last thing I needed was someone attempting to upend my life because it was their job to give a shit about me.

"Leave, Rae. I'm serio—"

"Cleaver!?"

I closed my eyes and quickly dropped her wrist. I stuck my tongue into the inside of my cheek as Roy pried the door away from my hand. I sighed as Rae's eyes flickered over to him, and he pushed his way beside me, chuckling. I'd tried to spare Rae from my best friend, but it had been her choice not to fucking listen.

Why the fuck did she never listen?

Roy laughed. "What the hell are you doing here, Cleaver Beaver?"

Rae rolled her eyes. "I could ask you the same thing, Roy Toy."

He shrugged. "I don't mind being a toy. Especially Marina's."

"Gross," she murmured.

I sighed. "I'm fine. Thanks for the homework, but it wasn't necessary. You've done your duty for the day. Let the school know I'll be back when I feel like it."

Roy scoffed. "Homework? This idiot thought you'd actually want homework?"

Rae grumbled, "I'm not an idiot."

"Goodbye, Rae."

"Wait a second. Rae?"

I saw her grow uncomfortable as Roy studied the two of us. She shuffled on her feet, her hands buried into the pockets of those faded brown pants of hers. I shoved Roy out of the way with my hip, going to close the door.

But it was too late.

"Hold up. Hold up, hold up, hold up. I know what's going on here."

Roy's voice filled my ears as panic flooded Rae's eyes.

I growled. "Roy. Cut the shit."

He barked with laughter. "Ho-lee shit. Are you fucking kidding me? You got it on… with *her*?"

Roy threw his head back with laughter as Rae turned bright pink. I looked over at her, trying to tell her how sorry I was with my eyes. But all she did was look down at her feet.

"Glad you're doing okay," she murmured. Then she turned on her heel and walked down the porch steps.

Roy slapped my back. "Holy fucking shit. That's a serious trophy, dude. Was she still a virgin? Does she shave? I feel like a girl with the last name 'Cleaver' either shaves everything, or shaves nothing. Come on, man, you can tell me. Wait a second, why the fuck didn't you tell me in the first damn place? We've got so much to talk about!"

I slammed the door closed and whipped around on him. I glared at him through my good eye, backing him slowly into the living room. He held up his hands in mock surrender, furrowing his brow deeply at me.

Then I licked my lips. "That was some bullshit you just pulled back there."

He scoffed. "And?"

"You were an ass. And you had no right to be."

"Oh, come on, Clint. There's plenty of bitches in the sea, dude. Don't waste another minute on the likes of that stuck-up snob. She'll end up like her mother, and you'll be glad you got rid of her when you could. You know they all end up like their parents."

I wanted to strangle him. I wanted to rip his tongue straight from his head. But I didn't. I drew in a few deep breaths before pushing by him, then scooped up my game controller. I fell against the couch and sighed, closing my eyes as a headache spread along the back of my skull. My mind conjured the face of Rae. The embarrassed look in her eyes. The bright pink tint of her cheeks. Maybe this was for the best. Maybe she was embarrassed, having been with me.

I mean, I was the school bully, after all. The big, bad, manwhore wolf. The man who couldn't even stand up to his father for fear of losing his own fucking life.

I certainly wasn't some prize to take home to Mommy.

"You ready for another race?"

My good eye flew open as Roy flopped down beside me. His Coke sloshed over the side, falling to my jeans with a cool splash. I slowly looked down at it, then glanced at him as he took a sip.

"You gonna cry over spilled Coke? Or are you gonna fill me in on the dirty, nasty details of the school slob?"

I quirked an eyebrow. "There a third option?"

Roy clicked his tongue. "Come on. Really? You're gonna hold out on me like that? I tell you every little fun detail with Marina, but you're not going to tell me about bagging the school sass-mouth? That's just wrong, dude. On so many levels."

"How is Marina doing, anyway?"

"Oh-ho-ho, she's fantastic. Really taking a liking to the taste of my dick after her lunch banana."

And as he launched into his latest escapades with

his girlfriend, I started up a new race for us, hoping it was enough to distract him from the fact that I'd never divulge those details with him.

Because I sure as hell didn't need the questions that would conjure.

23

RAELYNN

I pulled my ponytail out and ran my fingers through my hair while Allison fixed her makeup beside me. I'd been spending lunches in here with her, especially since I hadn't been hungry. All this week, I'd been worried about Clint. Worried he was hurt, or in the hospital, or worse. And when I showed up at his house yesterday after school, I got shooed away and laughed at.

I wondered if he was embarrassed of me. It sure seemed like it, with how quickly he tried to get me to leave.

Allison sighed. "How are things with your mom?"

I rolled my eyes. "About as good as you can expect."

"Didn't D.J. show up last night? I think that's what you said before you hung up the phone."

"Yep. To apologize, like always. He brought flowers

for Mom. A nice dinner I was forced to sit down and have."

Allison scoffed. "What was his present for you this time?"

I shook my head. "Money. Money I didn't want to take, but Mom made me. I've got it in my wallet, but I don't even know what to do with it. I'm thinking about slipping it in my mother's purse later."

"Why don't you use it to get ahead on your lunches? So you don't have to keep using your money from work."

I shrugged. "I might just put it in my savings account. Get me a hundred dollars closer to my goal."

She paused. "He gave you a hundred dollars? Just like that?"

I nodded. "Yep. Just like that. And now, it's simply a game of wait until they fight again. Which should be soon. They can't go more than a couple of weeks without repeating the cycle."

"You know you're always welcome to come over. My parents love you. For all they care, you could live with us."

I giggled. "Don't say shit like that. I might just take you up on it."

"How do my eyes look?"

I grinned. "Like Michael wants to get lost in them."

I watched her blush a bright shade of pink and I thought it was the cutest thing. This crush going back and forth between her and Michael was awesome to watch unfold. I mean, I knew he'd had the hots for her ever since eighth grade. All this time, I'd been telling him she might never return his affections. Allison had always been driven by her future. By school. By her architecture and her life's aspirations. As far as I knew, she hadn't even been kissed.

Because if she had been, I'd certainly know about it.

"Want some?" she asked, holding out her mascara.

I scoffed. "And who the fuck would I be wearing that for?"

"I don't know. Maybe Clint Clarke?"

Marina's voice wrapped around us as my eyes fell onto her reflection. I watched her walk out of one of the stalls as Allison's jaw dropped open. Holy shit, she'd been in there the entire time. Listening. Eavesdropping. Learning shit about my life I certainly didn't want her to know about.

Marina giggled. "Sucks about your mom. But money talks. And good dick."

Allison snarled. "What the heck do you want?"

Marina grinned. "Such harsh words. Might want to tone it down there."

"What, Marina?" I asked flatly.

She smiled sweetly before she came over to the sink beside me. She washed her hands with meticulous precision, cleaning underneath her fingernails. I slowly looked over at Allison, watching my best friend silently glower at this girl. Whatever was coming, it wasn't good. And with Roy finding out about my affair with Clint yesterday, it didn't shock me that I was now having a run-in with his girlfriend.

Marina reached for the paper towels. "So I heard a little rumor."

I rolled my eyes. "I'm sure you did."

Allison scoffed. "What rumor, Marina?"

She smiled brightly. "A rumor that says your friend is fucking the brains out of Clint Clarke himself."

I peeked over at Allison and watched her face pale.

I sighed. "I take it you heard this from Roy?"

Marina wiped her hands off. "Let's just say a little birdie told me."

"A little birdie you're fucking around with."

She threw the paper towel away. "What's it to you if we are?"

Allison went to say something, but I held up my hand. It would be nothing but wasted energy. And this was my fight, not hers. I didn't know what Marina had up her sleeve. I didn't know what she was trying to do. But I didn't want Allison caught up in it. I wanted her to enjoy her senior year.

Not be dragged down by a decision I'd made in a moment of weakness.

"What do you want, Marina?"

She giggled. "I just want to hear it from you. That's all."

"Well, then you're barking up the wrong tree."

She snickered. "Figures. You'll freely talk about your mother hoeing around. But you certainly don't want to talk about you doing it."

Allison took a step forward. "That's enough."

I turned around, pressing my hands against her shoulders. I leveled my gaze at her as Marina threw her head back with laughter. I shook my head. The last thing we needed was some girl fight where we pulled at each other's hair and eventually got expelled. Michael had almost blemished his perfect record with the fight against Clint. I wasn't about to let Allison throw her acceptance to UCLA away because she wanted to claw this bitch's eyes out.

"Let me handle this," I whispered.

Then I turned around to face Marina.

"I'll ask you again. What is it you want?"

Marina leapt for me, getting into my face. "I'll tell you what I want, you little slut. I want you to know your place. I want you to know exactly where you stand with a man like Clint. You're nothing compared to him. He's got the world at his feet, and you'll be drowning in squalor. Fucking men in an effort to pay your bills. Whoring around like your mother does. We already see you turning into her. You look like her. Smell like her. Talk like her. Walk like her. And soon, you'll fuck like her, too. The town mattress, ready for a good ride whenever you're drunk enough."

I shrugged. "Too bad I don't drink."

Marina scoffed. "Just like Clint beat the snot out of your friend, I've got no problems beating the snot out of you. Or your little friend behind you. You think you're tough, but you're nothing, Cleaver."

I grinned. "If I didn't know any better, I'd say this was coming from a place of jealousy."

She paused. "So the two of you are fucking."

I shrugged. "Why do you care if we are?"

Marina lunged at me and I heard Allison squeal.

But I held my ground. I didn't flinch. I didn't blink. And I sure as hell didn't move. Marina ran her eyes down my body before moving along beside me, brushing her shoulder against mine.

"I'll be watching you, you piece of trailer trash," she said.

I snickered. "I'd have to live in a trailer for that title, Marina. Or do you not know the difference between a house and a trailer?"

"I don't know. Maybe I'll get Clint to educate me this weekend at my pool party. You know, once he's done making out with the girls in the hot tub. That's his favorite pastime. And it really is a treat to watch once those girls get to grinding in his lap."

I bristled at her words as she left. I heard her giggle fade down the hallway, her heels clicking against the tiled flooring. I slowly turned around to Allison, who was visibly trembling with anger. The embarrassed tinted blush of her cheeks had turned to a full-on crimson rage, her fists clenched at her sides.

"Allison, breathe. She's not worth the effort."

She shook her head. "She is an absolute, raging bitch."

My eyebrows rose. "I think that's the first time I've ever heard you use that word."

"Well, it's true. Marina's nothing but a—a sleazy, good for nothing rollercoaster boys can have a good ride on before bouncing to the next one!"

I giggled. "Wow."

"What?"

I paused. "I kind of like this side of you."

"I sucked down what happened with Michael. I mean, he's a guy. He can take care of himself. But watching it happen to you? That's completely different. I'm done with this… this stuff. I'm done with Clint and his cronies screwing around with you just because he's—"

I held my hand up. "Allison."

She sighed. "Sorry."

The two of us turned toward the bathroom exit.

"What the heck was that all about anyway?" she breathed.

And as my mind swirled with the encounter, my shock turned to rage. I knew exactly what it was about. I knew exactly where that information had come from. Though I didn't want to admit it—nor did I want to believe it—I knew what was happening. I knew what Clint was doing.

"It was a wake-up call, Allison. That's what it was. And it's time I finally listened to the alarm."

It was time for me to accept that my weakest moment would now be used against me. Especially if my suspicions regarding why were correct.

I turned to Allison. "Is Clint at school today?"

She paused. "Yes. He was in first period math today with Michael."

"Good."

I started out of the bathroom, feeling Allison trail behind as I turned my attention to him. That boy. The boy I had a strong feeling had been manipulating me from the beginning.

It was time for me to get some answers.

24

CLINTON

Marina choked down that damn banana like she probably choked down Roy's fucking dick. She sat on his lap, giggling and kissing the tip of his nose like the innocent girl Roy wanted her to be. He had a sick sense of humor, wanting to destroy innocence like that. I liked my women primed, though. Already knowing what they wanted, and ready to bestow their talents upon me.

Then again, I hadn't thought about any girl since my encounters with Rae.

"Oh, Clint. Where'd you get those bruises?"

"Here, let me help."

"Can I do anything for you?"

"Do you want me to get you some ice cream?"

I looked over at Roy and he winked. He was right. Women couldn't resist a guy with bruises on his fucking face. But if they knew how I'd gotten those bruises, it would be a different story. The line of girls coming up to me asked me where I got them, and each time my fight story became a little more dramatic. It went from some kid on the side of the road to some kid picking on a girl on the side of the road. Then, it morphed into some college kid on the side of the road picking on his fiancée before I offered to show her what a real man could provide.

It was the first time in my life I ever felt pathetic for it.

"Clint!"

Rae's voice pierced through the cafeteria and my eyes fell upon her. She strode with intensity in her movements and a sour expression on her face. The girl at my side, trying to practically spoon-feed me ice cream, got up and stepped off to the side. Roy chuckled and out of the corner of my eye I saw Marina's lips curve into a wide grin. I spread my arms out, letting my knees fall apart in the stance I was known for.

Spreading myself wide for all to see.

Gotta keep up appearances.

Rae stopped in front of me. "Fancy seeing you at school."

I shrugged. "Can't keep everything hidden forever."

She grinned. "No, you can't."

I flickered my eyes over to Allison and saw her staring at Marina. I didn't know what the fuck that bitch had done, but it had certainly pissed the two of them off. Rae had her hands balled up into fists. Hell, so did Allison. I narrowed my eyes softly—well, my good eye. The other one was still too swollen. I tried to read her, to figure out why the hell she was storming up to me in the cafeteria on a whim.

I mean, I had to give her props for her balls. Especially after the encounter with Roy the other day. But what was her problem?

I licked my lips. "Can I help you?"

Marina giggled. "Yeah, Rae. Can Clint help himself to you?"

Roy let out a bark of a laugh as the rest of the guys around us chuckled. But Rae didn't bat an eye. She kept staring at me. Glaring at me. With those fists balled up, ready to fly.

Then she pointed her trembling finger at me.

"I'm only going to tell you this once, because I'm done with your antics."

Marina smacked her lips. "Oooh, scary. Practically a haunted house."

Roy wrapped his arm around her waist. "I bet her house is one."

Everyone snickered again. But Rae didn't move. She stood strong, and I admired her for that. Because my friends could be ruthless when they chose to be.

I sighed. "What is it, Cleaver?"

Her eye twitched. "If this is the kind of bullshit I have to put up with to be friends with you, then it's not worth it. Do you hear me? I'm not going to be cornered in a bathroom and teased relentlessly for shit I'm trying to do to help you. To befriend you. To see the decent fucking person beyond the shitstain that is the boy that walks into this school every day."

I watched her shoot a killer look at Marina before her eyes came back to mine.

"So if these are the lowlifes you're going to hang out with? These stubborn, ignorant, pig-headed, ugly people? Then we're through. You and me, and whatever this is, it's over."

I blinked at her, not knowing what to say. Did she really expect me to make a choice right now? In front of my friends? When our fuckable encounters were nothing more than rumor at this point? I looked over at Marina, watching her practically foaming at the mouth. What the hell had she done to these two girls?

I cast a glare at Roy before my eyes panned back to Rae.

She furrowed her brow. "I guess I have my answer then?"

What the fuck did she really expect me to do? I mean, I knew we had something special. A connection I'd never shared with anyone else. She got me, and I got her. And when I was with her, the rest of the world faded away. But when she wasn't around, when we weren't behind closed doors, the world existed. Sure, it was only high school. And yeah, I hung around shitty people. But I sure as hell wasn't going to spend my senior year—the last glory year of my life—fucking around in the shadows and having spit balls stuck to the back of my head.

She's the only person who doesn't make you feel like shit, Clint. Don't do this.

"Well?" Marina asked.

I kept staring at Rae as I answered her. "Put a cock in it and shut up."

Everyone snickered again behind me except Roy. He didn't stand up for her, but he sure as hell didn't buck up to me. He knew his place.

Like everyone else.

You don't have to put on a show with Rae.

"Well?" she asked.

I didn't know what to do. Things with her were so new. I mean, days old kind of new. And it was terrifying. What was I supposed to do? Toss the entirety of my reputation away on a girl I'd fucked around with for a few days? She wasn't just any girl, though. Even I knew that. But was I ready for a move like that? Was I ready to abandon my post as top dog of this school and attempt something else with her? Something that wasn't guaranteed?

For all I knew, this was a ploy of hers. A ploy to peel me away from my throne so she could wreak revenge and havoc on my life. I mean, we had a history, she and I. And not simply a sexual one. I'd made her life a living nightmare freshman year. And she'd been my target on and off for the rest of high school.

For all I knew, this was her revenge. Her plan. And with Allison at her side after what I did to Michael? It wouldn't have shocked me one bit.

I'm not ready to take that chance yet.

Rae sighed. "You did this on purpose, didn't you?"

Marina giggled. "You mean, did he do you on purpose?"

I grumbled, "Put a muzzle on that girl or get her the fuck away from this table."

Roy scoffed. "Say what now?"

Rae sighed. "It's fine. Just don't play stupid. I know they know. I've accepted that. But at least give me the satisfaction of confirming the nightmare I've already come to terms with."

I shrugged. "Not sure what you mean."

Roy chuckled. "She means, did you fuck her in order to use it against her? Because honestly, if you did? Fucking props to you. Because that's some lowdown shit and I love it."

Marina cackled. "Cleaver Beaver the Dick Eater. Has a nice ring to it."

Roy threw his head back in laughter and the gang behind me joined in. I sat there, staring up at Rae, and I saw Allison tearing up, getting emotional for her. It was the first time I'd ever felt guilty for teasing someone. For pushing someone around. I wanted to apologize to them for what happened with Michael. I wanted to apologize for the unhinged animals behind me, cackling and barking with laughter like feral fucking animals.

Rae nodded. "This was always going to be used against me, wasn't it?"

Her voice was so soft, it almost got swallowed up by the laughter around me. And yet I heard it. Loud and clear. Like a fucking bullhorn. How the fuck could she even think that? Did I come off as that terrible of a person? That much of an asshole?

Because that was some shit my father would have pulled in his younger years.

Holy shit, I'm turning into my father.

Allison sniffled. "Come on, Rae. Let's get out of here. None of them are worth it."

Marina snickered. "Not what Rae thought when she was spreading her legs."

"Can it!" I roared.

The entire fucking cafeteria came to a grinding halt as I looked over at that bitch.

"What the fuck has your boyfriend, on numerous occasions, told you about that disgusting mouth of yours? Either keep it closed or take Roy somewhere and stuff it full. Got it? Holy fuck, Marina."

Everyone's eyes went wide as I turned my attention back to Rae. But, try as I might, I couldn't bring myself to address the issue at hand. She shook her head side to side, then allowed Allison to turn her around. She peeked over her shoulder at me as a sadness filled her stare. Then she stopped and turned around to face me.

"Thank you for giving me the answer I needed," she said.

I paused, then sighed. "You're welcome, I guess."

The cafeteria returned to its dull roar as Allison shook her head. I saw Rae's chin trembling and it broke my fucking heart. I turned my eyes out toward the window, where some of the nerds sat on the back patio doing homework while eating their fucking lunch. I couldn't stand to look at her. I couldn't stand to look at myself.

You're a sorry excuse for a human, Clint. Just like your father.

"You all deserve each other, you know that?"

I snickered at Rae's voice. "Yeah, I guess so."

And I watched as Allison physically pulled her out of the cafeteria, leaving me surrounded by a bunch of brainless, nitwitted assholes I wanted nothing more to do with.

Fuck my life.

25

RAELYNN

I sat at my window as the thunder rolled. The snacks under my bed were long gone, but I wasn't hungry anyway. Not after my encounter with Clint at school today. I placed my elbow on the windowsill, resting my chin in my hand. I saw lightning crack the sky, illuminating the world around me. Black outlines of decrepit houses came into view. The rolling green hills of the rich beyond ignited, taunting me with what I'd never have. The storm rolled in, bringing the pitter-patter of rain. I watched it come, a shower of greatness. Here to wash away the stench of our garbage-laden street.

It didn't wash away the hurt in my heart, though.

"Fuck Clinton Clarke."

The rain battered against my window as lightning pierced the sky overhead. The clouds hung low, pregnant with rain. They were so close I imagined I was almost able to reach up and touch them. I placed my forehead against my window, the same window I'd crawled out of that night I first slept with Clint. I closed my eyes and reminisced about how much I'd hated the fact that he'd found me. How much I'd enjoyed opening up to him. How wonderful the bike ride had been and how kind he'd been.

How gentle he was.

"Stop it," I muttered. "You're torturing yourself."

Tears rolled down my cheeks with every flash of lightning. And as the thunder crashed, I let my sobs run free. All day, I'd kept them in check. Throughout history, where I felt Clint staring at me. Throughout P.E., where I saw him in the bleachers watching me from beyond his sunglasses. I dealt with the snickers and the names murmured under people's breath as I passed by. Cleaver Beaver the Dick Eater. How quickly shit like that worked its way around the school.

I wondered if I was turning into my mother.

"Shit."

I put my head in my hands and cried. I didn't try to hold it back any longer. The thunder covered up my sobs and the lightning heated my tears. And as the rain battered harder against my window, it was almost like the storm was trying to wash my sins away. Wash my tears away. Cheer me up with its furious might. I was envious of the storm. How strong it was. How it could rage, and people didn't bat an eye. If anything, they cowered away. Respecting it. Admiring it. Sitting out on the porch and watching it in a mesmerized sort of awe.

Now I know how Clint feels.

I didn't know which was worse, being invisible to

the masses or being seen only for my greatest mistake. But the truth of the matter was that I still didn't regard Clint as a mistake. I never could. What we'd shared was tremendous, even if he didn't feel it. Even if it was faked on his end. Even if he completely fabricated his words and his actions and his emotions, I hadn't. I didn't. And I never would.

"That's what makes you better than him."

I sat up from my arms and dried my face. I sniffled until my nose was clear, then went back to watching the storm. I'd had my moment of weakness, and now it was time to press onward and forward, like nothing ever happened. It was all I had, and it was all I'd use. Because in the end, that made me better than them. They could flash their money around and ride in their expensive cars and wear their designer clothes to school. But, in the end, what made me better and stronger than them was my ability to persevere.

Whereas they broke down over a scuffed tennis shoe. Or a broken nail.

Except Clint.

I shook the thought from my head. He was like them. Just like them. He wasn't different. He showed me that today. There was no use in crying over him. He was nothing but a cup of spilled, spoiled milk.

I hated that I'd fallen for it, though. I was angry at myself for falling for his tricks. His ruse. Not seeing through the wolfish grin long enough to latch onto his plan. His ultimate plan to destroy me. His ultimate plan to play the best trick this fucking high school had ever seen.

Fucking around with the school charity case before exposing her to be like every other girl who wanted to ride Clint Clarke's cock.

It was genius. And simple. And I'd fallen for all of it.

I sighed. "You're such a fool, Rae. Holy shit."

A knock came at my door and I shot up from the windowsill. I dove back into my bed, covering myself up as I tried to make myself look presentable. The last thing I needed was my mother knowing any of this, for more shame to come down onto the people in this family. I called out for her to come in, hiding my reddened cheeks with my pillow.

When the door slowly swung open, she arched her brow at me.

"You okay in here?"

I sighed. "That obvious?"

She snickered. "I may or may not have been standing here for a few minutes now."

"Oh."

Mom walked into my room and closed the door behind her. She came and sat on the edge of my bed, patting my leg. I didn't like her seeing me like this. I had to take care of her. That was how this dynamic worked. That was how it always worked with us.

But I needed my mom, too.

"You wanna talk about it?" she asked.

I rolled my eyes. "Just some stupid boy at school."

Mom sighed. "I'm familiar with those."

I paused. "How far do you think a bully would go in order to get a rise out of someone?"

"Why do you ask?"

"I think a bully at my school has gone a little too far with some stuff."

"Would this be the stupid boy at school?"

I scoffed. "Aren't all stupid boys eventually bullies?"

She paused. "You have a good point."

The two of us shared a brief moment of laughter before Mom took my hand.

"Has he hurt you, sweetheart?"

I sighed. "Not physically."

She nodded. "Okay, good. I mean, not good with the hurt. But—"

My eyes widened. "Oh, no no no. Nothing— nothing like that. Nothing like what you're thinking."

"You'd tell me though? If it was?"

"I promise, everything that happened wa—"

Mom raised her eyebrows as I caught what I was about to say.

"I, uh…"

She giggled. "Sweetheart, I was much younger than eighteen when I started having sex with boys."

"Mom."

She smiled. "I'm not going to go into that. We had that talk when you were much younger. But let me see if I can piece this together. You fell for the school bully, had some romantic moments together, and now he wants nothing to do with you. Right?"

I paused. "Don't tell me you've experienced some- thing like that, too."

She shrugged. "It happens sometimes. Maybe not

quite like that, but it does happen. And it sucks. And I kind of want to wring his throat."

I giggled at her words as the pillow slowly slid away from my face.

"What do I do?"

She sighed. "There's nothing you can do. You can't change a man. So you can't let that man change you. Bad boys are just that. Bad. Bad for you. Bad for themselves. Bad for anyone who comes into their lives."

I nodded slowly. "People at school will know soon enough."

"And all you can do is stand up to them. Stand your ground and don't let them beat you into it. High school is relentless. There isn't a person on this planet —rich or poor—that would do it all over again. I'm here for you, no matter what. And you can talk to me about anything, okay?"

I smiled softly. "Thanks, Mom."

She tucked a strand of hair behind my ear. "I guess we both have a tendency to go for the wrong men."

I giggled. "Yeah. Fuck D.J."

Mom laughed, covering my mouth with her hand. "Fuck D.J."

"Did something happen?"

Her hand fell away from my face. "Isn't something always happening with him?"

"I thought you two just made up, though?"

She shrugged. "Maybe I didn't want to make up this time. Maybe I'm ready to let him go."

"Wait, seriously?"

"Seriously."

I paused. "You're done with him? I mean, for real this time?"

She nodded. "For real this time. I have to stop this cycle, Rae. I didn't realize the damage I was doing to myself. Or to you. Or to us. I'm sorry, sweetheart. I'm sorry I've set this kind of example for you. I'm sorry I raised you in all this. I'm so—please forgive me, honey."

"Of course, Mom. Of course I forgive you."

She started crying and I pulled her closely to me. I wrapped my arms around her, silently thanking any god that would listen. Maybe this was it. The breakthrough my mother needed in order to see the life she had carved out for herself. I cried along with her, burying my face into her hair as she scooped me into her lap. I hadn't been in my mother's lap for years. Since I was nothing but a child who stood tall enough to wrap my arms around her hips. She held me close, rocking me side to side as the two of us grieved with one another.

Grieved for our broken hearts and minds.

Mom kissed the top of my head. "I love you so much, sweetheart."

My breathing shuddered. "I love you, too."

"It's done. I promise you, it's over. He's never coming back around. You have my word."

"Thank you, Mommy. Thank you so much."

She whispered. "I've missed hearing you call me that."

Mom held me as the rain continued to batter against the window. Even though the thunder rolled away into the distance, the rain continued to flood our front lawn, drowning the grass seeds Mom and I always attempted to plant and grow during the summer months. I sighed as I pulled away, falling back to the mattress of the bed. And as Mom stood up, she reached for my hand.

"Want to watch a movie and make a pizza delivery guy drive out to us in this nonsense?"

I smiled. "Oh, hell yeah."

She leveled her eyes with me before soft laughter fell from her lips. I took my mother's hand, and together, we started down the hallways. We slipped down the stairs in our socks, laughing and picking at one another as we crash-landed into the foyer. Mom went to grab her cell phone while I picked out a movie, and the only thing that raced through my mind was how things felt normal again.

How things felt good again.

"Pepperoni and pineapple?" Mom called out.

"And mushroom!"

Mom barked with laughter. "Thanks for the afterthought, kid."

I giggled. "You're welcome. Especially after you see what I'm gonna make us watch."

"Please tell me it's not another Rocky movie."

And instead of answering her, I simply let the opening song do it for me.

Mom poked her head around the corner. "I'm ordering brownies instead of cinnamon bites for that one."

"Hey," I protested. "I like their cinnamon bites!"

She winked as she ducked back around the corner, wrapping up the order for our meal of the night. I sat down on the couch, watching my favorite Rocky movie make its entrance. But the second Mom came back into the room, a knock sounded at the door.

"Huh. Bit fast for a pizza guy, don't you think?"

I shook my head, smiling. "I'll get it. You sit down and watch this cinematic marvel."

Mom groaned. "We're watching The Notebook after this."

"If I can stay awake through it, I'll even promise to act like I'm paying attention."

"Ha. Ha. Ha."

I threw my head back with laughter as my mother's voice. I hadn't felt this carefree with her in a long time, and it felt wonderful. The last time we had a true girls' night like this, I was just starting seventh grade. We'd watched Beauty and the Beast while wolfing down pasta from her favorite Italian place up the street, and ended up falling asleep together on the couch halfway through the second movie.

I couldn't wait to do the same thing tonight.

I reached for the doorknob as the rain finally slowed to a trickle. I smiled brightly as I greeted whoever the hell was at the door at six in the evening on a Thursday night. I expected it to be a few people. Allison, coming over to check on me. Clint, coming to grovel at my feet before I curb-stomped his face. Even Marina, coming to take another jab at me before she went and got off with her boyfriend.

But, I sure as hell didn't expect to see Michael.

Soaking wet. Dripping with venom from his lips and angry eyes that widened as I appeared at the doorway.

"You hooked up with Clinton Clarke? Are you fucking kidding me?"

And just like that, things were not-so-good again.

26

CLINTON

"Shot! Shot! Shot! Shot!"

The crowd chanted as another double shot got shoved into my hand. Girls reached out for me as Roy slapped me on the back, cheering me on yet another time. I'd lost count of how many of these I'd had. I didn't have a damn clue how full my stomach was of vodka. The only things I was aware of was the smell of Marina's backyard pool and the chanting, laughter and clapping as I drank all these assholes under the damn table.

I had numbed myself so I wouldn't feel the pain of losing Rae.

"Yeah, Clint! Get it!"

Everyone clapped as I threw back the clear liquid. I opened my throat, allowing it to slide directly into my stomach without so much as swallowing. Fucking hell, I'd gotten too good at that. And it felt marvelous. Kind of. In a way.

Why didn't this feel as good as it used to?

"Care for another one, big boy?"

"Eat some peanuts first."

"Want a sip of my margarita? Tequila always gets me ready for another round."

"Woo! Clint! Come jump in the pool with me!"

I felt someone tugging at me and I ripped back. I leaned against the bar counter with a smirk on my face, gazing at the horde of people around me. Girls in their bikinis and their barely-there tits. Girls with slim hips and tiny waists and long legs ready to wrap themselves around me. Dyed blond hair flashed, as the alcohol-soaked girls that had come to have a good time and be admired preened and strutted.

And yet, my mind still drifted back to Rae.

It's better this way.

"You can do one with me, right?" Roy asked.

I felt him shove another shot in my hand before he raised up his own. We clinked our shot glasses together before throwing them back, and I felt my world tilt in on itself. For a split second, I stood on the sky, looking down at the stars and the cloudy night before gazing up at the pool, the grass, the concrete and the people walking around.

You're gonna be sick tonight, jackass.

With a blink of my eye, the world righted itself. But my stomach didn't feel well. I drew in some deep breaths, trying to keep it all down and not get sick on myself. This crowd of assholes would spread it around school come Monday. I slumped against one of the bar stools as the girls walked away, jumping into the pool and shrieking in delight. Marina beckoned for Roy, swaying her hips and jiggling those small tits of hers, and Roy clapped me against the shoulder as he headed for his lay of the night. I sat there with thoughts of Rae floating around in the alcohol that swirled around my brain.

She deserves better than you, dickweed.

I scoffed as I closed my eyes. I swallowed hard a few times, trying to settle the bile creeping up the back of my damn throat. I mean, how long could I have expected us to last, anyway? Rae would have left me the second something better came along. I knew how women worked. What they wanted out of life. They were all the same, once I stripped back the clothes and the soft demeanors. And knowing my luck, something better would have come along sooner rather than later.

Just when I'd started to fall for her.

Get up, asshole. You need water.

But I didn't want to get up.

"And this is Clint," Roy said.

The giggle that filled my ear caused me to open my eyes, and I found myself staring at a very pretty girl. Short red hair. Freckles all across her face and bright brown eyes. A slim figure not at all concealed in a string bikini. She looked like the rest of the girls here. A bit too long-legged. A bit too buck-toothed. A bit too much waterproof makeup and absolutely no curves in sight.

I nodded. "Hey there."

The girl giggled. "Hi."

Roy smiled proudly. "This, my friend, is Lindsey."

I licked my lips. "Nice to meet you."

She nodded. "You, too. I, uh, saw you over here. With those shots."

I quirked an eyebrow. "You like what you see?"

And when she blushed, I had my answer.

Roy cleared his throat. "Well, I'll let you two get to know one another. Clint."

"Yep?"

"Don't do anything I wouldn't do."

I rolled my eyes as the girl let out another soft giggle. A forced one. One that probably got her into Roy's good graces in the first place. I appreciated the effort, but I wasn't into it. Lindsey was a pretty girl, but she wasn't Rae.

Still, though, she sat next to me at the bar.

"Do you come to these parties often?"

I slowly panned my eyes over to her. "Yep. You?"

She shook her head. "No. First time ever being invited."

"Is it everything you could have hoped for, and more?"

"That depends. What are you doing later on?"

My cockeyed grin spread across my face, but I didn't make a move for her. She wasn't my type. Wasn't my style. And I had no issues letting her know it. I lobbed my head over to see her and found her blushing again. Tainting that creamy skin of hers that, in any other world, would have had me on my knees ready to give her the attention she wanted.

Tonight, however, was different.

I chuckled. "I'm sleeping off this alcohol and

trying not to wake up with a bleeding hangover in the morning."

Lindsey's face fell. "Oh."

"That's the price ya pay for shooting vodka all night."

"Guess it's rough being the entertainment."

And as she snickered, her words slapped me across the face.

Entertainment.

I was nothing but the entertainment?

I heard her say something, but I didn't catch it. I felt her kiss my cheek as her hand lingered against my thigh, but I hardly felt it. And as she walked away, I didn't even steal a glance at her barely-there ass. My mind had latched onto that word. That phrase. It parsed out every syllable and bounced around in my head. Taunting me. Lashing out at me. Encompassing the whole of my high school career.

Entertainment.

My eyes slowly focused on the crowd around me as images of a trained monkey rushed through my mind. Being slapped around and whipped by trainers before being put in front of a crowd and expected to obey. It was an apt description. One that made my stomach turn over on itself. And as I sat there on the sidelines watching everyone else party, I wondered how I'd gotten there.

Here.

At this dumbass party with these dumbass people.

Do I even like these people?

In a flash, I was unsure of everything in my life. As

I slid off the barstool and made my way for the patio doors, I felt people clamoring for my attention. Women tugging me over to the hot tub and guys trying to get me into the pool. Roy tried sliding my leather jacket off, but I simply shook him off me.

"The fuck, man? I set you up with a good catch."

"You good? You need some water?"

"Give him some space. I think he's gonna puke."

"Hey! Clint! What gives?"

I ignored all of their comments and questions as I lumbered into Marina's parents' house. I slid the patio doors closed behind me, seeking solace in the ice cold air conditioning of their kitchen. I walked over to the fridge and pulled out a bottle of water, chugging it back as it filled my stomach. I backed it up with another. Then another. And slowly, I felt my veins being freed of the alcohol I'd pushed through them.

Which freed my mind up to roam even more.

"Clint! The fuck!"

Roy's muffled voice hit my ears and I turned around. I saw him banging his fist on the kitchen window before he shrugged at me with an attitude I didn't like. I held my bottle of water up to him before drinking the rest back, but Roy wasn't a fan of my actions. He looked pissed. Though I didn't know why.

I mean, did he sell his soul to Satan in order to get me that girl?

Terrible exchange.

I tossed my third empty bottle of water into the trash can, then grabbed a fourth. And as I cracked it open, I started walking through the house. It was small, compared to my father's. But there was a lot of love in this place. I felt it. The walls bled with it. And it made me smile. The sounds of the party fell into the background as I walked down the small hallway. I stood in the living room, gazing out at the front lawn as whispers of happy secrets puffed up from the plush carpet I stood on.

You don't belong here.

My eyes fell onto my bike and I felt myself gravitating to the front door. I slid my bottled water into my leather jacket pocket, making my way outside. My feet carried me toward my bike as I drew in a deep breath. And as I slung my leg over the side, I reached for my helmet.

Drink the water first.

"The fuck are you doing!?"

Roy's voice caused my head to whip up as I held my helmet in my hands.

"You leaving already?"

And as my best friend came closer to me, something happened. Something changed. Something shifted.

For the first time since I'd started high school, I wanted as far away from Roy as I could get.

27

RAELYNN

"Now, class, make sure you read the labels on your beakers and bottles carefully. I understand we have a shower in the back, but that doesn't mean I want to use it today."

The class let out a soft titter, but I kept my eyes trained on my hands. I wrung them in circles, taking deep breaths as I kept reliving that moment. The look on Michael's face a few nights ago when he strolled up onto my porch during that thunderstorm. The anger in his eyes. The heat in his voice. The way he scoffed at me before stalking away, not giving me any time to craft any sort of a response.

Just an accusation and my guilty face staring back at him.

Allison nudged me "You listening?"

My head whipped up. "Sorry. Yeah."

"If you're listening, what did the teacher just say?"

"He doesn't want to use the shower today."

"That was seven statements ago. So you're not listening. Good. At least I know now."

"You know damn good and well why I'm not listening."

The teacher cleared his throat. "There something you want to share with the class, ladies?"

Allison shook her head. "No, sir. Nothing."

And when he looked at me, all I did was shake my head.

"Good. Now, one last thing. Once you document everything you see from your experiment, I want you to keep your notes with you until tomorrow's class. We're going to be taking three sets of notes and comparing them for grades at the end of the week. So make sure not to get any liquids on them."

I sighed. "Great."

Allison giggled. "I'll help you out as much as I can. I know you're not the cleanest person around."

"Thanks? Maybe?"

"Hey, at least you were listening this time."

I shot her a look, but all she did was giggle. Our teacher released us to the hounds, allowing us to conduct the experiment in front of us with very minimal instruction. I hated chemistry. Science had been the bane of my existence ever since middle school. But it was required, and if I took it now I wouldn't have to take it in college.

Good for you, thinking about the future.

Allison and I worked in silence for a few minutes. We poured chemicals into beakers together and documented what we witnessed. We combined elements that made a sort of putty mixture before melting into a pile of goop. Which was weird and utterly unexpected. I was almost certain we'd done that particular facet wrong. But what really felt odd was standing with Allison in complete and utter silence.

So I took a leap of faith.

"You know, don't you?"

She sighed. "It's not hard to pinpoint. Especially since Michael didn't want to walk with us this morning."

"Has he talked with you about it?"

"No. He hasn't so much as looked my way."

I sighed. "I'm so sorry, Allison."

She shook her head. "Nothing to be sorry about. If anything, you should apologize to him for keeping it from him for so long."

"Thanks."

"Just trying to tell it like it is."

I paused. "He was so angry, Allison. I mean, just furious. Standing on my porch, drenched in water. Fists clenched. Teeth grinding together. I mean, I didn't even get a chance to respond before he stormed back off through my drowned front yard. I've never seen him like that before. I'm worried about him."

"He probably feels betrayed."

"And I feel like shit for that."

"How are we doing back there, ladies?" our teacher piped up from across the room.

I tried my best not to sigh. "Doing great, Mr. Abernathy."

He nodded. "Wonderful. Now get back to work."

Allison picked up her pencil. "Right away, Mr. Abernathy."

We kept our heads down with the experiments and the descriptions until his attention was off us. Then, Allison flickered her eyes over to me. I felt her studying me. Trying to figure out what the fuck to say next. And I hated it. I hated all of this. I wanted to talk with Michael. I wanted to explain what had happened, to tell him the kind of life Clint actually led, because I knew Michael well. I knew if *he* knew, he'd look at this differently. Despite the fight. Despite the blood. Despite the anger.

Then I felt my cheeks flush with red.

"I'm so embarrassed, Allison."

She rubbed my back. "He'll come around soon enough. He has to."

I scoffed. "Does he, though? Because right now, I'm the all-around shitty friend."

"He just doesn't get it right now. He needs to cool that hot head of his, and then yes. He'll come around. He always does."

"Have you ever seen him this upset before?"

And when I looked over at her, she shook her head.

"I haven't, no. But, I know what he's like when he gets frustrated with schoolwork. Or his parents. He loves you. Just like I do. And when he's done pitching his fit, he'll come around. Trust me."

I shrugged. "If you say so."

"Boys just don't understand this kind of thing."

I scoffed. "Well, add me to that bunch. Because I don't get it either."

She sighed. "Look, in the end, it doesn't matter. It's over, right? So just give Michael some time and he'll bounce back eventually. I'm sure of it."

"I really hope you're right."

"If you'd like to share with the class, I'm sure all of us could take a break to listen."

I bit down on the inside of my cheek as Mr. Abernathy's voice rose above the class. My eyes locked with his, and I saw him staring at me with a cool look on his face. He thought he was clever. Smart. Observant. But all I did was smile politely at him before drawing in a deep breath.

"No, sir. Just talking about the experiments and how they relate to real life. You know, like how I'd enjoy melting a very specific boy I know into a puddle of goop just by pouring this blue substance over his head."

"Rae," Allison hissed.

Mr. Abernathy's eyes widened. "A boy?"

I nodded. "Mm-hmm. Boy troubles during science experiments. I think I've got a new podcast, don't you? That's what I was talking about, by the way. Podcasts and boys."

The classroom snickered and laughed as the teacher's face fell.

"Ah, well uh. Just—keep your head focused and in the game. You've only got fifteen minutes left in class and I expect the two of you to be through that list of experiments."

Allison sighed. "This is our last one, Mr. Abernathy."

He nodded curtly. "Well, good then."

I shook my head as our very uncomfortable teacher hunkered his way down into his chair. He crossed his arms over his chest, glaring at us from beyond his invisible-framed glasses. I wasn't convinced by Allison's reassuring words, but it didn't stop me from hoping she was right. I mean, I couldn't bear to lose one of my best friends over this stupid thing. This stupid, idiotic boy thing.

Stupid and idiotic. Sounds like something you'd get yourself into.

"You think I should go over to his house after school sometime this week?"

Allison poured the clear liquid into the beaker. "I don't think that's a good idea."

"Why not?"

"Look, it's bubbling up."

I watched the bubbles turn all sorts of fluorescent colors as it climbed up the neck of the glass beaker. It overflowed and we quickly moved our notes before jotting down what we'd witnessed. I kept stealing glances over at Allison. I watched her pen move quickly across her notepad. Something looked different about her. I couldn't place it, but I knew it.

She was hiding something from me.

"Allison."

"Hmmm?"

"What aren't you telling me?"

And when her pen faltered, I knew I had her.

"Rae, don't do this now. Okay?"

I scoffed. "So you have been talking to Michael."

"Rae—"

"Just tell me the damn truth, Allison."

I kept my voice at a hushed volume, but I still felt people's eyes on me and Mr. Abernathy lingering around us. I still felt as if the world was shining its great, big beacon directly into my fucking face.

And after Allison was done jotting down her notes, she turned her attention to me.

"No, Michael hasn't talked about the incident between you two. But yes. We've talked, a lot, over this past weekend. Which was the first reason I knew something was up. He called every day, multiple times a day. Came over a few times. He talked about anything and everything other than this one thing, and you know Michael. You know he's just not like that. He's not a chatterbox about his life."

I paused. "Is he okay?"

She nodded. "He's fine. He's angry. He's hurt. He's upset, clearly. But he's fine. So, when I tell you to give him time, that's what you need to do. From someone who spent practically all damn weekend with him? Give. Michael. Time."

Then the lunch bell rang, causing the class to scatter and rush for the hallways.

Just like the entire world seemed to rush around in my mind.

28

CLINTON

I sat in math class staring out the window onto the school lawn. The weekend had been rough. Solitary. Filled with a lot of sleeping and multiple hangover cures. Roy ended up pulling me back into that fucking party of Marina's, where I ended up getting so shit-faced that I passed out on the porch. The fucking concrete porch. I woke up the next morning to Marina shaking me like a damn blender, telling me to wake up and get out before her parents got home. I drove back to my place tipsy and tired, trying my hardest to keep my bike steady on the road as I chugged back the lukewarm bottle of water still stuffed down into my pocket somehow.

Only to be met with my father at the front door.

My neck still hurt from that encounter. But as far as brushes with my father went, this one was pretty tame. Cecilia pulled him off me, which was a first. And to punish her for it, my father left a few hours later for a business trip without her. Left her behind in the house to mope around in her heels and her perfectly-mani-cured fingernails.

Making me feel like a stranger in my own damn childhood house.

The rest of the weekend was spent in my room. I hoarded food there like a wild animal and didn't come out until it was time for school this morning. I skipped Monday. I didn't like Mondays, anyway. I called in for myself, actually. Made a few retching noises. Let loose a few burps. Talked to the school nurse. And in the span of ten minutes, I had a free day from school without a phone call to my father.

Which was the last thing I needed to happen right now.

I slept all day yesterday, and as I sat there in my boring as hell math class, I wished to be sleeping again. In the comfort of my own bed with music softly playing in the background. But no. I had to be here. Because the school breathed down our throats and sent out needless phone calls to parents if we didn't show up. Like I still wasn't some legal-ass adult at eighteen. I mean, everything happened at eighteen. I could buy cigarettes. Doctors didn't have to go through my parents anymore. I could schedule my own medical shit. Fill my own prescriptions. Buy fucking nose medi-cine over the counter with my I.D.

So why the fuck didn't schools stop calling parents when we turned eighteen?

If the doctor couldn't do it, why could they?

Makes no damn sense.

"Mr. Clarke?"

I whipped my eyes to the front of the classroom, where Miss Abigail was staring at me from beyond her black-framed glasses.

"Yeah?"

She pursed her lips. "What's the value of 'x'?"

I shrugged. "Depends on how you dumped them, I guess."

But, instead of the class laughing like they usually did, I watched them shake their heads and scowl at me. A couple of the girls from the party at Marina's rolled their eyes before passing notes to each another. I felt like that monkey again. Only now I was failing at my job. And if I wasn't here for entertainment and laughter, then what the fuck was I here for?

I suddenly felt out of place at school, too.

Like I had at home this past weekend.

"Very funny, Mr. Clarke. Explains why you haven't done your homework in a week, too."

And with that, Miss Abigail turned her attention away from me. A flippant response before paying attention to the students that were really important. The students that made teachers like her proud. The students teachers like her wanted to mentor. Wanted to remember. Wanted to mold and shape.

Just another retired circus monkey.

I felt something hot against the nape of my neck and turned around. And it didn't shock me one bit when I found Michael mean-mugging me from behind. He'd switched his seat in class to sit behind me instead of in front of me after that schoolyard fight. Why he'd done it was beyond me, but it wasn't something I cared about debating. Every time I saw that squirrelly little fucker, he made it a point to glare in my general direction.

Only his glares had gotten hotter with each passing day lately.

I blew him a kiss before turning around, then slumped into my seat. I let my eyes fall back out the window, gazing out at the green grass and bright blue sky as Miss Abigail's voice faded into the background. Classes changed and I gathered up my things. I went and flopped myself down in English class and saw Allison continuously stealing looks in my general direction. I didn't pay it any mind, though. I didn't give a shit about Michael or her. The only person I gave a damn about was Rae.

And I couldn't even get her to look at me.

I saw her in the hallways and tried to meet her eyes, but she always turned her back to me. I tried scanning the cafeteria at lunch time, trying to catch where her and her friends would park it. I wanted to hear her voice again. Even if it was in anger, cursing me out before slapping me across the face. Yelling at me was better than the whole barrel of 'nothing' she was tossing my way now.

And when I saw her walk into the cafeteria, hope ignited in my chest.

I stood up from my chair as Roy rattled on about some stupid-ass nonsense. Marina nibbled at her banana, keeping the trend of her starving herself going. I stood there, listening as voices faded into the background. And as Rae's eyes found mine, I saw her lips turn down at the sight of me.

Then she turned around and walked back out of the cafeteria.

"You good, Clint?"

Roy's voice pulled me back from the brink, as I felt my fists balling up, my arms shaking, every part of me tensing up as Allison and Michael appeared in the cafeteria doorway. Michael had a scowl on his face before he walked up to the lunch line. Allison rolled her eyes at me, the two of them moving in the opposite direction of Rae. That made me even more furious. Why the fuck weren't her friends with her during a time like this?

Roy tugged on my leather jacket. "Dude, sit down. I was getting to the best part. Marina did this new thing that—"

"I don't give a shit what your girlfriend does to your dick, dude!"

I whipped around, glaring at him as the cafeteria came to a grinding halt.

"I don't give a shit how she kisses you, or how she sucks you off. I don't care how much she puts out or the new shit you can get her to pull. I literally give no fucks about any of it. And you want to know why?"

Roy grimaced. "The hell's wrong with you?"

I chuckled bitterly. "I don't give a damn about it because I know you only do it to be cool. You do it to get attention and to try and be the big man, when you're not. It's pathetic. And you really need to stop, because you look like a shithead."

Roy slid Marina off his lap before he stood up, standing toe to toe with me. And despite the fact that I towered over him by almost five inches, he held his ground. Which was impressive, but stupid.

"You wanna run that by me again?"

I licked my lips. "I don't know. Were you dumb enough not to hear it the first time around?"

Marina hissed. "The two of you, shut up. Teachers are coming over."

I jumped at Roy, causing him to step back before I grinned at him. And as teachers in the cafeteria came to settle down the riff-raff, I strode to the cafeteria door. I wasn't hungry. I wasn't thirsty. The only thing I felt was anger. Frustration. Confusion. The three-course meal I'd been dining on for fucking days. I marched right out of that damn cafeteria, ignoring the teachers that called out after me. I got around the corner and charged for the glass double doors, slamming into them with a pop.

And when my eyes gazed down onto the football field, I saw three senior students from the school down the road laughing and joking around, and dumping shit onto the grass.

Perfect.

I made my way for the field, practically leaping down the stairs. I heard them laughing as one of them whipped out their cocks to literally piss on the painted outlines of our mascot on the green turf. I whistled to myself as my fists unclenched. I breathed a sigh of relief as their laughter came to a grinding halt. I hopped over the fence, touching down onto my feet as I smiled broadly at them.

"Afternoon, boys," I said.

And I chuckled as my victims cowered in their own fucking boots.

29

RAELYNN

I got halfway down the hallway before I rounded around the corner. I didn't want to come into contact with Clint. Not now. Not when things were so rough with, well, everything else. I waited for a few minutes, listening as Clint's voice boomed across the cafeteria. I didn't know what he was saying, but I knew he wasn't happy. I heard Roy's name tossed into everything, then I saw teachers getting up from the corner. Part of me wanted to rush to Clint, to help him calm down before he really got himself into some trouble.

But then his heavy footsteps faded away before the slamming of a door echoed in the distance.

I heard teachers fruitlessly calling out his name as a dull roar rose from the crowd of students in the cafeteria again. And after a few deep breaths, I made my way inside. I took my seat quickly in the corner, like I always did. The place where Michael, Allison, and I always sat. The place where Allison had kept me company yesterday while Michael strode past us, making his way for the outside patio.

Only this time, he slammed his tray down beside me just as Allison sat in front of me.

My eyes widened as I turned my body to face him. I peeked over at Allison, watching as she nodded toward Michael. I licked my lips, feeling the whole of my body lock up as my eyes met his.

This was the first time he'd so much as acknowledged my existence since his appearance on my doorstep. And I wasn't sure what to make of it all. He looked angry, but also tired. He looked frustrated, but also worn. Frazzled. Part of me wanted to reach out and hug him. But the rest of me knew better.

He sighed as he rested his elbow on the table.

"Look. I'm still pissed off. You hid this from me, and I don't get why you went for Clint of all the guys in this school. I don't get it, and I never will. But I want to put this behind us. Can we? Please?"

My jaw dropped open. "I, uh… don't know why you're asking me. I'm not the one to make that decision."

Michael snickered. "You have just as much of a choice about it as I do."

"I mean, not really. I'm not the one hurt. I'm the one doing the hurting."

"It's clear you're hurting, Rae. Just in a different way."

I paused. "Maybe so."

Allison darted her eyes between us. Michael sighed as his free hand settled against my knee. I looked down at it and smiled with tears in my eyes, then settled my hand on top of his. It felt good, having him back. Having him talk to me. Having him near me. I'd missed my friend, my confidant, my cheerleader and my guiding moral light.

I nodded as I held back tears. "I'd really like to put this behind us, yes."

Michael took my hand, ripping me out of my seat. And as he wrapped his long arms around me, I squeezed him around his waist. I giggled breathlessly as he nuzzled against me, trying to soothe my invisible wounds. I heard Allison get up before a soft pair of arms wrapped around both of us, causing Michael to chuckle to himself.

"Had to get in on the action, huh?"

Allison smiled. "I mean, I can never resist a good happily ever after."

I rolled my eyes. "You've been watching Disney movies again, haven't you?"

Allison scoffed. "Just let me say, 'And then everyone lived happily ever after, the end'."

Michael laughed. "Okay, but only this once."

All of us gave one last big squeeze, then we unraveled ourselves from one another. We sat down and started unpacking our lunches, smiling and talking like we used to do. It felt nice, having some semblance of normalcy around this table again. And it felt really good to hear Michael's lame jokes as I talked about Mom and D.J. I rehashed the conversation, telling them about my mother's decision. How I really felt she was serious this time. How it felt like things might actually be different.

But soon, I felt my eyes scanning the cafeteria.

"He left."

Michael's voice pulled my eyes back to him, and he gave me a knowing look.

"What?"

Allison giggled. "Oh, come on, Rae. Don't play that game."

Michael shook his head. "Lying's what got you into this mess, you know."

I sighed. "No, omitting information is what got me into this mess."

Allison smiled. "So, you admit you're lying now?"

I paused. "I plead the fifth."

Michael scoffed. "He left, and he hasn't come back yet."

I shrugged. "Oh, well. His loss. I was going to throw a Cheeto at him."

"Uh huh," Michael said as he spooned a bite of chicken pot pie into his mouth. "Sure, you don't."

I rolled my eyes at him before focusing on my peanut butter and jelly sandwich. Mom had actually packed me a lunch today. For the first time in years, I came downstairs to a brown paper bag that she handed off to me with a big smile on her face. And thinking about it made me smile with every bite. Mom looked radiant lately. Like a weight had been lifted off her shoulders. I mean, I knew she'd end up stressing herself out over money and bills. But being free of D.J. looked good on her.

I really hope it stays this way.

"So you actually told your mom about Clint?"

Allison's question made me nod as I swallowed my sandwich.

"Mm-hmm. I did. And I'm actually glad I did. It's been a long time since I've really been able to talk to her like that. And, despite the hiccup of that evening, we still enjoyed our pizza and movie marathon."

Michael grinned. "Shame you didn't invite me in for pizza."

I giggled. "You didn't stick around long enough for us to get to that point."

"You have a decent argument there."

"It's not an argument, it's just the truth. Nothing more, nothing less."

"Refreshing, coming from you."

I playfully glared at him. "That one feel good?"

Michael nodded. "Actually, it did."

"Good. Because it's the only one you'll get."

The three of us laughed again before a commotion started in the back of the cafeteria. Kids rushed to the windows and poured out onto the patio, their hands clapping and cupping over their mouths. I furrowed my brow deeply as I craned my neck, trying to figure out what the fuck was going on.

Then, I heard it. I heard what they were chanting.

"Fight! Fight! Fight! Fight!"

Allison's face fell. "Uh oh."

Michael shook his head. "Shit."

And as a sinking feeling filled my gut, I felt myself standing from my seat.

Clint.

I abandoned my lunch and pressed myself between Michael and the wall. I slipped away, listening to them yell at me as I headed for one of the windows. I pushed people out of the way, trying to catch a glimpse of what they were looking at. And when I saw a towering black mass dancing around on the football field, I felt my lunch creep up the back of my throat.

Shit.

I pushed away from the window and charged for the cafeteria exit. I had to navigate the masses, since they had already started rushing out the door. Teachers were trapped. The principal was stuck at the back of the hallway. It took all the effort I had to shove people to the concrete in order to get ahead of them.

And all the while, Allison and Michael yelled for me to come back.

30

CLINTON

I took a blow to the jaw and stumbled back. Actually stumbled. On my feet. That hadn't happened in a fight in quite some time. Usually, it was only my father that made me stumble backwards. These boys fought harder than I'd originally given them credit for. And I was happy for it. The pain gave me something to focus on. Their beady, disgusting little eyes gave me targets for the fury in my fists. I felt blood pumping through my veins and fire coursing through my bones. I felt alive. More alive than I ever had before.

Except with Rae.

"You're fucked, you little piece of shit."

I grinned. "Gotta take me down first."

I hooked my arm around his neck and bent him at the waist. Throwing my head back, I cracked the other guy in the nose behind me as he growled and cursed to himself. I laughed as I choked off the boy's air supply before an elbow came down into my back.

And as I dropped to my hands and knees, it gave me the perfect angle to wrap my arm around some other boy's legs.

I didn't even know who was who. At this point, it was kill or be killed. Just like in my house.

And I sure as hell wasn't on the menu tonight.

"Fight! Fight! Fight! Fight!"

I heard chanting kids racing for the field. A crowd gathered as I shoved myself up off the ground. My jaw was swelling, my lip was busted, and one of my eyes was already swelling shut. More decorative scars and colors to go along with the ligature marks that took me for fucking ever to cover up this morning.

"You're dead," the kid snarled.

I simply smiled before I charged him.

"Clint! Clint! Clint! Clint!"

I yelled out as I tackled him to the ground. I straddled him, throwing punch after punch before his buddies dragged me off him. I slung my fists around like wildfire, feeling them connect as the crowd's chanting grew to a dull roar. I smelled their blood. Felt their fear. And it fueled me forward as I fisted a handful of hair and pulled some dude's head back.

"This is for fucking around with our field."

I punched him in the nose before someone tackled me to the ground. Kids cheered and girls cried out for me to stay safe as I rolled around on the turf with him. I smelled that piss growing closer. My eyes widened as we kept rolling around. I slid off his body, gripping his coat as I dragged him through the grass. Through the mud.

Right through that fucking urine stain his buddy left behind.

"What the——?"

I chuckled. "Tell Mommy Dearest that hot water really helps get out the stench of piss."

I tossed him off to the side before whipping around. One of the gangly boys charged me, and one knock of my fist had him on the ground. I clotheslined the other boy barreling for me, reveling in the glory as people chanted my name. This was where I excelled. This was my golden goose egg. I dabbed at the blood trickling down my chin as I turned toward the crowd, tossing my fists in the air.

Thankful for the distraction from all the misery that had been sinking me into the trenches.

"Watch out!"

The girl shrieked just before I got knocked to the ground. The asshole had me pinned, his fists flying in my general direction. And without thinking, I took a play out of Michael's book. I crossed my arms over my face, deflecting his pathetic attempts at being a man before I had the strength to roll him over.

Before someone gripped my jacket and pulled me off him.

"Clint! Stop it! Right now!"

A familiar voice rose from the crowd as the boy holding me tried tossing me to the ground. But, really, all he did was cause me to stumble around a bit. My eyes darted about, looking for that familiar voice. Listening out for the booming tones that echoed over the chants. Over the screams. Over the warnings from other girls that would surely pour themselves all over me to help clean up my cuts and scrapes.

"Stop this right now!"

Rae's voice pierced my fog of anger and helplessness as she appeared at the fence line. My eyes found hers, and I felt my heart leap in my chest. She was saying my name. Calling out for me. It was the first time I'd heard her voice in days.

"Rae," I whispered.

Then I got clocked. Right in the fucking jaw.

"Stop it! Please, Clint!"

Her voice spun around in my head as my back hit the ground. I felt my mouth pooling with blood as those three assholes danced around me. Swirling, like vultures, ready to strike the second I got up. I rolled over and planted on all fours as I spit out a mouthful of blood.

Then I felt someone drag me to my feet.

"That all you got, boy?"

"You're pathetic, you piece of shit."

"Looks like someone already got to him once, though. Serves him right, needing a reminder."

Those words lit my world on fire, and I wrenched away from the guy's grasp. I whipped around, clocking him with my fist straight into his gut. He doubled over and I threw my elbow back, connecting with someone's ribcage before I heard something fall to the ground. I turned around, bashing my head into the other guy's nose and watching blood pour down his face before I turned my attention back to the boy who was doubled over.

"Ready for the final countdown?" I asked.

I brought my knee up into the boy's forehead, watching him drop to his knees. The crowd erupted in applause as teachers tried pushing their way through, and then I heard it again. Rae's shrieking voice. Her words were muffled as adrenaline pumped through my veins. I twirled slowly, taking in the three boys who were flat on the ground at my feet.

I took a moment to revel in my victory before I felt someone tugging at my arm.

"Clint. That's enough. Stop this bullshit."

I looked over and saw Rae. Her voice pierced through my anger and my red-dripped vision slowly filtered back into regular color. Her eyes stared up at me. Her hands felt soft around my arm. She tugged me away from the circle of assholes I'd laid out on the football field, her eyes filled with frustration and fury.

And a bit of worry on the side.

"Rae," I said.

She huffed. "Come on. We have to get you out of here."

"What are you doing?"

She shook her head. "Keeping you from making anymore dumbass mistakes. Just leave those boys alone. Come with me. Please."

She tugged me a couple of steps away, but I heard the crowd gasp. I heard people calling out my name and it caused me to whip around. My arm wrenched away from Rae and I felt her trying to grab me. Her hands wrapped around my waist, trying to tug me off the field. I heard her pleading with me. Begging with me. Calling out my name just to get my attention. But all I saw were those three assholes charging me again. Stumbling on their feet and coming for more.

Which was something that made me smile.

"Give me a second, Rae."

"Clint, no!"

One of the guys attempted to sucker punch me in the gut, but I caught his wrist. I twisted his arm behind him before kicking him to the ground, then whirled around and trained my sights on the other two. I reached out for the next one that came for me, wrapping my large hand around his neck. I squeezed until he started beating his fist against my forearm, and I felt it again.

I felt Rae's hands fisting my leather jacket.

"We need to get the fuck out of here. Cut the shit, Clint!"

When I felt her hands fall away from me, I heard her yelp.

"Get the fuck out of my way, bitch."

My hand dropped the guy's neck as I slowly turned around. I vibrated with fury as I came into contact with the jock I had just kicked to the fucking ground. Rae lay there, gasping for air as she tried to roll over onto her stomach. And as my eyes slowly lifted to the jock that was standing beside her, he tossed me a wild grin.

"Getting your bitches to do your fighting now?"

I snarled. "You pathetic little fuck!"

I saw nothing. My vision tunneled, and the only thing I saw was his face busted into pieces on the ground. I snapped, lunging at him, wrapping my hands around his throat as I wrestled him back to the ground. I heard Rae whimpering, still telling me to stop, even as she gasped for her own air. I straddled the fat bastard and landed punch after punch, refusing to listen or stop. Refusing to cease my movements until this asshole stopped breathing.

I'd kill him for laying his hands on Rae.

He rolled me over and the fight changed. His blood dripped down onto my face as he punched my gut. I braced my abs, conserving my energy as he wore himself out. But, four punches in, he was ripped from my body. I saw him flying through the air like a bird in the sky before a familiar figure came into view. I looked over and saw Allison scooping Rae off the ground. I quickly got up, trying to figure out whether or not Rae was all right before I heard footsteps rushing up behind me.

"Oh, no you don't."

And as I turned around, I saw Michael land a punch straight on the fucker's nose.

Then he turned his anger onto the boy who'd put his hands on Rae.

31

RAELYNN

"Hey, Rae. You okay? Can you talk to me?" I finally caught my breath as tears rushed down my cheeks. I nodded, but I didn't want to speak. I'd landed my back directly on a rock, and it knocked the wind clear out of me. Allison tilted me to the side, raising up my shirt to see if any damage had been done. I felt her fingertips against my skin as the fight raged on, making me angrier with every punch I heard landing in the distance.

"You're bleeding. Hold still."

I drew in a shuddering breath. "Make him stop."

Allison didn't answer me and it forced my eyes closed. I felt her wiping something across my skin as sirens sounded in the distance. Fucking hell, that was becoming the school song at this point. With Clint's fighting and Michael's temper, they probably had the damn police on speed dial. It seemed like the entire fucking high school had gathered for this fight. And why Clint was fighting them, I could only theorize at this point. My back hurt. My wrist hurt. My head felt swimmy, and I wanted to go home.

And finally, the fight drew to a close.

I heard grunts and groans of the three guys lying on the ground. I had no idea why the hell the teachers weren't intervening, but I figured they'd given up on this point. Given up on Clint. On his fighting. On trying to rein him in. It made my heart sick for him, but I also couldn't blame them.

"Heads up," Allison murmured.

I felt her smooth my shirt down before a hand came into my watery view. I slowly raked my eyes up the arm, taking in the worn leather jacket before my eyes found his. Clint stood above me, concern filling his eyes. It was the only reason I took his hand, why I wanted to touch his bloody skin.

Because he genuinely looked worried.

"You're an absolute numbskull, Clint. You know that?"

Michael's voice filled my ears, but I was paying too much attention to Clint. His hands cupped my wrist, inspecting it before slowly turning me around. I felt him inching my shirt up before a smack resounded. I felt Clint's hand fall away from my body, and I closed my eyes, readying my ears for the punch I knew Clint would toss Michael's way.

But a punch didn't happen.

"I'm just making sure she's okay," Clint said.

Michael scoffed. "She would've been fine had you not gotten into the fight in the first damn place."

Allison sighed. "She didn't have to follow him on the field, though."

Michael's voice grew louder. "You know how she feels about this asshole! Of course she would!"

And then, Clint shocked us all into silence.

"You're right."

I slowly turned around, trying to make sense of what I'd just heard. I gazed up into his eyes, seeing nothing but remorse filling them. I peeked over at Michael and Allison, and even they were shocked. The kids fell silent behind us, waiting for something else to happen. Waiting for the sirens in the distance to come screaming into the parking lot behind the school.

"Principal! Scatter!"

Roy's voice boomed over everyone's heads and Clint reached out for me. Before I could even react, he took my good hand, tugging me alongside him as he ran off. I heard Michael yelling after me. I heard Allison calling out for me. But I didn't stop. I threaded my fingers with Clint's and ran alongside him, despite the pain in my back.

"Fine! I'll fucking cover for you assholes!"

I giggled and shook my head as Michael's voice filled my ears. Clint slammed through the gate at the end of the football field, pulling me behind him. We took off for the front of the school as the principal yelled after us. I knew teachers were running for us. But I also knew they wouldn't catch us.

"You're such an asshole, you know that? And stop pulling me, fucking hell, Clint. My wrist hurts."

He stopped in his tracks. "This is your bad wrist?"

I shook my head. "No. But that doesn't mean it doesn't fucking hurt."

"Then, come on and shut up before we're both in a hell of a lot of trouble."

I scoffed as he took my hand again. "We wouldn't be in this damn situation had you not fought in the first place!"

"No one asked you to intervene."

We started running again. "Yeah, well. Fuck me for caring, I guess."

We kept running until we got around the front of the building. Among the chaos and the insanity, the pain in my back and my wrist grew. I was pissed off at the entire world. For Clint and his bullshit fighting ways. At those boys for whatever the hell they'd been doing on the football field. For that asshole that actually knocked me down.

I'd never been knocked down before.

Clint makes you weak.

Ain't that the fucking truth.

We didn't stop running until we got to his bike. He tossed me a helmet and I slid behind him, wrapping my arms around his waist. I tried to ignore how wonderful it felt as he cranked up the engine. And just as the police were speeding into the back of the school, we sped out of the front.

"Hold on. We're gonna take these corners a bit sharp."

I wrapped my good hand into his leather jacket and let my hurt wrist fall between his legs. I closed my eyes, taking deep breaths of the wind as it swirled around our bodies. It felt like I was inches away from the asphalt as he careened out of the parking lot. It felt like we were breaking the sound barrier as we sped off into the distance. Even with my eyes closed, I knew where we were headed. I had the turns and directions memorized.

And when the stench of my neighborhood wafted under my nose, I felt my stomach clench.

I sighed as Clint pulled into my driveway. He put his kickstand down and turned off his engine, but he didn't move. I rested against the breadth of his strong back. I felt tired. Anxious. And yet, happy.

Happy to be against him again.

"Why are you such an idiot?" I whispered.

Clint cleared his throat. "Your mom home?"

I shook my head. "She's out putting in job applications."

"Good for her. Let's get you inside, then."

"You're coming with me?"

"I'm sure as hell not leaving you in this condition, no."

He slipped off the bike, then eased the helmet off my head. He smoothed my hair down around my face, then tucked some loose strands behind my ear. His touch ignited a fire in my gut. I didn't even understand how much I'd missed it until I felt it again. I let out a soft sigh, wishing for nothing more than his palm against my cheek.

But he pulled his hand away before he caved to the temptation.

"You need help?"

I scoffed. "I'm good. Thanks."

"Just a question, Rae."

"And a dumb one, at that. I can hold my own, Clint. Despite the fact that that douchebag knocked me off my feet."

"I should've killed him for that."

"And spend the rest of your life in jail? Nice."

"Does anything ever make you happy?"

I planted myself on my feet in the driveway before my eyes met his.

"Yeah. I've got plenty that makes me happy. But bullshit boys and their stupid fights don't happen to be one of them."

I turned on my heel and made my way for the porch, figuring he'd leave, drive off into the distance and never come back. So imagine my surprise when he stayed behind me, following me into the house. He closed the door behind us as I made my way to the couch. I watched as he found his way into the kitchen, and I wondered what he was doing. I started to stand up to go find out, but he must have heard me.

"Stay there, Rae. I'm coming with ice."

I leaned back into the couch with a sigh before I winced. I felt like utter shit. Clint came around the corner and sat down beside me. He reached for my wrist and slowly molded the ice pack to it. I watched him work, his bruised eye trained on my swelling skin. He helped me lean up before he slid my shirt up again, taking stock of the small wound on my back. And when his fingertips fell against the dried blood, I flinched.

But not because it hurt.

"You'll be bruised. The cut's only topical, though. We'll give the ice a few minutes on your wrist, then we'll move it to your back."

I nodded. "Okay."

He leaned me back into the couch before settling into the cushions beside me. I couldn't take my eyes off him. Couldn't stop looking at him as his hands fell between his legs. He stared hard at the wall, licking his lips, which were cracked open and bleeding. I wanted to lean against him, but wasn't sure if it was a good idea.

"I'm sorry."

Clint's words pulled me from my trance and I furrowed my brow.

"Wait, what? Why?"

He sighed. "I'm sorry for getting you hurt."

I shrugged. "Well, you didn't hurt me. So, yeah."

The pain that rose up in his eyes left me breathless.

"No, I didn't. But, I was reckless. And *that* got you hurt."

I had no rebuttal to that statement, either. Because he was technically right.

"How about we deal with one blow at a time, Clint. Okay?"

He nodded slowly. "Deal."

He moved the ice pack from my wrist to my back, leaning me up just enough to slide it between my skin and the couch cushions. I shivered at the cold as he leaned me back. Then he reached for my swollen wrists.

"Let me know if any of this hurts," he said.

And one by one, he began to softly massage the joints of my fingers.

32

CLINTON

I mindlessly massaged her fingers as she relaxed further into the couch. One of the few times Cecilia and I had ever interacted with one another was the one time my father ever did any real damage to my body. He had dislocated my wrist to teach me a lesson, then popped it back in once I agreed to clean up my bathroom. Cecilia had come in and help me clean it, then massaged my fingers before wrapping my wrist in an ace bandage to heal.

To this day, I can fully remember just how amazing that massage felt.

Rae sighed with relief as I slowly popped every knuckle. One by one, down her finger, until I'd traced all five of them. I massaged her palm slowly, being careful with the bones in the top of her hand. I worked my way toward her wrist, getting lighter and lighter until she flinched. Then I began backing up, making my way down the hand, back into the palm, and up to the tips of her fingers.

Giving myself time to process everything I thought. Everything I felt. Everything I wanted to do, but couldn't.

"You wanna tell me what this fight was all about now?"

I settled Rae's hand against my thigh, feeling her heat penetrate my jeans. Did I want to come clean? Did I want to open up to her? Did I want to let her in again?

Yes. Yes, I did.

I licked the blood off my lips. "This weekend was rough. Dad came home."

She paused. "What did he do, Clint?"

I shrugged. "The usual. Cecilia stepped in this time, though. And he wasn't happy about that."

"Is she okay?"

I snickered. "He punished me with a hand wrapped around my neck, and he punished her by leaving her behind while he jetted off on yet another business trip. Yeah. I think she's okay."

"So you lashed out at those guys because you needed… an outlet?"

"It's the only thing I know how to do when I'm confused and angry. It's the only way Dad ever taught me how to deal with shit."

"And you think that's productive?"

I shrugged. "Maybe not."

"I wouldn't think so either. Since you weren't doing a very good job of fighting."

I grinned as a soft chuckle bubbled up the back of my throat. I looked over at her, finding her smirking at me as her hand moved down to my knee. She squeezed it before moving it again, and I ached for her touch against my body again. I loved how she made me smile. How she had this ability to light up my world, even at a time like this.

"Don't be a smartass. It's not a good look."

She giggled. "And yet, it's in my blood."

I quirked an eyebrow. "I don't think it's genetic more so than a chromosomal defect."

"I'm shocked you even know what that is, considering you almost flunked out of sophomore science."

"And here I thought you never paid attention to me."

She snickered. "The only thing I paid attention to during that class was Mr. Blackman's ass. He had a nice one."

"And you weren't staring at my ass? How rude."

"Yours wasn't very nice back then."

"So you were looking."

And all at once, her face flushed red. It trickled down the nape of her neck, forcing me to swallow back a growl. I enjoyed bantering with her. I enjoyed making her flustered. The big, bad, tough girl from the wrong side of the tracks, melting into a puddle of embarrassment.

It looked spectacular on her.

"Well, Rae. The good news is that your wrist isn't broken."

She rolled her eyes. "I could've told you that."

"I'm sure. Can you tell me what it actually is, then?"

She glared playfully at me. "It's sprained, jackass."

I patted her head. "Good job, Rae. You get a gold star."

"You're a dick."

"And you love it."

Her eyes whipped up to mine and I saw something flash behind them. Something hot. Something passionate. Something way too fleeting for the moment. She looked away from me, casting her eyes down into her lap. So I decided not to back her into a corner over it.

I mean, I'd already gotten her to admit she enjoyed staring at my ass.

"Here. Let me get that ice pack real quick."

My hand pressed against the back of her shoulder and she leaned up. I heard her groaning a bit, which meant her muscles were already stiffening from the jarring impact. I stood up and took the ice pack back into the kitchen, tossing it into the freezer. Then I rummaged around for a washcloth.

"Time for some heat," I murmured to myself.

After drenching the washcloth in hot water, I wrung it out. I walked back into the living room, watching as Rae's eyes found mine again. I felt her studying me carefully. Trying to figure out her next move. I motioned for her to sit up and placed the washcloth against her bare skin, and the hiss that left her lips filled my ears.

"Does that hurt?" I asked.

She shook her head. "No. Just jarring, after the cold."

"Do you need a couple minutes?"

"No, no. I'm good. You can leave it."

"All right. Lean back for me. Like you did with the ice pack."

And after sliding her shirt down, she eased herself back into the cushions.

I sat down next to her. "You never should've charged that field, Rae. The hell were you thinking?"

"I was thinking about you, and how stupid you looked."

"You put yourself in harm's way for nothing. You know I can handle myself."

"And so can I, believe it or not."

"Says the girl who got knocked on her ass with one push."

She scoffed. "What? You saying I'm not tough?"

I growled. "No. I'm saying you could've gotten much worse, and I don't like the thought of you getting hurt."

"Well, I'm already hurt."

"I mean *more* hurt, Rae. Stop twisting my words and accept the fact that I give a shit."

She giggled. "How does that feel to admit?"

I grinned. "Probably more painful than that wrist of yours."

"You sure about that? Because it's a pretty gnarly sprain."

"Gnarly? You been surfing lately?"

She shrugged. "And if I have?"

I smiled. "I'd tell you I'd love to see you in that body suit sometime."

"And here I thought you liked me naked."

"I never said anything about not taking it off."

She blushed again, deepening that color against her beautifully-tanned body. I loved watching it. I adored everything about her reactions. The way she made her hair fall into her face to draw a sort of curtain between us. The way she shivered as I tucked that same piece of hair back behind her ear. The way she turned toward me, begging me silently with her eyes to touch her.

I especially liked the way she nuzzled against my palm, too. Once I offered it to her.

"I've missed you," I whispered.

Rae's eyes fell closed as I cupped her cheek softly. "I know."

"I'm sorry for not having the balls to choose you over Roy and the others. I should've had a different answer when you confronted me."

She nodded softly. "I know, Clint."

"You deserve better, you know."

She opened her eyes, locking them with my own. She lifted her head from my palm, leaving me wanting more of her heat. More of her skin. More of her body against mine. She scooted closer to me, letting her hurt hand settle against my thigh again. I swallowed hard, watching her face slowly gravitate to mine as the wash-cloth slid out from her shirt. Her eyes held me. Pinned me. Rooted me to the couch. And as her breath pulsed against my lips, she shook her head.

"Now *that* I don't believe."

I snickered. "You should. I'm not good."

She shrugged. "Neither am I."

"Don't you dare talk about yourself like that. You're the best, Rae."

"Then so are you."

"No, I'm not."

"Aren't you the one that pointed out just how much we have in common? You know, back when you stalked me at the park."

I chuckled. "I didn't stalk you."

She smirked. "You stalked me a little bit."

"I really didn't. I honestly found you by happenstance out there."

She shrugged. "It's fine. You don't have to admit it. But you're the one who said we were more alike than we seemed. So, if I'm worth it, you're worth it. Logic dictates it."

"Logic, huh? You a fan of all that nonsense?"

"Am I a fan of basic arguments and winning them? I mean, I am a girl."

My eyes fell to her lips before I licked my own again.

"Yes. You are a hell of a girl, Rae."

She scooted closer to me, our thighs pressed together. Heat crept up the nape of my neck as her hand slid up my thigh. Up my abs. Up my chest, until it settled against my shoulder. She had her arm almost around me. Almost giving me permission to wrap her up and pull her into my fucking lap.

Then her eyes fell to my lips.

"Do you have them now?"

I paused. "Do I have what?"

She giggled. "The balls, silly. Do you have the balls now to make the decision you should have made?"

"Depends. Are you giving me a second chance at the choice?"

And as she nodded, I wrapped my arms around her, pulling her into my lap as our noses nuzzled softly together.

"Yes," I whispered.

33

RAELYNN

I furrowed my brow. "Yes?"

Clint nodded. "Mm-hmm. Yes."

I grinned. "I mean, positive answer. But you might have to be a bit more specif—"

His lips crashed against mine and I slid my fingers through his hair. He tasted like metal and blood and sweat. The grass from the football field wafted up my nose as he tightened me against him. I felt his chest heaving, gasping for the air I robbed him of. And while I knew I needed to still be mad at him, I wasn't. I should have still been mad at him, but I couldn't be. He was an ass, yes. He had been an ass today, and he'd be an ass tomorrow. Starting a damn fight like that.

But…

"Oh, Rae," he growled.

Our lips kept connecting, cutting off our words. I wanted to taste more of him. Feel more of him. His tongue felt like silk and his body ignited an electrical storm in my mind. I couldn't think. Couldn't breathe. Couldn't process anything else other than the feel of his lips.

Which felt fantastic.

All at once, he whipped me around. My back lay against the couch cushions, my legs spreading to accommodate him. He fell against me, like a weighted blanket, comforting me as his hands explored what they wanted. He sucked on my lower lip and I arched into him, feeling fire rush through my veins as my legs began trembling. I slid his leather jacket away from his shoulders, not wanting any layers separating us any longer.

Even though I was still upset with him.

His words were punctuated with kisses. "I. Choose. You."

I sighed. "Say it again."

"I. Choose. You. Rae."

I moaned as his lips fell to my breasts. The way he stripped me of my clothes seemed effortless. The way our clothes mingled on the floor was like a song to our ever-uniting bodies. The warmth of his skin made me shiver. The heat of his tongue iced me over. I slid my hands down his back, feeling the pebbled muscles underneath his taut skin rolling for me as he sank in between my legs again. Our bodies clad in nothing.

Except one another.

He grinned. "And here I thought you hated my guts."

I scoffed. "Oh, don't get me wrong. I still hate your guts."

"Uh huh."

"I really do. You're a dick who pulled a dick move today. I hope you know that."

He nodded slowly. "I do. And you should hate me. You should always hate the kind of person I am."

"Now, get back down here and let me taste you again."

That cheeky little grin crawled across his face as I fisted his hair. I brought him back down to me, allowing his tongue to fill my mouth. I wrapped my arms around his neck and held him close, rolling my hips against him and feeling him growing against me. His hands ran over my waist, massaging my hips, exploring my thighs, cupping my breasts. I rolled us off the couch as my giggles filled the back of his throat. He held on tightly to me, catching me as I fell on top of him. And with a grunt, I straddled him. Placed my hands against his chest and leaned up to get a good look at him.

I smiled. "Wouldn't hurt so much if you hadn't gotten your ass beat."

He shot up, wrapping his arms around me. "You should see the other guys."

"Guys, huh? Sounds hot."

"You into that sort of thing?"

"Guess you'll never know."

He smiled before our lips collided again, only this time his hand slid through my hair. He pulled my head back, exposing my neck as he kissed down my skin. His teeth raked along my pulse point. I felt myself warming for him. Wetting for him. Ready for him. I whimpered as he kissed down the valley of my breasts, making his way to the pert peaks before he stopped.

I panted. "Clint."

He cupped the back of my head, slowly raising my head up until our eyes connected.

I paused. "What is it?"

His thumb smoothed along the tendrils of my hair. "You mean a lot to me."

I saw the sincerity in his eyes as he brought our foreheads together. I closed my eyes, feeling him slowly moving once more. He held tightly onto my body as he whipped me around, placing my back against the carpeted floor. I gazed into his eyes as he reached between our bodies. I licked my lips as I felt him seated against my entrance. I nodded softly, letting him know it was all right. And all at once, he filled me, shaking me against the carpet as our bodies became one.

"Clint, yes."

But he only shook his head before our lips fell together again.

I wrapped myself around him, holding on for dear life as he rolled against me. My legs locked around his waist. My arms went around his neck. I kissed his shoulder and nibbled his neck, allowing him the opportunity to take me to heights I'd never experienced before. He rolled faster, thrusting harder, stroking parts of me he hadn't touched yet. And as my eyes rolled back, I arched into him. I felt it coming, bubbling up. And the faster he moved, the more prone I was to succumbing to his assault.

His beautiful, salacious assault.

"Yes. Yes. Clint. Oh, shit. Clint, yes! Right there! Right there!"

"That's it, Rae. Let go. Do it for me, beautiful."

"Oh. Shit."

The words came out as whimpers. Broken syllables that fell from my lips. I felt myself vibrating around him, clamping down on him as the whole of my body lost control. He didn't stop, though. His face dropped to my neck and he kept on going. Kept on filling me. Kept on rolling and thrusting as I raked my nails up and down his arms, trying my best not to blow through the roof in ecstasy. I locked myself around him and managed to roll him over. I straddled him, my hands pressed once again into his chest. I gazed into his eyes as I swiveled my hips, feeling his hands grip them, guiding me. Teaching me with his movements how to please him. How to make him feel good.

How to make him soar.

"That's it, Rae. Perfect."

"Clint. I want you to feel good, too."

He reached up, cupping my cheek. "I always feel good when I'm around you."

I fell against his body, his hands cupping my ass cheeks. Our tongues twined together as I rested against him, feeling him hold me while he thrust. His hips rose, filling me and releasing me. Filling me and releasing me. And soon, I was on my back again, my legs in the air and tossed over his shoulder before he bent me in half.

"Oh, fuck!"

He grinned. "There's the spot you love so much."

"Shit. Shit. Shit. Shit."

"You'll say my name before it's all over."

The world slowly tunneled. All I saw was his face. All I felt was his body. All I knew was the scent and sounds and smells of him. My heart surged with delight. My soul welled with a happiness I'd never experienced before. And suddenly, I felt myself come alive. For the first time in my entire life, I knew what it felt like to be praised. Enjoyed. Cherished. Wanted. As my knees pressed into my chest and Clint drove himself deep into my body, I knew what it felt like to be prized.

I drew in a shuddering breath. "Thank you, Clint."

He ceased his movements and I opened my eyes. Well, the tunneling lifted as the electricity let go of its grip on my brain. His brow furrowed deeply as he rested there, on the backs of my legs. I smiled as I lifted my head to capture his lips softly before I nuzzled my nose against his.

"For what?" he asked.

I giggled. "For making me feel important."

My legs slid from his shoulders and his hands found mine. I lay there, our fingers threaded together as he pinned them above my head. Our eyes connected and didn't let go. Our hips moved in tandem and didn't let up. We breathed one another's air and shared one another's pleasure. I bucked when he rocked, and I jumped when he thrust.

And soon, we fell over the edge together.

With each other's names being chanted like breathless prayers on the cusp of the wind.

34

CLINTON

I stood on Rae's porch. "You sure this is something you wanna do?"

She shrugged. "Why not?"

"I mean, we could still take my bike. Ride in like a couple of badasses."

"Or we could park it here and walk to school. Giving us a little more time to spend with one another."

"Rae..."

"What?"

I sighed. "You know Allison and Michael aren't going to want to talk to me."

"We won't know until we give them a chance, you know."

"I know this. Michael doesn't like me."

"Michael fought alongside you yesterday."

"Yes, for you. Because you got hurt. Not because of me, or some brotherhood or some shit."

She rolled her eyes. "Come on. If we don't get started, we're going to be late. You can come home with me after school and get your bike."

I grinned. "Oh, really now? Will your mother be home?"

All she did was giggle, giving me an answer that suddenly made me want this entire school day to be over.

We walked hand in hand through her neighborhood, and I got a good look at it. There was trash lying around in the streets. The lawns were filled with dirt and mud rather than freshly-trimmed grass. The homes had crooked porches and dilapidated roofs. Rae and her mother honestly lived in the best house on the block. Which still wasn't saying much. It gave me a glimpse into the life Rae led. The dark shadows that shrouded this place. The smell that hung in the air around the homes, no matter how hard the wind blew.

But, once we got to the exit of the neighborhood, I paused.

"What is it, Clint?"

I licked my lips. "This could ruin my image, you know? Walking to school with some girl. Not riding in on my bike waiting for all the girls to flock to me. It's hard work being a bad boy, you know."

She snickered. "Well, your image sucks and could do with some damaging."

But when I looked down into her eyes, I knew she understood how sincere my words were. This was a big step for me. Something different. Something I didn't know how to navigate. And she gave my hand a comforting squeeze before leading the way. We started out of her neighborhood, holding hands tightly as we walked up the block. Hell, even the sidewalk changed from a darker tinted, cracked concrete to the nice, white, smooth concrete I'd taken advantage of my entire life.

Then we stopped.

"Allison! Michael! Hey!"

Rae's voice filled the air and I looked up from the concrete, watching as confusion rolled over their faces. Allison trotted toward us, with that confusion morphing into surprise. Michael didn't seem the least bit entertained by the idea of seeing me.

I didn't blame him.

Allison stopped in front of Rae. "Hey there. What's going on?"

The two girls hugged one another, forcing Rae to drop my hand. Michael walked up and stood beside Allison, squaring off with me like he was ready for another fight. And what was worse was that he didn't look as if he'd been in a fight. He had no cuts. No scrapes. No bruising. Nothing. Whereas my eye was still swollen a bit, I had a black eye underneath it, and the cut on my lip had bruised up.

Michael scoffed. "Yeah. What's going on?"

Rae took my hand again. "Nothing. Just walking to school."

Michael darted his finger between the two of us. "He's walking you to school."

Allison shoved him with her shoulder. "Michael."

Rae shrugged. "He's walking with us to school. Got an issue with that?"

I looked over at her warily before I cleared my throat.

"Hey, Mike. I just wanna—"

He cut me off. "It's Michael, thanks."

I nodded slowly. "Michael. I'm sorry, you know, for the whole fight and everything. It happened at a time where I was angry at shit in my house, and I took it out on you."

He nodded. "Anything else?"

I paused. "Well, thank you for jumping in yesterday, too. You've got some serious fight, and I was impressed."

"Well, I didn't do it for you. I did it for Rae. But you're welcome. For not letting you get killed out there."

Allison swatted at his arm and I looked slowly over at Rae. But again, all she did was squeeze my hand. Like that was supposed to reassure me things would be all right. She stepped closer to me, leaning her cheek against my arm. And as I turned my head back to her two friends, I saw Michael's eyes ignite with anger.

While Allison's eyes filled with happiness.

Michael rolled his eyes. "Will he be walking with us every morning?"

Rae shrugged. "I don't know. Part of that is up to him. But I'd really like it if you two gave him a chance."

Michael scoffed. "He attacked me, Rae."

I nodded. "And I apologized for that. I got some shit going on at home and—"

He cut me off again. "We've all got shit going on at home."

Rae stepped in. "He's got my kinda shit going on, Michael."

And that quickly shut down the conversation. Though I wasn't completely happy with Rae blurting that out. Or equating my home situation to hers. Or talking about my home situation in general, like I was some fucking charity rehab project.

Rae sighed. "Anyway, please give him a chance. For my sake. I'll be spending more time with Clint now, and I'd like there to not always be this fighting and tension."

Michael grumbled. "Of course."

Allison linked her arm with his. "What he means is that of course, we'll give him a chance. For both of your sakes."

As the four of us walked to school, it was quiet. Rae didn't speak with them, and they didn't speak with us. Lines had been drawn in the sand, and we had our respective corners to stand in. And I didn't want it to be like this for Rae. She deserved better.

So I cleared my throat.

"Looks like you got out better from that fight yesterday than I did, Michael."

I looked over at him, but all he did was nod.

"Guess that's what happens when you don't run into a gaggle of guys without a plan."

I nodded. "Gaggle of guys. I like that. Especially since that one looked like a goose."

Allison giggled. "That's bad, Clint."

I shrugged. "Well, he did! And the way he announced his charges every time with that yell of his. I was waiting for him to fluff his feathers out and start chomping at me with his beak."

Rae laughed. "Have you ever been attacked by a goose? There's one that roams our neighborhood. I swear, it's hellbent on terrorizing every little kid in that cul-de-sac of ours."

Allison rolled her eyes. "I wake up to the honking of geese every morning, courtesy of the stupid pond Dad wanted to live beside when we first moved."

Michael chuckled. "Harsh words coming from you, Ali."

Rae paused. "Ali?"

We all stopped just outside of the school's front doors with Rae having a tight grip on my hand. While things had flowed in conversation well enough, now it came to a grinding halt. We all stared at one another, like four dumbasses all lost in the same math class. But as Allison's arm quickly fell from Michael's, I knew exactly what was happening.

And neither of them had told Rae yet.

Allison giggled nervously. "Um, we'll talk at lunch. Okay? When it's just the three of us?"

Rae's lips parted in shock. "I mean, I thought maybe—"

I butted in. "Of course. Just the three of you at lunch. Sure."

Michael snickered. "At least someone gets it."

I shot him a look as I squeezed Rae's hand. She nodded slowly, then the two of us ventured toward the doors. But as she pulled them open, I felt my nerves getting the best of me.

And I quickly dropped her hand.

She furrowed her brow. "What?"

I shook my head. "This isn't a good idea."

"Look, Clint. I'm not gonna force you to do something you don't want to do. But if you can't do this, that means you can't do us. I'm not your dirty little secret. I'm not just some rest stop you can park at sometimes. At least, that's not what I want to be."

"That's not what you are, Rae. Never. It's just all happening so—"

"Fast? Quick? Like lightning? Trust me, I get that. But I'm also not a slave to my image at school. I think we both know that. So, time to choose which one you want more. Your image or me."

I watched Michael and Allison slide past as Rae kept the door held open. Allison tossed me a wary look, but Michael could have killed me with the one he gave. Rae deserved better than this. She deserved better than me. But if I was the one she wanted, then I had to do my best. Right? I mean, I understood her position. I couldn't keep us in the shadows simply for the sake of some fucking high school bullshit.

So I squared my shoulders and stood tall.

"Fuck 'em, right?"

Rae smiled. "Yes. Fuck 'em. Now let's go before we're late for homeroom."

I reached for her and tugged her into the school. She giggled as she rested against me, her cheek pressed against my arm. We walked through the front foyer of the school together, in front of everyone. For all to see. I strutted my shit. I felt as if I were growing taller with every step I took. I walked down the main hallway before Rae took the lead, showing me where her locker was.

A locker I intended on walking her to every morning.

As she worked the lock, I started looking around. I took stock of the students. The teachers. Hell, even the principal. And while I assumed everyone's eyes would be on me, I didn't see a single soul looking in my direction. Not even in my general direction. I furrowed my brow as I found Roy slobbering all over Marina in a corner. I scanned the room and found the redhead from the party a couple weekends ago pressing herself against one of my other boys. No one had their eyes on me. No one gave a shit who I'd come into school with.

No one except me.

35

RAELYNN

*Raelynn*One Week Later

"Welcome to Grady's Groceries. May I interest you in a—?"

The man waved his hand in the air. "Just ring me up. I'm in a hurry."

I forced a smile. "Of course, sir."

I scanned the groceries as quickly as I could, then bagged them. Cold items in the blue bags, regular items in the yellow ones. Eggs went down first, then the loaf of bread sat on top. Chips in the same bag. Apple juice in another bag. With the frozen vegetables, ice cream, and pint of milk in the last one.

"That'll be $18.7—"

The man tossed a twenty-dollar bill at me. "Keep the change. I gotta go."

It bounced off my chest and fluttered to the belt as he scooped up his bags. He lumbered away, murmuring to himself as he walked straight out the doors into the pouring rain. I shook my head as I picked up the bill, cashing him out and setting the change aside. I slipped it into the manilla envelope I had at my register for the manager to collect. Extra money for the store without disrupting the balance of the registers at the end of the night.

I sighed. "I really hate this job sometimes."

Grady's Groceries was a small store in town that serviced a very specific group of people in the area. It wasn't a chain. It wasn't some big-box store. But it always had quality, fresh items. And it seemed as if people were always willing to pay for fresh and quality. Of course, there were items like frozen vegetables and things of that nature. However, that didn't stop the all-natural crowd from coming in and making my life a living nightmare.

Is this made with gluten?

Is this made near gluten?

Was someone thinking about gluten when they made this?

"Rae!"

My manager's voice ripped me from my trance. "What's up, Bryan?"

"We need help stocking. You up for a change of scenery? It'll be counted on your paycheck."

I smiled. "You know I'm always up to help."

"Great. Get back to aisle four. Dani's struggling with the lower shelves. Back's acting up again."

"Got it."

I logged out of my register and practically broke into a dead sprint for aisle four. Dani was the resident grandmother. Worked part-time in order to have more money to spoil the eight grandchildren she had. But sometimes she needed a bit of help. And I was more than willing to provide that help if it meant not having to interact with the pompous, arrogant customers that seemed to be out in full force today.

"Hey there, Dani."

She sighed. "Hey, Rae. Sorry for pulling you away."

"Now, you know good and well I don't mind. Whatcha stocking?"

"This damn cake icing. Why is it on the lower shelf? I keep telling Bryan cooking supplies need to be more accessible to people of my age because we're the ones that do most of the baking."

I took the icing from her hand. "And I'll make sure the suggestion is heard."

I crouched down and began unpacking the items while she took a break. I sat on the floor, divvying everything up and secretly wishing I could pop open a container of icing and start eating it. I unloaded one box before Dani scooted another toward me with her foot. Together we got the baking aisle restocked. Took about two hours, but we handled it.

Then it was back to my post and dealing with customers.

"Do you have this, but in blue?"

I paused. "You want a blue ice cream carton?"

"Yes. Everything has to be absolutely perfect for this party I'm throwing. Everything has to match. I like rocky road, but I can't find a rocky road in a blue carton."

"Sure, just give me—"

"Miss?"

I whipped my head around as Miss Blue Ice Cream scoffed. "Yes?"

"Is the bakery going to be making any more cakes? I need a freshly-baked carrot cake for something tonight."

I shook my head. "We stop producing cakes at seven."

"So no more cakes."

"No, ma'am."

"What if I pay for the cake?"

"There isn't anyone to make the cake right now. The bakery's completely shut down."

"What if I wait for a bit?"

I paused. "Waiting won't do you any good. There's no one here to make your cake."

"Well, can you call someone in?"

"To make your cake?"

"Yes. Aren't you listening?"

Miss Blue Ice Cream Spoke up. "I need help. This is melting, and I need you to help me."

I sighed. "Then go put it back so it won't melt. I can be there in a second to help you track down some rocky road in a blue container."

Mrs. Carrot spoke up. "Oh, a blue container? If you like non-dairy products, there's a rocky road in a nice light blue container at the end of the aisle, on the left. It's tucked beside the sherbets."

Were these people fucking serious right now?

Thankfully, Bryan came over and busted up the convention. Which enabled me to check out the three customers that had gathered around my register. I checked them out, moving as quickly as I could while Bryan dealt with the crazy that had been dumped into my lap. He checked them out personally, thank fuck. Before disappearing into his back office to take 'a breather.'

Like he'd put in some hard work for the day or some shit.

"And here I thought I'd find you smiling."

The second I heard Clint's voice, a massive smile did cross my face.

"Just like that one, actually."

I giggled. "What the hell are you doing here?"

He leaned against my kiosk. "Maybe I came to see a gorgeous girl. Or maybe I came to pick up an apple."

"Or maybe you came to distract yourself because your father's back home."

"Maybe you're smarter than you look."

I laughed as he leaned over, kissing me on the cheek. Thankfully, we were tanking into my last hour of work before the store had to close down. Which meant not many more people would come in. I leaned my hip against the register, gazing into Clint's eyes. I enjoyed having him there. He'd already popped in on me a couple of times to say 'hello' and grab something for Cecilia. But he hadn't ever stuck around.

Until now.

I licked my lips. "I take it you have nowhere else to be?"

He winked. "You mean, other than home? Come on, don't you remember? I reorganized my priorities. I'm a brand new man."

I rolled my eyes. "Until your father leaves to go back out of town."

He shrugged, and it made me shake my head. He was relentless in all the best ways. I reached out for his arm, patting it softly before his hand fell on top of mine. He brought my hand to his lips to kiss, sending goosebumps traveling up my arm.

And I watched his eyes follow their trail.

"It's okay, Clint. You can stay as late as you want. I won't tell anyone you hang out at Grady's Groceries in your spare time."

He chuckled. "Bless your heart."

"It needs some blessing. It's been having some inappropriate feelings lately."

He quirked an eyebrow. "Oh? Care to share with a curious ear?"

"That depends. What are you willing to do for them?"

"Oh, I like a good barter."

"You curious enough to do my homework for me?"

He smiled. "Not on your life. But, I can hold you close while you do your homework after your shift."

"And let your wandering hands distract me? Hardly. I'd end up flunking all my classes."

He shrugged. "I don't do my homework and I don't flunk classes."

"Because the teachers don't wanna hold you back and deal with you another year."

"Potato, po-tah-toe."

I snickered. "To answer your question, no. I don't have much homework to do after my shift. I usually get it done during my breaks on nights like this. Why?"

"Well, I was hoping I could sweep you away and steal some alone time with you. You know, if your attention doesn't have to be elsewhere."

"Oh, alone time. That sounds nice."

"I could make it real romantic for you. A shoulder massage. With some nice lotion."

"Can you make that a foot massage? My heels are killing me."

"Rae, I can make it a full body massage, if you want."

He winked at me and my stomach flipped over with desire. My heart skyrocketed to a rate that threatened to burst the blood vessels in my head. I licked my lips, watching his eyes rake over me before a soft chuckle fell from his lips. And while I still had a bit of history reading to do, I could also do with some one-on-one time with Clint.

Especially after this shift.

"Hey, Rae!"

I looked up. "Yes, Bryan?"

"Got a family emergency, I need to leave. Can you lock up the store? I sent Dani home to get some rest. She couldn't get back up on her feet after the incident in aisle four."

Clint quirked an eyebrow. "Incident?"

I nodded. "Yes, sir. I can do that."

"Good. I'll count the registers when I come in. Just wipe down your area, sweep up a bit, and make sure all returned groceries are back on the shelves."

"I hope everything's okay!"

"Me, too!"

I watched my manager zoom out of the grocery store, leaving me and Clint completely alone. I looked over at the clock, then groaned when I saw I still had forty-five minutes.

"So, what's the plan, Stan?"

I giggled. "If we don't get a customer in five minutes, I'll start shutting this place down."

Clint grinned. "Anything I can do to help?"

"You can keep your hands to yourself until we can get out of here."

"And here I thought grocery aisle sex sounded kinky."

"Not with video cameras recording us."

He shrugged. "I mean, I'm down for it."

I scoffed and swatted at him as giggles fell from my lips. And as we continued to talk, no one came in. Not a soul. With forty minutes left in my shift, I felt confident that if I shut things down, we wouldn't lose one single customer.

So I grabbed the paper towels and the cleaner fluid to start cleaning.

36

CLINTON

Despite Rae's protests, I jumped in and helped her. While she wiped down her register or whatever, I grabbed a broom and swept up some of the bigger dirt piles. I rolled the cart of returned groceries over to her, and together we started down the aisles. She handed me things and I placed them back on the shelves. And every once in a while, I stole a kiss for myself. The camera, too. But, mostly for myself.

Rae giggled. "You're gonna get me fired."

I grinned. "I mean, all I hear is more time with you."

"And what am I going to do when I graduate high school and don't have the money to move out on my own like I want?"

"Eh, we'll figure something out."

I stole one last kiss from her before I let her push me away. I chuckled as we continued walking up and down the aisles, putting back everything from all-natural peanut butter to gluten-free snack items. She gave me a kiss on the cheek before she shooed me outside, telling me she had to lock everything down from the inside out.

I headed over to my bike to wait for her.

Nighttime had settled over Riverbend. And in our little side of town, there were more stars in the sky than usual. I stared up at them, my arms crossed over my chest. I found myself discovering more things like this. Like the stars overhead. Or the beauty of a sunkissed horizon. I'd been writing more and more lately. For the first time in over a year, I had to go buy a new notepad. My muse attacked me at all times of the day and night, waking me from a dead sleep and forcing me to write things down so I didn't forget them.

And while I still struggled with this whole thing between Rae and me, I knew it was due to her.

She was my muse.

"You look lost in thought, handsome."

Rae's voice ripped me from my trance and I found her staring at me. Leaning against me. Sliding her arms around me with her lips only inches from mine.

"And what if I am?"

She smirked. "Well, I'd say 'penny for your thoughts,' but I think that price is a bit steep."

My lips puckered. "Oh, you're gonna pay for that one."

"Really? How—ah!"

I smiled as I slapped my hands down against her ass cheeks. The resounding crack made her jump closer to me, and I felt her chest pressing against mine.

I captured her lips, swallowing her moans and protests as I massaged her butt. We leaned against my bike, our tongues intertwining, her soft whimpers of frustration turning into moans of pleasure.

I never wanted it to end, either.

"You really need to get a car."

I nuzzled my nose against hers. "A car? What on earth for?"

She kissed my lips softly. "They're much easier to make out in."

I chuckled. "Actually, that's the most convincing argument to buy a car I've ever heard."

"Does that mean you'll buy one?"

"That means I'll think about it. But only if you promise to break it in with me."

"Sounds like a good time."

"Sounds like a good promise."

She giggled before her lips captured mine again. Only this time, she stepped between my legs. Her body molded to me as I cloaked her back with my arms, trying to feel as much of her as I could at once. Her tongue slid across the roof of my mouth and I felt my cock aching for her beyond my jeans. My hands slid from her back to her ass, down her thighs and back again. I gripped her hair and pulled her head back softly. I licked down her pulse point, hearing her gasp softly as my name fell from her lips.

"Clint, oh."

That never ceased to make my heart skip a beat.

I buried my face in her chest. "What kind of trouble should we get into tonight?"

Her hands raked through my hair. "The kind of trouble that continues this saga."

I kissed her skin. "Mm, you had me at 'oh.'"

I hoisted her against my body and threw my leg over the bike. I settled her down against it, feeling her legs lock around me. Her hands clung to my leather jacket, pulling me closely against her. And as we sat in the shade of the trees planted specifically for this little shopping complex, I felt myself give way to her.

"Shit, Rae."

My hands slid up her shirt. I cupped her breasts, teasing her nipples through the padding of her bra. She rolled against me, my bike holding us steady as her tongue explored my mouth religiously. I wrapped my arms around her, running my palms along her bare skin, feeling her shake and shiver as goosebumps poured over her skin. I sucked on her lower lip and she kissed across my cheek. I felt her nibbling on my earlobe, causing me to growl out as my cock jumped with need for her.

Then she pressed her lips against the shell of my ear. "We really should get out of here."

"You don't have to tell me twice, beautiful."

It pained me to feel her slip away. But I knew it was headed toward something more pleasurable. More beautiful. More amazing than I could have ever expected from tonight. I handed her the helmet I'd dug out for her all those weeks ago, then slid my own over my head. I flipped up the visor, then reached out and flipped hers up. She gave me a massive smile as her cheeks flushed, then she inched her way onto the back of my bike. She was getting better at it. More steady, if that made any sense. Usually, she teetered, almost tripping over herself trying to get on.

But she'd gotten the hang of it.

I liked that.

I cranked up the engine. "Ready to get out of here?"

"What was that?"

"I said, are you ready to get out of here?"

Before she could answer, a set of headlights filled the parking lot, causing Rae to curse. They come straight for us, pulling up to my bike, blocking me in between the car and the tree that sat behind us.

Rae clung to me. "Who's that?"

I shook my head. "Probably Roy. But he can piss off. There's nothing to see here."

I slipped my helmet off and got off my bike. I kept my voice raised, hoping that Roy and the goons from school would buzz off and leave us the fuck alone. I hung the helmet on the handlebars, but felt Rae reach out for me. She pulled me back to her, so I wrapped my arm around her waist, trying to comfort her as she sat on the passenger's seat of my bike, pressing closer into me.

She was scared. And I couldn't blame her for it.

"I don't think that's Roy, Clint."

As the car door opened, I squinted my eyes, trying to figure out who the fuck was beaming us down with their high-beam headlights.

"Fucking cars," I murmured.

All at once, I saw the darkened outline of four

guys. Two in the front, and two in the back. They leaned against the hood of the car, their silvery outlines looming over us. Once they stepped closer into the light, leaning against the hood of the car, I recognized them. Well, two of them.

From the football field last week.

Shit.

They stood there, looking at us. Like fucking goof-balls with their arms crossed over their chests. They tried puffing out their muscles to look bigger, but I swear they were gangly little fucks. Rich bitch boys who didn't have a hope or a prayer in this world of stacking on muscle. And yet, I remembered the fight clearly. All three of those gangly assholes had a mean punch to them. They had been much stronger than they looked, and I'd be a damn fool to assume these other two fuckers would be any different.

"What do you want?"

My voice filled the space between us, but they didn't move. They didn't speak. They just stared at us with dumbass smirks on their faces. Rae pressed closer into me, and I felt her trembling. Shaking with fear. That pissed me off. No one scared my girl. No one rolled up on us and intimidated her like that.

She leaned into my ear. "Let's get out of here, okay? Speed away on your bike?"

I didn't answer her. I didn't want my answer to scare her. While motorcycles were fast, we didn't have time or space to get away from them. I wouldn't even get situated on my bike before they rammed into both of us, pinning us to the tree behind us. And I couldn't put Rae in danger like that. I couldn't let her get hurt again.

Which meant running wasn't an option.

"Please, Clint."

Hearing her beg made me sick to my stomach, but I shook my head. I felt her disappointment as she leaned her head against my shoulder, silently begging me to step down. But there was so much to this inter-action she didn't understand. So many ways for her to get hurt that she didn't realize.

And if she had a chance to get hurt, it meant that option wasn't really an option at all.

37

RAELYNN

The more the men came into view, the more of them I saw. They were lean, but tall. Three of them as tall as Clint. Easily. They all had beer cans in their hands and the glossy look in their eyes told me they'd been drinking. Probably all night, up until this point. I felt sick to my stomach. The smiles on their faces were wicked. The palms of their hands dwarfed those regular-sized beer cans, and the way they looked at me was frightening.

Their eyes darted between Clint and me, but they kept resting their gazes on me.

I gasped. "Clint."

He pressed further back into me. "It's gonna be all right, Rae. Just do exactly as I ask."

I wasn't so sure about that, though.

Each of them leaned against the hood of the car, blocking out parts of the high beams that shone against us. And when the blind spots faded from my vision, I found all four of them licking their lips. Staring at me. Raking their eyes up and down the parts of me they could see. I slid off the bike, staying behind Clint. I fisted his leather jacket, drawing him closer as his arm wrapped around behind me. He tapped my waist, trying to comfort me as the boys started laughing to themselves.

Then one of them finally spoke up.

"You look scared."

I narrowed my eyes. "You think?"

Clint squeezed my side, telling me to stop. And for once, I listened. I didn't like the way they were looking at me. I didn't like the way they slowly boxed us in. They all pushed off the hood of the car, stalking toward us. Making their way for us. Eyeing me hotly as Clint tried obscuring their view. Clint stood his ground, despite the fact that I knew we needed to run. He locked eyes with the boy in front, who stood a little over an inch taller than him.

I still felt the other three boys staring me down. Looking at places on my body that made me want to punch them straight in their noses.

I snarled. "Fuck off."

Another boy snickered. "She's got spunk. I like spunk."

The boy staring at Clint grinned. "I hate spunk."

Clint grimaced. "Good thing it isn't up to you either way."

"Oh, yeah? And what makes you think that?"

I giggled bitterly. "Because you don't get to control me."

All four of the boys looked over at me and I clung tightly to Clint. I didn't know what to do. I didn't know what the right move was. Mom taught me to always stand up for myself. But what the hell was I supposed to do in a situation like this? I didn't want to run. I didn't want to abandon Clint. And yet, I knew I was the target. I knew if they got through Clint, I'd be in a hell of a lot of trouble.

I whispered. "What should we do?"

Clint peered over his shoulder. "Stay there and do as I ask."

One of the boys grinned. "An obedient girl. I like that in my women."

I scoffed. "Good thing I'm not your woman, then."

"I think we could change that. I hear you like bad boy dick."

"I guess that takes you out of the running, then."

The boy lunged at me and Clint jumped in the way. He stood toe to toe with him, staring him down as his chest puffed out. The other three guys started laughing, filling the air with the smell of beer. I rested my forehead against Clint's back, feeling him stiffening, tightening, shaking with fury. His fists balled up at his sides and the staredown began, each party waiting for the other to make a move.

Was it possible to stare them down until they sobered up? Until they got back into their car and left?

Where the hell is the patrol car that always comes through?

"Clint," I whispered.

One of the boys chuckled. "Think your girl's calling you."

Clint nodded. "And don't you forget who she belongs to."

"I don't think she belongs to anyone. She's a free-spirited girl, right? The one who ran to your defense?"

"And if I remember correctly, you're the asshole that knocked her down. Hurt her. And mark my words, you'll pay for that."

"Oh, she's got some fluff. She's good."

I felt Clint lunge and I gripped his leather jacket. I pulled him back to me as the boys erupted into laughter. He shrugged me off, whipping around and glaring at me. I glared right back, silently screaming at him, telling him there was no way on fuck's green earth he'd be able to take all four of them in a fight without them dragging me off in the process.

And when he drew in a deep breath, I watched his eyes soften.

"Look at that, boys! He's whipped already."

I heard the drunk assholes making whipping noises as they twirled their hands around in the air. Clint's face flushed with anger and he grew another two inches as fury filled his veins. He whipped back around and I tightened my grip on his leather jacket, trying desperately to keep a hold on this situation. I had my purse with me. It hung off my shoulder. And if I slipped my hand in there, I could press the emergency button on my phone, calling for help before this escalated.

Clint growled. "The four of you need to leave. Now."

Main Boy shook his head. "Eh, that doesn't sit well with me. I mean, what if the little lady's in trouble?"

I snickered. "I'm not. The only people I'd be in trouble with are the four of you."

"But it would be the best kind of trouble."

Clint grinned. "She gets plenty of that with me."

"And from the looks of her curves, there's plenty to go around. Sharing is caring, Clarke."

I wrangled Clint back again, feeling him trying to tug away from me. I slipped out from behind him and pressed my hands into his stomach, getting him to back up. I almost had him backed up, too. Until I felt a pair of hands on my hips. A pair of hands that weren't Clint's.

And he lost his fucking mind.

"What the fuck are you doing, touching my girl?"

"Clint! No!"

He lunged around me, slapping the boy's hands away. I whipped around with wide eyes, watching as Clint went straight for the boy's neck. His three goons wrapped their arms around Clint, dragging him back before tossing him onto the ground. And as I stood there, with a gasp falling from my lips, Main Boy looked straight at me.

"You ready to try a real man?"

Clint shot up from the ground. "You don't speak with her. At all."

"That right, sexy? You don't wanna talk to a man like me?"

I scoffed. "Hardly."

"Even if I know I can throw it down better than your measly little man here can?"

My eyes narrowed. "Sex isn't what I'm after."

The boys laughed at me as they leaned back against their car. Clint got in front of me again, blocking my body from their reach. I turned a little to the side, concealing my hand as it slipped into my purse, silently rummaging around for my phone.

Main Boy grinned. "So, entertain me. What is it you're after?"

I shrugged. "Not you four, that's for sure."

"And what about us do you not like?"

"Other than your overall assholeish nature, your ugly looks, your disgusting demeanors, and your pompous attitudes?"

He shrugged. "Yeah. Sure. Other than those."

I grinned. "I don't like small dicks."

Main Boy lunged off his car and Clint stepped in front of him, toe to toe again, though I knew he was upset with me. I pulled my hand out of my purse quickly, sliding my phone into my back pocket. Then I dropped my purse to the ground, trying to act like I was scared out of my mind to conceal what had just happened.

Just a few more shielded seconds, Clint. Work with me here.

I saw Clint's shoulders stiffen but his hands slowly unclenched. As he backed away from the guy, making his way back for me, I caught his eyes and saw the nervousness growing in them. His eyes darted around in the darkness, looking for a way out. He hugged me close and kissed the top of my head, then moved his lips to my ear.

"I'll pay for this statement later, but keep your fucking mouth shut, Rae."

I had a bad feeling about this. And so did Clint. He was nervous, which made me even more nervous. He turned back around, giving me darkness to stand in. And slowly, I slipped my hand around my back.

Main Boy's voice boomed. "You know what I think?"

Clint sighed. "What do you think, dickweed?"

"I think we've been chatting long enough. I came here for a good time, and I'm not leaving until I get one."

Then, as my finger found the red emergency button, I watched Main Boy rush for Clint.

38

CLINTON

I reached my arms out and fisted the guy's shirt as he came for me. I backed him all the way up to his car as Rae let out a yelp. I had to get these guys away from her. They were predatory, and they announced it well enough with their eyes. My bike was close. Really close. And the key was already in the ignition. I pinned that asshole to the hood of his car to give myself time to think. A well-placed knee to the groin turned his buddies' attention away from Rae and to me.

"Get him, guys."

As they ambushed me, I heard Rae calling out. The crunch of dead grass could be heard, and I hoped she was climbing into that fucking tree, doing her best to get away from these assholes. They ripped me away from the guy I had pinned to the hood of the car, tossing me back to my bike. And as I fell to the concrete, I gazed up at my getaway, hoping with all my might they'd follow me and leave Rae alone.

Piss them off first. They'll follow you then.

"That all you got?" I asked.

I leapt off the ground, poised for a fight as their main guy hunched over, grabbing his balls like a little bitch.

I grinned. "Because if that's all you got, there's no way in hell you'll please a girl like Rae. She needs something a little... thicker."

"Clint! Shut up and come on already!"

Her voice sounded far away, and I hoped that meant she was running. Another guy rushed toward me and I clotheslined him, preparing myself to throw another punch. The fight began and I hit them everywhere I could, making sure not to leave my bike. They kept coming at me with punches. With elbows. With snarky remarks about all the things they'd do to Rae once they got their hands on her.

I wasn't having any of it.

I ran myself into one guy's stomach, picking him up off the ground. I body-slammed him into the hood of the car, then moved just before another one kicked me. I heard the headlight shatter before the lighting dimmed around us. A yelp told me that glass had raked right across someone's skin. I chuckled to myself as I whipped around, lifting my legs to donkey kick the asshole headed for me.

And since I couldn't see Rae, I took that as a good sign.

"You guys really are pathetic!" I grunted. "This is easier than last week!"

"You're gonna die tonight, asshole."

The growling voice told me it was time. I bolted for my bike, praying to any god that might be listening for help in abating Rae's anger. Because I knew she'd be angry at me. Spitfire angry. But I had to get these assholes away from her. I had to keep her safe.

And whatever that took, I was willing to do it.

"Oh, no. You're not getting away. Get in the car, boys! We got ourselves an asshole to run down!"

"Clint!"

Her voice seemed so far away, but that was the point. Give her a chance to run before leading these guys off somewhere else. I threw my leg over my bike, not worrying about my helmet. I cranked up the engine and sped out of the parking lot, hearing my gear shifter groan and flailing my leg to get the kick-stand up as I took off.

It worried me when I didn't see that headlight turning toward me in the rearview mirror.

"No!"

Rae's shriek told me everything I needed to know. I whipped around, revving my engine as I raced down the road. I saw the car hopping the curb, blowing past that fucking tree. I saw it racing up the street before the headlight illuminated Rae's form on the side of the road. She was climbing the chain-link fence around the elementary school playground, hopping it before the boys even got out of their fucking car.

I grabbed my helmet off my handlebars and pulled up behind their car, whipping the helmet at their rear windshield and shattering it into a million pieces.

That got their attention.

"You son of a bitch!"

Rae yelled, "Clint!"

"Get him!"

"You're dead tonight, fucker! I just replaced that damn thing!"

I laughed. "Gotta catch me first, assholes!"

Rae cupped her hands over her mouth. "Clint! Don't do this!"

"Get yourself safe, Rae. For fuck's sake, just stop fighting!"

I saw the car back away and turn around. It swerved, showing that the boys were more drunk than before. I turned and raced off, letting Rae's voice fade into the background as we peeled away from the grocery store, weaving in and out of the small parking lots. I didn't want to take this shit to the main roads. I didn't want anyone getting hurt. I just wanted to cause enough ruckus to get someone's attention. Anyone's. A police car driving by. Some innocent bystander who would call 9-1-1. I'd gladly go to jail and do time as the adult I was if it got these drunken, horny bastards away from my girl.

I wasn't sure if I'd ever be able to fix my relationship with Rae, though.

After something like this.

I felt an empty beer can clink against my bike and something wet sprayed my back. The car's engine revved, catching up with me. I throttled it through a parking lot and hopped another curb. My bike went airborne for a second before landing onto a small back road. I heard the car behind me practically falling apart in order to keep up with me. I knew if I looked back, I'd see something hanging off that piece of shit.

I tried looking around for Rae, but it was no use. I circled back to the grocery store but she wasn't near the elementary school or back inside the store. I didn't see her walking along the streets or heading into the gas station. I had no fucking clue where she'd gone, which meant I now had to solve the other issue on my hands.

"I see you!"

The four fucking maniacs chasing me in their rundown car.

The main roads were empty at this time of night. Half past ten, in the middle of the work week. I blazed a trail up the main roads, trying to get away from the goons. I soared through yellow lights and took sharp turns on red lights, hoping and praying to trigger a cop from out of nowhere. But, of course, there were none to be found tonight. Fucking hell, I'd torn through this town and gotten clocked by more cops than anyone else. Yet the one damn night I needed them to clock me, they weren't anywhere in sight.

That's some fucking karma, if I've ever witnessed it.

The closer they got to me, the more panicked I became. Rae was safe, and as long as they were tailing me, I knew she'd stay that way. They were drunk. They'd probably been to some dumbass party of hoes and gangly dickweeds from their high school. But I knew how volatile guys were when drunk. Roy and I had destroyed many lives while drunk. We'd wreaked many hours' worth of havoc with alcohol in our systems. And it seemed that no matter how hard I pushed my bike, they pushed their car just a tad bit harder.

The only way I stayed out of their reach was to take sharp turns.

Because their car couldn't handle them.

We blazed a trail through town before I took a sharp right. I rumbled over some abandoned railroad tracks and blazed into the darkness. A massive stretch of road that didn't have lamps hanging overhead. Nothing but dilapidated houses and abandoned parks where children used to get their kicks before growing up and moving away. I heard the car behind me sputtering as they continuously threw beer cans and bottles at my fucking wheels, trying to get me to career off the damn road. And when that didn't work, they moved over into the other lane in my rearview mirror, approaching me with their windows rolled down.

"Nice bike you got there!"

I peeked over at the guy who had tossed Rae to the ground last week.

"Think I could fuck your girl on it?"

I reached out with my hand and hooked my fingers up his nostrils, pulling at him until he was hanging halfway out of the car, screaming as the driver started swerving, trying to see what was happening. His hand wrapped around my wrist, clinging to me for dear life as he yelled in horror. I chuckled and smiled widely before releasing his nose, shoving him back into the car with my hand.

Then I slammed on the brakes of my bike, whipping a U-turn and kicking up burnt rubber before speeding off in the other direction. And for a while there, the car wasn't even in my rearview mirror. Did I shake them? Were they gone? I had enough time alone to breathe a sigh of relief.

Until I saw a light click on in the corner of my eye.

"Holy shit!"

"You motherfucker!"

I heard the boy behind the wheel of the car screaming as he careened out of the fucking woods. I slid my bike close to the asphalt, twisting away from him as he shot himself across the damn street. It took me a few seconds to get my bike back underneath me before I sped off again, and it was those few precious seconds that enabled them to catch right back up to me. On my tail again, like they had been.

And for the first time in my life, I had no idea what the fuck to do to shake these assholes.

39

RAELYNN

"Clint!"

I watched his bike speed off into the distance with the car behind him. I rushed across the elementary school playground, doing my best to try and figure out where the fuck he was headed. My lungs burned. My legs ached. I clutched my purse, wrapping it around my neck and shoulder before reaching for my phone. I pulled it out to see if anyone was listening.

But all I saw were a bunch of random numbers pressed into my phone.

"Shit," I hissed.

I could have sworn I'd pressed that damn red emergency button. Fucking hell, did I have to screw every little thing up? I kept running, feeling my purse slamming against me as the revving of Clint's engine started coming closer to me.

And as it barreled by the elementary school, I was still half a football field away from the road.

"Clint!" I roared.

I felt my voice growing hoarse. I saw the car rush by just as I got past the school building. I bent over, panting for air as I watched the car full of angry drunken idiots swerve down the road. Were there not any cops out tonight? At all? The hell was that about?

I had to get to Clint.

I fumbled with my phone as I stood up, throwing my head back, trying my hardest to catch my breath. Even for someone who enjoyed P.E. and sports, I still couldn't keep up. I grumbled to myself as I clutched my phone. I looked down, hovering my finger over the red emergency button. The dial-out to 9-1-1. The number that would surely bring people to help out this situation.

But then I heard laughing in the distance. I heard Clint's bike revving before the rickety sounds of the train tracks were heard.

If I called the police, would Clint get in trouble, too?

"I can't get him in trouble for this. It's not his fault," I murmured.

Instead, I dialed Michael's number. Hoping beyond all hope that he'd pick up the phone. I knew he was done with my shit. Done with me and the idiocy surrounding Clint and me. But Michael was the one with the car. Allison hadn't gotten her driver's license yet because of some weird fear of making herself motion sick, so her parents still carted her around.

I put my phone to my ear, listening to it ring as I started jogging toward the road that connected the parking lot of Grady's Groceries and the elementary school.

Michael chuckled, answering the phone. "Hey, Allison and I were just talking about you."

I panted for breath. "Michael. Please. I need your help."

"Wait, what? Rae, what's wrong?"

"Me. And Clint. It—I'm at the—"

"Clint? What the fuck has he done?"

I shook my head. "Nothing. He—he's in trouble and—"

"Why are you out of breath?"

I groaned. "Do you have your car at Allison's?"

He paused. "Uh, yeah?"

I drew in a deep breath. "Please. I need you to come get me. I'm standing outside of the elementary school. We have to go after Clint. It's important."

"And why should I give enough of a damn about him to do something like that?"

"Look, I know you're sick of his shit. And my shit. I know you're sick of me, despite the makeup session we kind of had in the cafeteria. But I need you to come get me. It's a very serious emergency, and explaining it only wastes time."

"You make it sound like he tossed himself off a bridge or something."

I yelled, "Damn it, Michael. I need you right now. My best fucking friend. Please. If you come get me, I'll leave you alone. For good. I won't talk to you. I won't approach you. I won't bother you with Clint shit ever again. Just please, this once, come get me and stop asking questions."

"I don't want that, and you know it."

"Well, you're sure as hell acting like it!"

I heard his bike revving off in the distance. Coming closer, only to fade back. And I could have sworn I heard the skidding of tires. The sound made me sick. So sick that I actually heaved. And when I did, Michael sighed.

"You said you're at the elementary school?"

I sniffled. "Yes."

"Are you crying?"

"Just shut the *fuck* up and get here."

"Fine. I'm on my way. But I'm leaving Allison behind. She doesn't need to get involved with his shit. Just like you shouldn't have."

"Spare me the lecture, please?"

"Stand on the curb so I can spot you. Bye."

I hung up the phone call and stood there like a damn idiot. The sounds faded into nothingness for a few seconds, and it forced tears down my cheeks. I knew the first question Michael would ask the second I got into his car. He'd want to know if I called the police. And if I didn't, he'd chastise me for it. He'd tell me I was turning into Clint, and I'd really risk losing my friend then.

So as I stood there waiting for him, I pressed that little red emergency button on my phone screen.

"9-1-1, what's your emergency?"

"Hi. Yes. I'd like to report an… ambush?"

"An ambush, ma'am?"

I cleared my throat. "Yes. An ambush. My boyfriend came to—"

Boyfriend? Is that what Clint was to me?

The word made me smile.

The operator cleared her throat. "Your boyfriend came where, ma'am?"

I shook my head. "Yes. Sorry. My boyfriend came to see me at work. We were standing in the parking lot after I locked up, and four drunk guys in a car pulled into the parking lot. Started harassing us. Calling us names. Throwing beer bottles and things at us. They were trying t—"

I heard the operator typing in the background as tears rushed to my eyes again.

"They were trying to what, ma'am? Where are you currently?"

I sighed. "I'm in Riverbend, in front of the elementary school beside a place called Grady's Groceries. I don't have any other address other than that. You guys have to hurry. My boyfriend started fighting with these guys so they wouldn't get to me. They were talking about things. Taking advantage of me and all that. He got on his bike and rode off, and a car full of drunk teenagers are following him. He's in a lot of trouble. Please."

"All right, ma'am. I want you to stay calm. About how old do you think the boys are?"

"No more than eighteen. They go to Lincoln High School."

The operator hummed. "Do you know what the car looked like?"

I searched around for Michael's SUV as I racked my brain.

"Uh… it was a low-riding car. Like, not like the usual way a car sits on its tires, if that makes any sense. And it was white. A white, low-riding car with tinted windows. I don't know anything other than that, though. I'm sorry."

"It's fine. It's okay. Just take some deep breaths for me. You're panting pretty hard."

Was I?

Shit, I was.

I drew in some deep breaths. "I don't want my boyfriend to get in trouble. He only fought against them and sped off to get them away from me. They were grabbing for me. There are parking lot cameras at Grady's Groceries. The footage should show—"

The operator cut me off. "It's okay. First we get everyone safe. Then we figure out who's at fault. But, from one woman to another, I believe you. Okay? Just stay where you are."

But just as she said that, Michael's SUV pulled up to the curb.

"I'm sorry, I have to go. Please. Send someone out here. Hurry. I think my boyfriend and those goons have raced across the railroad tracks. And there's a lot of trees and overpasses and things for them to get hurt on."

"Ma'am. Do not go after them. Please, stay on the line with me and wait for—"

I hung up the call and ripped Michael's door open. I climbed in, slamming the door closed as I buckled my seatbelt. I dropped my purse to the floorboard and slipped my phone into his cup holder. Then I looked him straight in his eyes as he waited for an explanation.

I sighed. "I've called the police. But we have to find Clint. He's in a lot of trouble. Serious trouble."

Michael scoffed. "Shouldn't shock you one bit."

"He's in trouble because he saved me from a group of drunk guys who wanted to take me, Michael."

"Take you? What the hell do you mean, ta—"

I leveled him with a stare that told him everything he needed to know. Finally, he pulled away from the curb and whipped a U-turn.

"I take it the revving engines beyond the railroad tracks are them?"

I nodded. "Yes. Please. Thank you."

"And you said you called the police?"

"I did. I told the 9-1-1 operator as much as I could remember. I just hope Clint doesn't get into too much trouble for helping me like that."

Michael paused. "What did he do, exactly?"

I shrugged. "What he always does. Harassed them to get their attention so I could run and hop the chain-link fence of the playground back there."

Michael nodded, but he didn't say anything. And for some reason, I wanted to know his thoughts. I wanted him to talk to me, even if it was in anger.

"Does he know the guys or anything? Or was it just a group of random guys?"

I winced, knowing how he'd react to the answer. "Two of the guys were from the football field fight the other day."

He scoffed. "See, Rae? That's what I'm telling you about this asshole of a dude. He's always in trouble. That's why you never should've gotten involved with him in the first place. You're a good girl. You're not the kind of girl who throws it all away on some dickhead with a nice face."

I gritted my teeth. "I know you're pissed off at me. And rightfully so. And yes, you're also probably right about Clint and this entire scenario. About a lot of things. But he did what he did tonight to protect me. I need you to trust me on that. So spare me the lecture and give it to me some other time. You know, when we figure out whether Clint is dead or not."

"Would do the world some good."

"Michael!"

"I don't like the dude, okay? He's an absolute maniac. Has been our entire high school career. Those comments he made about Allison? Absolutely unacceptable, whether he's screwing my friend or not."

I bit down on the inside of my cheek. "Just fucking drive."

"Fine by me."

40

CLINTON

*A*t least *they're far away from Rae.*

It was the only thought that filled my head as I sped down the back roads. The further we got away from the railroad tracks, the worse the road conditions got. And suddenly, I understood where that phrase came from: 'The other side of the tracks.'

I'm not ever using that fucking phrase again.

I zoomed by crumbling neighborhoods with broken porch lights and cars propped up on cement blocks. I weaved in and out of abandoned neighborhoods, cursing how those assholes kept up with me. These guys were bad news. They had every intention of doing harm tonight. And with the endless supply of beer bottles and cans being tossed at the wheels of my fucking bike, they were still drinking.

Which meant this would only get worse for me if I couldn't shake them soon.

I whipped a U-turn and headed back for the railroad tracks. I felt my phone vibrating in my pocket, and I knew damn good and well who it was. Rae. Probably calling to see if I'd gotten away yet. Wanting to know if I was fine. If I was hurt. If I needed anything.

Fucking hell, she deserves better than all this.

"We're coming for you!"

"You won't get out of this alive!"

"You're an asswipe, and you'll stay an asswipe until we side-swipe your ass!"

They yelled at me. Taunted me. Actually made me fearful of what was to come. I turned back around, soaring away from the railroad tracks again as the car skidded to a stop behind me. I grinned as I threw it into gear. I felt my bike rumbling underneath me as my speed picked up. Sixty. Seventy. Eighty miles an hour. The wild whipped around me, cradling me and harboring the fugitive I'd become during this entire debacle.

God, if you get me out of this alive, I'll stop fucking around.

I was desperate. Because as I heard that bullshit white car gaining on me, I wondered if I'd ever shake them. If I'd ever get them off my damn tail. If there was anyone on this planet that wasn't in God's good graces, it was me. Well, my entire family. Because let's face it, my father needed to be included in that group. But, if he or she was listening—and he or she believed in mercy—I needed a massive chunk of it right about now.

"Come on," I growled.

As I soared over the Adderscape Bridge, I breathed

a sigh of relief. The Riverbend outer city limits ended about a mile up the road. Which meant nothing but clear, straight roads for miles. I looked down at my gas tank and smiled. I still had three-fourths of a tank. And there was no way in hell those idiots would outdrive me in the gas-guzzling low-rider they had. If anything, I could keep traveling from city to city. Heading nothing but north until they ran out of gas or pulled over for some.

So, with that plan in mind, I set my cruise control to eighty-five.

Because even if I'm clocked for speeding, those fuckers will be, too.

I shook my head. "You never should have picked that fight, Clarke."

It never should have happened. The second we hit my bike, we should have been on it and headed somewhere else. I made us sitting ducks with my inability to do anything but devour Rae's body. Rae's presence. Rae's giggles and her curves. By sitting out there in an empty parking lot, I made us vulnerable to attacks. Attacks I was all too familiar with.

I sighed. "You're a fucking idiot."

And truthfully? The last thing I needed right now were more enemies. I had Roy and that asshole ex-posse back at the school. Because I knew damn good and well they weren't friends of mine anymore after my outburst. And while I didn't mind ditching those little bitches for something better, it'd make the rest of my senior year a pile of steaming shit. They'd torture me. Roy would take my place, so to speak, puff out his chest, and target me just to look like the big man on campus.

The question was, would I let him attack me? Or would I retaliate?

And outside of all that, Rae's friends hated me. Allison and Michael. Hell, my own father hated me. The only person right now other than Rae who put up with my presence was Cecilia. And that's only because she had to. My life was fucked, and I knew it. All because of some girl. Because of some night where my mouth started running and some girl started opening up and then my dick slipped and fell between the sweetest pair of legs to ever wrap around me.

Because you love her.

The thought startled me so badly I felt my bike wobbling. The motion snapped me from my trance, and I heard the car of idiots behind me laughing. I turned off the cruise control and swerved off the road, giving myself a second to catch my balance. Catch my breath.

Love?

Had I really fallen for Rae Cleaver?

"Get him, boys!"

I heard car doors open and I pushed off the grass. I got my bike back onto the road and took off, only I wasn't going in the right direction. I didn't care anymore, though. I'd stayed stationary long enough for those assholes to get out of their fucking car. That was something I could capitalize on.

"See you later, dickweeds."

I flew back in the opposite direction, approaching

the bridge again. I forced my mind to concentrate, but it still had a tendency to wander. I mean, when the fuck was I going to catch a breath with people? When were the people in my life going to stop beating me up and start enjoying me? All I wanted was for my father to stop being such an asshole and my stepmother to actually give more a shit, instead of stepping in when she thought my father was hitting me a little *too* hard.

When would the school stop giving up on me and start trying to help me?

Gotta start helping yourself, Clarke.

I sighed as I felt the rumbling patches underneath my tires signaling the expanse of the bridge in front of me. I took a look in my rearview mirror, keeping an ear out for the sound of the car. But it was nowhere to be found. I didn't hear the guys yelling. I didn't feel them throwing bottles and cans at me. I even let off the gas, trying to see if I could hear them off in the distance.

There was nothing.

I sighed. "Holy shit, I think I actually lost them."

Relief washed over my body. I shook my head as the rumbling patches gave way to the reddened concrete that signaled bridges in our area. I slowed my pace down, giving my bike a chance to breathe as I drew in the nighttime air through my nose. Everything was silent. Everything felt peaceful. I pulled over on the side of the bridge, turning off my engine as the trees around us shaded me.

"Silence," I whispered.

There was nothing but the sound of the wind rustling the trees. Nothing but the sound of water rushing underneath the bridge. I peeked over the edge, seeing a great expanse of black with small caps of dark blue where the water rushed over smooth rocks at the bottom of the river. I'd completely forgotten this place existed. This small slice of country paradise on the outskirts of one of the biggest cities in the country.

I need to bring Rae here sometime. Have a picnic.

I smiled at the thought. The idea of bringing Rae here and sitting on the bank of the river. Our feet in the water. Our eyes, watching fish swim upstream, trying to fight the current. Our hands, interlaced as we looked out over the nature that surrounded us with full stomachs and a peaceful presence.

I let myself dream about it for a second before my mind took the helm again.

Sitting duck, Clarke.

Adrenaline rushed through my veins again. I cursed myself as I struck my bike's engine back up. It was happening again. Me letting the thought of Rae distract me. I had to keep moving. I had to get home. I had to get back to the school and the grocery store and see if Rae was all right. I needed to go by her house to make sure she'd gotten home. And if she wasn't home, I had to go out on a search for—

"Look who's the sucker now!"

My head whipped around as the blaring headlight of the car filled my vision. Their horn blared over the sound of their disgusting laughter. I felt a glass beer bottle slam directly between my eyes. And as my head fell back, the sound of screeching tires filled my ears. The smell of burning rubber wafted underneath my nostrils. I heard metal crunching against metal, alerting me to the imminent threat.

Get off the bike. Get off your fucking bike.

I moved my leg just before it got pinned. I lunged for the hood of the car, trying my best to avoid what was happening. I heard my bike slam against the metal railing of the bridge before the car backed up. I took off running, leaving my bike behind, darting for the trees. They were thick around these parts. No way in hell that car could navigate woods like that without being totaled.

But the throbbing in my forehead was too great.

"Geromino!"

It was the last thing I heard before I felt a searing pain waft up my side. I stumbled off my feet, hearing the laughter from those boys fill my ears. The car slammed into my side, shoving me toward the metal railing. And as I lost my balance, I felt myself teetering over the edge. Flailing my arms. Crying out for help. With tears threatening to burst from my eyes as the sky quickly came into view.

Before fading away into nothingness as my body slammed into the river.

41

RAELYNN

Michael white-knuckled his steering wheel. "Do you have any idea where the fuck they are?"

I shook my head. "No. Just keep driving."

"For all we know, he's back home. Safe and sound. While we're out here—"

"Just drive, damn it!"

I slid to the edge of the seat as Michael put on his high beams. We'd only just crossed the railroad tracks, and I already saw burnout marks on the asphalt of the road. There were patches of grass that had one-tire and two-tire streaks in them. I had Michael pull over on the side of the road. I hopped out and started looking around. I ran to the bridge, fearful that the worst had happened. I bent over the edge, looking for his bike. Looking for him. Looking for any signs of wreckage.

To my relief, there was none.

"Ready to keep going?"

I hopped back into his car. "Yes. Sorry. Thank you for stopping."

"Not a problem. Didn't think I'd actually see tire tracks out here."

"Do you believe me now?"

And when I shot him a look, all he did was purse his lips.

"How far out do you think they drove?"

I shrugged. "I figured we'd follow the tire tracks until they stop."

"Fine by me."

Every half-mile, we came upon them. Some of the tire tracks led into abandoned neighborhoods I'd only heard rumors about. But I kept my focus, not wanting to get off track. We had to find Clint before these guys did. Otherwise, he'd be in a lot of trouble.

Michael sighed. "You know the police won't find us all the way out here."

I nodded. "I know. If Clint and those boys are back there, they'll find them. Which is why we have to search back here. If there's any sign of them, I'll have to call 9-1-1 and update them. Or something."

"Yeah. Or something."

I ignored his remark. I was growing tired of Michael's attitude anyway. I mean, I wasn't pissed off at the fact that he wanted to fuck around with my best friend. The girl I'd known since elementary school. If anything, that should have pissed someone like me off. But it didn't. Because I wanted their happiness.

Why didn't they want mine?

Michael throttled it out of the neighborhood. "We're almost to the city limits."

I paused. "Adderscape Bridge?"

"That's the one, I think."

"Head there."

"Why?"

Worry filled my gut. "Please, just head there. I just... want to make sure."

"Whatever you say, Juliet."

I rolled my eyes at his comment as he blazed a trail down the road. There was no one back here. No lights. No animals. No people. No police. If Clint had raced himself into this territory, he didn't have any help at all. No hope of ever having someone come upon him to help. That was why I wanted to check every inch of this back road. Especially if the tire tracks were still fresh.

"How much further?"

Michael shrugged. "Two, three miles?"

"Can you go faster?"

"Just because Clint wants to break the sound barrier for you doesn't mean I do."

I scoffed. "You know what? Go ahead and stay angry with me. I don't care anymore."

"You sound more and more like him every day."

"I'm sorry that you don't like the fact that I'm dating some guy that punched you in the face. I'm sorry that you think he's an asshole. But when you take into account the fact that his father literally throws him around the house on a daily basis, and you take into account the fact that I should be pissed off that you're in love with my best friend, you don't have a leg to stand on."

"And why's that?"

"Because as Allison's girl, I should be pissed off that you want to screw with her. Fuck her. Or do whatever it is you want to do with her. But I'm not. I want you two to be happy together. I want her to see how you feel about her because I think you two would be great together. Because you're alike. Because you're similar. Because your lives mesh. Just like mine and Clint's do. So, if you expect me to be okay with the fact that you're slowly but surely macking on my best friend, get your fucking act together and suck it the hell up."

Michael put the pedal to the metal as we careened around the corner. The last turn before the straightaway over the bridge. His high beams pointed straight ahead, and I saw fresh tire tracks on the bridge.

As well as Clint's motorcycle crunched against the railing.

"Michael, stop!" I shrieked in his car. My voice filled the space around us as he came to a grinding halt. I ripped my seatbelt off and slammed out of the car, rushing toward the edge of the bridge. My heart leapt into my throat. Tears burned the backs of my eyes. I stumbled over to his bike, taking in the broken rearview mirror and the bent handlebar.

But, all things considered, it looked intact.

"Clint!"

My voice echoed off the trees and into the darkness of the water below. The metal barrier was bent. Fractured. Bowed, in some places. Then I saw the tire tracks right in front of the bike.

"They were here, Michael! They were here!"

Michael jogged up to me. "I'm checking the woods. Call the police."

"Michael, what if he's—"

"Just do as I'm telling you to do, Rae!"

I swallowed hard as I watched Michael rush for the woods. He darted into the trees before I turned my eyes back down toward the water. I didn't want to approach the edge. Flashes of the nightmare I always had before school came rushing back to me. My arms flailing as I fell over the edge. Darkness overcoming me just before I woke up. The smell of smoke. Of burnt rubber, singeing my nostril hairs.

Only this time, I wasn't sure if the smell was phantom, or real.

"Clint!"

My voice cracked before it gave out. I threw myself over the railing, gazing down into the darkened expanse below. I looked up at the sky, the starry sky that always permeated my worst nightmare. And as my eyes fell back down to the water, my stomach flipped over on itself.

A nightmare come true.

"Clint! Are you down there?"

My pathetic voice did nothing but hiss as I cupped my hands over my mouth. I heard Michael running around in the woods, calling out for Clint in the distance. Tears rushed down my cheeks. My hands shook. They gripped the edge with all their might, and

I didn't know what to do. I knew he was down there. Had he been washed away by the current? His dead, lifeless body, floating down river until his jacket snagged onto something?

I heard Michael trotting up to me. "He's not in the woods. And if he is, he's not in a position to call out for me. I don't hear a car anywhere, either. Those guys must've buzzed off."

Yeah. After they ran him off the road.

"Did you call the police?"

Holy shit. My phone. The light on my phone.

I ripped my phone out of my pocket and turned on the flashlight. I heard Michael scoff as he shook his head, but his eyes fell over the railing, too. Down into the deep, dark abyss of the raging river. I turned the flashlight on my phone up as bright as I could get it, then shined it down onto the water.

Michael sighed. "It's at least a twenty-foot drop."

"You think that's enough to kill him?"

He paused. "I don't really know, Rae."

I flashed my light against the water as Michael stepped off to the side. I heard him talking into his phone. Saying something about 'a prior call' and 'needing an ambulance.' His voice faded away after that, though. Because the second my light fell onto Clint's body on the side of the river, my voice reached another fucking planet with the octave it leapt into.

"He's down there!"

I took off running, only for an arm to wrap around my waist. I felt Michael pulling me into him as he continued talking on his phone, trying to give directions to whoever the fuck was on the other end of the line. I heard him talking about tire tracks, and a car of guys. A bike on the bridge and a body in the river. I cried out for Clint, raking my nails against Michael's bare skin. But, despite the pain I knew he was in, he didn't release his grip.

"Rae, you can't go down there. It isn't—Rae!"

I growled. "Let me go."

"Not on your fucking life. I'm not losing you, too."

"He's not dead! Don't say shit like that!"

"The bank is too steep. You'll hurt yourself traversing it at night. The police are a few minutes out. When they get here—"

My nostrils flared. "Let—me—go, you asshole!"

I struggled against him as I heard his phone drop to the pavement. He wrapped both arms around me, hoisting me off my feet. I cried out for Clint as my voice left me completely. Tears rushed down my cheeks as I tried prying Michael's arms from around my waist. He carried me back to the car, away from the bike. Away from the bridge. Away from Clint's body lying on the edge of the riverbank.

"Clint!" I called breathlessly.

"Come on, Rae. Let's get in the car. This is a crime scene. The police are only a few minutes out."

"No, Clint. Please. Don't do this to me, please."

"I'm sorry, Rae. I'm so, so sorry."

Michael set me down onto my feet and pinned me against his car. I bashed my head against the glass, only to feel his hand wrap around it. I sobbed out into the night, gazing up at a nighttime sky I'd come to hate as images of my recurring nightmare continued to bombard me. The squealing of tires. The crunching of metal. That dumbass smell of burnt rubber that still lingered in the fucking air.

I drew in a shuddering breath. "It's my nightmare come true."

And when Michael didn't say anything, I knew he'd been thinking exactly that.

How could this have happened? Things were finally going smoothly. Things were finally going well for me and him. I knew what I wanted. I knew what I needed. I knew what I wanted to do with my life and who I wanted to do it with. I'd found someone who got me. Who understood me. A guy who made me feel on top of the world, and absolutely gorgeous in his arms. I found someone who didn't only leave his judgment of my life at the door, but he literally understood my life. Understood the judgment that came with my life. I finally had everything I could have ever asked for.

Him.

And now, I felt it all slipping through my fingertips.

Michael kept me pinned. "Do you want me to call Allison?"

I shook my head, unable to speak.

"Do you want to get out of here?"

I shook my head harder, trying to give my voice a few minutes to return.

"Do you want to talk about it?"

My eyes whipped open as tears streamed down my face. I glared at Michael, hating him for everything he was suggesting. Oh, he wanted to be here now? After being an absolute shitbag for the past couple of weeks? I could have spat in his face. I could have slapped him right across that dumbass, concerned little furrowed brow of his.

But I settled for shaking my head as I leveled him with a DEFCON-5 stare.

"Fair enough. I deserve that."

I nodded curtly, trying my hardest not to say anything. Trying my best to save my voice so I could keep calling out for Clint. I had to wake him up. As long as Michael was here, he wouldn't let me down that bank. Yelling was all I had to get him to wake the fuck up and get back here.

Because he couldn't leave me. Not now.

Not when I finally had all I wanted.

42

CLINTON

I felt my head pounding. I felt disoriented. For some reason, I felt water rushing over my legs. And I had no idea why. I sniffed the air, groaning as my head pounded with frustration. I felt something sharp underneath my side, prompting me to move. So many things bombarded my senses as I slowly came out of it.

Came out of what, though?

I swallowed hard, tasting the metallic essence of blood. I smelled smoke. And oil. And dirt. Why did I smell oil? What was going on?

I thought people smelled toast before they had strokes, or some shit.

I tried opening my eyes, but I couldn't. I tried rolling over, but it was all for nothing. It was like this massive disconnect with my soul and my body was taking place. Like that paralyzing sleep shit. I heard bats fluttering around me. Or a winged animal of some sort. Water dripped in the distance and continued rushing over my legs.

I started shivering from the cold, which only exacerbated the pain in my back.

Fuck.

I swallowed again, but the reflex was daunting. It made my nose hurt, of all things. I didn't know what the fuck that was about, either. Wind kicked up around me, causing me to shiver and hurt in places I hadn't realized. Like my nose again. My shoulder. My ankle.

Why the hell did I hurt in all these random places?

"Clint!"

I could have sworn I heard my name off in the distance, called in panic. I heard it again. And again. I heard it again before something popped, then the sound went away. I was probably imagining it. Dreaming it, because of the pain I was in. Holy shit, I'd never experienced pain like this before. The way my body felt was nothing compared to some of the beatings I'd taken from my father over the years. I drew in a deep breath, reeling from the pain in my nose and forcing myself to lick my lips.

The taste of blood was strong.

Fuck me, this hurts.

Even though I still couldn't open my eyes, I tried getting my bearings. I heard a fight going on in the distance. Scuffling of feet, and all that. I tried opening my eyes to figure out what was going on. Was someone in trouble? Did they need something?

I heard a whisper in the wind that sounded like my name, and I thought I might be losing it.

Pull yourself together. Where the fuck are you?

It was a good question. One I wasn't sure how to answer. I mean, I was obviously on the edge of a water source. Rushing water. A brook? Or a river? I mean, the water came all the way up to my hips. My feet were actually floating in it. So a deep river. I focused on the sounds around me, hoping anything would trigger a flood of memories. Something. Anything. A flash of a picture in order to give me context to the hellhole I'd woken up in.

I let my mind do the seeing for me.

There's wind rustling in leaves. Lots of trees. I'm in a forest, possibly. And it's cold. So there's no sun. A river, so there's water. Which means the droplets of water are coming from… an overhang? A tree?

A bridge.

Images bombarded my mind as the word 'bridge' soared through my mind. The car. My bike, crunched against a metal railing. A bridge, tumbling out of view. The sky above my head as my hands reached out for it. All of them still images. All of them, bringing into focus moving memories and images.

Rae.

"Clinton Clarke! Are you down there?"

"I see him! Clint!"

"Clinton!"

Fucking hell, I hate being called by my full name.

Just as quickly as the pictures started, they stopped, taking with them the moving images as I tried piecing together my night. The fuck was my brain doing? Why was it struggling like this so badly? I tried opening my eyes again as a light quickly illuminated my face. I felt the quick warmth and saw the light behind my eyelids before it disappeared. I heard people screaming out my name. I heard footsteps along something above me.

The bridge. That's the damn bridge.

That word started up another barrage of still images. A grocery store. My hand reaching out to push open the door. A girl, standing behind the register. With thick, beautiful dark hair and brooding brown eyes. I felt my heart leap in my chest. I felt my cold legs warming at the snippets of memories. I saw myself leaning against the counter, watching her smile and quirk an eyebrow at me. Feeling my eyes slowly inch down her body, taking in her toned curves.

Rae.

A pain ricocheted through my head and I groaned audibly. The first sound I'd forced my throat to make since I woke up. I tried drawing in a deep breath again, but the pain was too much. I stopped it midway, trying to open my jaw. Trying to part my lips. Trying anything to get more air into my lungs.

I couldn't open my jaw.

I'm gonna die here.

"Clint!"

"We're coming down for you. Stay put."

"Clinton Clarke! Can you hear us!?"

Their voices drifted away as my mind ripped me back into memories. The pain in my head was excruciating, and it seemed as if my body was hellbent on torturing me. The images began to move. Snippets of memories slowly became chunks of time. I felt Rae's lips against mine. The warmth and wetness of her tongue pressing against my own. My hands twitched, moving at the phantom feel of her ass cheeks in my palms. What I wouldn't give to be next to her. What I wouldn't give to feel her pressed against me, ridding me of my pain and warming me as this water threatened to drag me into the deep.

Into the cold, dark depths of its deadly stare.

I heard footsteps off in the distance. I wanted to cry out for them, but I couldn't. My mind kept interrupting my need to survive. It kept bombarding me with memories I no longer wanted. Because it wasn't thoughts of Rae any longer. I saw snippets of that car. Those headlights. Those assholes, and everything they'd said to Rae. What their eyes insinuated. What the licking of their lips foreshadowed. I felt anger blooming in my chest and rage coursing through my veins. A searing pain unlike anything I'd ever experienced trickled all the way down to my damn toes.

No one hurts Rae. Not on my watch.

Then it happened. The entire replay behind my eyelids. I saw myself riding my bike. I heard the screeching of those tires and the laughing of the boys behind me. My mind replayed it all. From the first time I rumbled over the railroad tracks to the neighborhoods we'd zoomed in and out of. The entire world fell silent to my ears as my mind took me down that dangerous path. Took me down memory lane, where I even remembered the plan I'd come up with.

Cruise out of town until they run out of gas.

It had been the perfect plan. Run them out of

town. Get them away from Rae. And once they puttered over to the side of the road, speed off into the night. It was foolproof. It was perfection. So, how the hell did I fuck it up?

Because you're always a fuck-up, Clarke.

A fuck-up, Clarke.

A fuck-up, Clarke.

My voice morphed into my father's, and my mind held me hostage. I replayed the first time my father ever hit me. It was four months after he and my mother split up. We got into a fight because I wanted her to read me a bedtime story over the phone, like she used to read to me when she was still here. My father got angry with me. He thought I was accusing him of shitty stories. When really, all I wanted was my mother.

A small boy who wanted nothing but the comfort of his mother.

"Your mother's gone. She chose pills over us. So get used to it, or do without your stories."

Then he popped me on the side of the head.

A whimper bubbled up my throat. I begged my mind not to do this. I fought with myself, trying to stop the reel playing out in my head. But it was no use. My mind had fully run away with me, and there was nothing I could do to stop it.

Hell, I couldn't even move. The fuck made me think I could control my own mind?

I'm dying. This is what it's like right before someone dies.

My mind replayed the last time I'd ever heard my mother's voice. It was two years after she'd left, and she called me on a whim. On my birthday. I remember crying into the phone, I was so happy to hear from her. An eleven-year-old kid, with his first-ever black eye from his father. That had been my father's birthday present to me. A black eye, because I wanted a chocolate birthday cake instead of a strawberry one.

"Hi, Mommy. When are you coming home? Please come home. Please come get me."

"Oh, honey. I'm gonna be coming soon, okay?"

I remember her slurred words. How they seemed like the most amazing thing at the time, until I grew older. Until I realized she'd called me in the middle of one of her pill highs. Probably out of guilt for abandoning us.

"Please, Mommy. Dad hits me. I just wanna be with you. Why can't I be with you?"

"Oh, honey. Your father knows what's best, okay?"

"No, he doesn't. I know why you left, okay? I know it's because he wanted you to live this life you didn't wanna live. Mom, just come get me, okay? Please?"

"That's enough, boy. Give me that phone."

So much truth for an eleven-year-old boy. And yet, it was true. After dealing with my father's beatings every time I didn't act the way he wanted me to, I knew why my mother left us. Why she started downing pills until she had the courage to leave. Her postpartum depression got the best of her after having me, and instead of Dad being supportive, he ignored her. Told her to suck it up. Forced her to continuously go out to parties and get dressed up and accompany him on trips and continue to please him and be his trophy wife because that was what he expected.

Despite my mother's suffering.

The pills were to find the courage to leave, weren't they, Mom?

It's the only question I'd ask her. If I ever saw my mother face to face again, it was the only thing I wanted to know. Because deep down, I knew that was the reason she started popping them. Why she let them take over her world. Why she let them ease down her throat.

It was so she could ease out of this life and go on to the next.

But why couldn't you take me with you?

My mind played one last reel in my head. One reel that made me feel more alone and more empty than ever before. It was the last time I ever heard from my mother. A card, in the mail. A card my father was reluctant to give me. It was my fourteenth birthday, and it got delivered to the house without a return address. Dad tossed it to me, grumbling something about his 'good for nothing ex.' And as I opened it with trembling hands, I found myself repeating the words.

Because I'd damn near memorized that letter.

Clint,

You're fourteen today, and I can't believe how much time has passed. I think about you every day, wondering if I made the right decision for you. And I guess I'll never know. But I want you to have something. It's coming in the mail for you in a few days. I saved up a lot of money for it, so I hope you like it.

I love you. Never forget that, no matter what.

• *Mom*

Two days later, a leather jacket arrived in the mail. Much too big for me at the time, but it was there. It arrived while my father was on a business trip. Probably the only reason it had gotten to me in the first place. Hell, my father paid me so little attention once I became a teenager that he didn't question the jacket at all until almost a year later.

Just before I turned fifteen.

And now, my fucking leather jacket is getting wet.

Sounds meshed in my mind. I felt the headlights in my face again. I saw light beyond my eyelids. The smell of smoke became too much and the cry of Rae's voice in my ear made me sick to my stomach. I heard those boys laughing. I heard the tires screeching. I heard the crunch of metal as my body jumped. Twitched. Shooting pain up and down my arms and legs before my eyes slowly opened, for the first time since I'd come to.

And I was staring up at that bullshit sky.

My jaw unlocked and I drew in lungfuls of air. My eyes darted around as my body slowly came to life, with my toes wiggling in my boots. I turned my head enough to take in the bank I was lying on. And yes, I was sprawled out on the river's edge. I centered my head again, with the edge of the bridge in view. Holy shit, I'd tumbled over the edge. Dropped at least twenty fucking feet down to this water.

How the fuck had I not ended up in the river?

Flashes of that came back, too. How I got off my

bike. How I started running for the woods. How that damn car literally attempted to pin me to the metal railing.

Holy shit, those assholes had actually tried to kill me.

I need to call the cops.

"Clint!"

"Clinton!"

"Clinton Clarke!"

For some reason, I thought I heard Rae's voice. Among the foreign voices that somehow knew my name, I could have sworn I heard hers. But that wasn't possible. If this was the river-bridge combination I thought it was, I was damn near twenty miles away from her place of work. Where this shitshow kicked off.

She wouldn't have come that far down this road to find me.

Right?

I wondered what condition my bike was in. Fucking hell, it was probably totaled. Which Dad wouldn't be happy about. I'd get yet another beating for that shit before his guilt prompted him to buy me a newer one. A nicer one. That was how shit worked with Dad. He'd beat me, then feel guilty, then I'd wake up one morning to a nice-ass gift. And even then, it was only sometimes.

Only sometimes, he felt guilty for beating his son up.

I licked my lips again, tasting copper against my skin. I grimaced as the pain in my body slowly faded into the background. I felt myself growing used to it.

Numb to the pain, like I'd become numb to my father. Numb to my home. Numb to the absence of my mother. Numb to the anger I always felt. Numb to the insecurities I kept buried deep in the pit of my soul.

"Clint!"

I tried bending my arms, but it was no use. I tried using my legs, but to no avail. Moving hurt too much. And part of me wanted this river to sweep me away and carry me off to somewhere else. Another place. Another time. A place where my mother existed and not my father. A place where school existed, but not Roy and those assholes. A place where my bike existed, but not the car chasing me.

A place where Rae existed, without her bullshit life and friends.

Rae.

I closed my eyes, allowing her smell to wash over me. Allowing the feeling of her body pressed against mine to draw me back under. If this was it, dying with her memory on the tip of my brain was a nice way to go out. I felt myself accepting my death. Accepting how cold my body was growing. And while my father would surely call me a 'cop-out pussy' at my own damn funeral, it didn't matter.

So long as I had memories of Rae to keep me company.

I sighed as my jaw snapped shut again. Like my body had released itself, only to lock back up because it was easier to simply shut down. And all the while, I thought about how strange this was. How worried I'd been for Rae's safety. How worried I'd been that her friends wouldn't like me. How worried I'd been about some dumbass reputation being destroyed because she wanted to walk into school holding fucking hands.

None of that mattered anymore.

Because all that worrying had been for nothing, when this was how things were going to end.

I love you, Rae. And I hope you know that.

And as I felt myself slipping into the cold, dark expanse of the river, I could have sworn I heard Rae's voice ring out in the depths of my ears.

"Don't you die on me, Clinton Clarke!"

Thank you for reading PLAY WITH ME. Don't miss PROMISE ME, the next book in Rae and Clinton's love story, and be sure to join my email and SMS lists below to don't miss any of my future books!

Want to read an exclusive novella from Clinton's point of view? Check out CLAIMING ME.

Get an SMS alert:
Text REBEL to (844) 339 0303

If you want to support me, consider leaving a review on Amazon.
I'd love it!

REBEL HART

Rebel Hart is an author of Dark Romance novels. Check out all of her books at www.RebelHart.net/Stories. And don't forget to join her Readers' Group to chat with Rebel and other fans: facebook.com/groups/rebelhart

NEVER MISS A NEW RELEASE:
Follow Rebel on Amazon
Follow Rebel on Bookbub

Text REBEL to (844) 339 0303 to don't miss any of her books (US only) or sign up at www.RebelHart.net to get an email alert when her next book is out.

authorrebelhart@gmail.com

CONNECT WITH REBEL HART:

ALSO BY REBEL HART

For a full list of my books go to:

www.RebelHart.net/Stories

Printed in Great Britain
by Amazon

23355554R00199